Aubrie could feel him watching her.

She wouldn't give him the satisfaction of looking back. She got up to get a drink. She needed something to calm her nerves. On her way back from the bar, Terian sprang up in her path.

"We have nothing to say to each other."

"We need to talk about what happened."

She fought for calm. "It doesn't matter. You're still the same manipulative man I met in school. I know the real reason you're on the island." He wasn't just visiting on vacation. "You're looking at a property to open a restaurant."

Terian's eyes registered his surprise. "How did you find out?" Because the owner was a friend of hers—and Aubrie wanted the building for *her* restaurant. He suddenly seemed uncomfortable.

"I might as well tell you that you don't stand a chance of getting that place on Hibiscus. I'll simply outbid you." She wouldn't let him derail her future plans—never again.

Dear Reader,

I don't know about you, but I adore good food. My husband and I love trying new restaurants—for us, it's not just about the food but the dining experience. The Cheesecake Factory in Beverly Hills is special to me because it's where I got engaged. The Big Easy and Basilico Italiano in NC are where we would go on date nights. There are so many eateries across the country—restaurants where wonderful memories were born. All these recollections serve as the inspiration for *His Partnership Proposal*.

I had fun writing this story, which is the fourth book in the Polk Island series. Born in a family of lawyers, Aubrie DuGrandpre had to take a firm stand when she chose to become a chef. Terian LaCroix's background is quite the opposite. His father encouraged him to follow in his footsteps and work in the family restaurant. However, Terian has dreams of owning an award-winning fine dining establishment.

Terian steps out on faith to finally make his dream a reality. However, he and Aubrie are interested in the same commercial property. They strike a partnership, which is challenged by Terian's need to be the best and in control and Aubrie's fear of losing her heart to him only to have it broken a second time.

The story pairs well with baked chicken cooked in red wine, a cauliflower mash and roasted vegetables. As always, thank you for your never-ending support of the Polk Island series.

Jacquelin Thomas

HEARTWARMING

His Partnership Proposal

—

Jacquelin Thomas

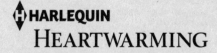

HARLEQUIN®
HEARTWARMING™

ISBN-13: 978-1-335-58479-3

His Partnership Proposal

Copyright © 2022 by Jacquelin Thomas

Recycling programs
for this product may
not exist in your area.

For questions and comments about the quality of this book,
please contact us at CustomerService@Harlequin.com.

Harlequin Enterprises ULC
22 Adelaide St. West, 41st Floor
Toronto, Ontario M5H 4E3, Canada
www.Harlequin.com

Printed in U.S.A.

Jacquelin Thomas is an award-winning, bestselling author with more than fifty-five books in print. When not writing, she is busy catching up on her reading, attending sporting events and spoiling her grandchildren. Jacquelin and her family live in North Carolina.

Books by Jacquelin Thomas

Harlequin Heartwarming

A Family for the Firefighter
Her Hometown Hero
Her Marine Hero

Harlequin Kimani Romance

Five Star Attraction
Five Star Temptation
Legal Attraction
Five Star Romance
Five Star Seduction

Visit the Author Profile page
at Harlequin.com for more titles.

Bernard, thank you for thirty-one years of wedded bliss, friendship and lots of laughter.

You are where my love story began...

CHAPTER ONE

Aubrie DuGrandpre stared out the window at the fifty or so guests milling around the massive backyard, made more beautiful by stunning views of the Atlantic Ocean. Although Polk Island was just across the bridge from Charleston, she didn't get there often because of the long hours she worked.

"Why are you in here?" her mother asked. "You should be outside greeting everyone along with your brother and cousins."

"This is a DuGrandpre Law Firm gathering," she responded. "I'm just catering the event."

"You are a *DuGrandpre*, dear. The firm is kicking off its weeklong sixtieth anniversary celebration with this private party for our high-profile clients. We're all expected to participate."

"Why aren't you out there?" Aubrie asked. "You're one of the senior partners."

"I'm on my way now," Rochelle stated. "I had a bit of a wardrobe mishap earlier. I've put on a few pounds, and I can't seem to get rid of them."

"Mom, you look great."

She smiled. "Thank you for saying that, but now I'm going to have to invest in some new clothes if I can't shed the weight."

"Maybe cutting out the desserts and pasta might help."

Rochelle frowned. "I know…it's just that I love them."

"Maybe don't eat them as much. Mom, why don't you start coming to the gym with me?"

"I might just do that, Aubrie."

Rochelle and her husband, Jacques, were senior partners in the firm which had a rich history in Charleston since the 1960s when Aubrie's grandparents relocated from New Orleans with their twin sons to open the doors of the DuGrandpre Law Offices. Etienne and Jacques shared control of the firm after their parents retired. Aubrie was the only one in their family who'd opted to become a chef instead of following tradition and becoming a lawyer.

At thirty-three years old, Aubrie was the proud owner of two restaurants: one in New Orleans and the other in Charleston. She'd recently investigated opening a third and considered an island location.

"I guess we'd better get out there," Aubrie said. "Looks like the family is gathering together. It's nice to see our New Orleans relatives here."

"Yes, it is," Rochelle agreed.

Aubrie followed her mother to the patio and into clear skies and bright sunshine. It was a beautiful day. She was looking forward to the start of summer, her favorite season.

They were met by her father.

"I was about to come looking for you two," Jacques said.

"I'm sorry, hon. I had trouble finding something to wear," Rochelle responded, giving him a tender look. "I've got to do something about my weight."

Aubrie smiled. "I told Mom that she looks fine."

"Yes, she does."

Taking Jacques by the hand, Rochelle said, "I guess we should make our rounds."

Aubrie navigated through the sea of guests, smiling and pausing every now and then to chat with a few. She made her way to the back where she had a clear view of the oceanfront.

I'd rather be out there swimming in the ocean than standing around at this party right now.

If she'd had her way, she would just attend the anniversary gala on the following Saturday. She didn't work at the law firm and didn't see the importance of having to be present for every event planned this week. Besides, there was always someone who inquired as to why she chose to be a chef instead of following in her family's footsteps. Aubrie didn't like feeling as if she had to defend her decision. She'd had to do this with her family in the beginning, but she refused to continue doing so with outsiders.

As she walked around greeting guests, she made her way to the gazebo overlooking the beautiful ocean. The view was simply breathtaking. She thought back to Jadin and Landon's wedding, which had been held at the estate. A touch of sadness swept through her. Seven years ago, she was planning her own wedding...

"Why are you standing over here by yourself?" her cousin Jordin inquired, bringing Aubrie out of her musings. "Are you okay?"

"Yes, I'm fine."

"Your mother was asking if there's more chicken in the kitchen."

"There is," Aubrie said. "I'll bring it out."

"Do you need any help?" Jordin asked.

"No, I can handle it."

"Where's Michelle?"

Aubrie glanced around for a sighting of her best friend. "I don't think she's here yet. Maybe it's a busy day for the shop." Her friend's tee shirt design business had really taken off.

"I know. Ethan wants to order tee shirts for his employees." Jordin's husband ran a gym on the island.

"That's great. She's going to be so excited. It's wonderful that you and your husband are being so supportive. Michelle was nervous about moving to a storefront, but she's doing well with her custom tee shirts."

"She does great work," Jordin responded.

A short time later, her friend arrived.

"Hey, I'm sorry I'm late," Michelle Chapman said. "I had a last-minute customer." Her gaze bounced around the surroundings. "Wow…this place is *amazing*."

"It belongs to my aunt and uncle," Aubrie said. "Growing up, Ryker and I spent many summers here."

"Where is your brother? I saw Garland when I got here. I don't think I've ever seen those two apart."

Aubrie chuckled. "He's probably somewhere inside." Ryker and Garland had been married for ten years and were the proud parents of three children: Amya, Kai and little RJ. It thrilled her to see her brother so happy.

She didn't think love was in her future and had made peace with that a long time ago. Aubrie was content with her life and her restaurants. She wouldn't ask for anything more…

Well, maybe another restaurant, she thought with a smile. Polk Island was beautiful and a popular tourist attraction.

The perfect place for my new venture.

"WHAT DID I tell you…this place is beautiful," Terian LaCroix said as he drove down Main Street. "Polk Island, South Carolina, is the perfect place for my restaurant." Elated, he glanced over at his twin sister. "What do you think?"

"Oh, I agree," Torrie responded. "I saw a café and one other restaurant during the drive over here, but they're nothing like what you have in mind."

"I found the perfect location near South Beach, a high-traffic location. This is it," Terian stated as he parked the car in the empty parking lot. "There used to be a high-end steakhouse here with two private dining rooms, but it closed for some reason. Capacity is one hundred fifty seats." The standalone building was surrounded by high-end homes.

"Ooooh, I can see the ocean from here," Torrie said. "We have to take a stroll on the beach before we leave the island."

He chuckled. "Sure." His sister loved the beach as much as he did. The May weather was nice, the temperature just right.

"This is the perfect place for what you have in mind."

Terian nodded in agreement. "Yeah, it is…"

Torrie played with a micro-thin loc. She'd been wearing her hair in locs for five years. She turned around to face her brother, gazing through hazel eyes that were identical to his own. "Are you absolutely sure about this? Striking out on your own. I don't doubt that you can do it—it's just a huge undertaking."

He had an indefinable feeling of confidence. "I am," he told her. "I've never been so certain about anything."

Torrie moved closer to peek through one of the windows on the side. "I love what I can see of it. The decor is a little dated though."

"I'm going to change all that," he responded.

She looked back at Terian. "So, what's next?"

"I'm going to submit an offer to the owner."

Her eyes widened in surprise. "I know we're here on this island, but I still can't believe that you're really serious about leaving New Orleans."

Terian nodded. "I am. I didn't expect all this to happen so soon, but I figure a place like this isn't going to stay empty too long." When he came across the listing while searching online, he had felt in his gut that this was the perfect building for his restaurant. He'd booked a flight to Charleston while still on the real estate website. Two days later, he asked Torrie to join him because he valued her opinion.

"Why not open a restaurant in NOLA? Is it because of Dad?"

"You know it is," he responded. "Pop would consider it a betrayal. It's going to make him mad that I left LaCroix to strike out on my own, but he'll handle it better if I'm not in the same city."

"You're probably right. He's not gonna be too happy about it either way."

They left the site and drove a couple of blocks away to the beach parking lot. Torrie was out of the car almost before he took the key out of the ignition.

Terian watched in amusement as his sister changed out of her sandals into a pair of flip-flops. She pulled her dark brown locs into a ponytail, before retrieving a bottle of sunscreen out of her tote and rubbing it on her milk chocolate–hued skin.

"Oh yes, the beach… I can't wait to dip my toes in the ocean."

"You're like a little kid," Terian teased.

"I don't care. I love the water."

"I do, too. I'm hoping to find a place to live within walking distance to the beach. I can train for the 5K run I signed up for. If you were going to be here—I'd have put you down for it. It's to raise money for breast cancer research."

"I'm doing a 5K run with Luke next month."

"I've been replaced," Terian said and pretended to wipe away a tear. He and Torrie had always been close—she was his best friend. While he was happy for her, there was a part of him that worried how her marriage might affect their own relationship. He liked Luke well enough, and he believed the man truly loved his sister. She was starting a new season in her life. Terian felt it was time that he did the same.

"No, you haven't," she responded. "You'll always be my running buddy, but I figure I should do at least one 5K with my fiancé. Especially since that's how we met last year."

"I suppose you're right."

During their walk along the shoreline, Torrie asked, "How do you think Aubrie DuGrand-pre is going to react when she finds out you're opening a restaurant so close to Charleston?"

He shrugged with nonchalance. "I don't know, but it shouldn't matter. She opened her first place, Manoir Rouge, two blocks from our restaurant in New Orleans, when she could've opened it here on the island. The way I see it—it's her loss."

"Is this your way of getting back at her?"

He eyed her in disbelief. He'd never expected

his sister to ask such a question. "No, it's nothing like that, Torrie."

She scrutinized him. "Are you sure?"

"You should know me better than anyone else."

"I do," she responded. "That's why I'm asking. I know how competitive you are. You always want to be number one—the best. When we were growing up, you had to be the best at checkers, the best in sports. You started running because I was getting accolades and you couldn't stand it. You had to best me at that."

"I'm my father's son," he said. "You know Pop won't accept anything less than being the best. He made me this way. He's the reason I had to be the best in sports. Pop wanted you to be a princess...pretty and pampered."

"True, but there comes a point when you must be your own person. I'm not the princess type. You have to live your life for yourself."

"Pop's not as hard on you. He wanted me to prove myself worthy of running LaCroix Restaurant while he's willing to just turn the reins over to you without question."

Torrie stopped in her tracks. "Wait...are you saying I don't deserve to run LaCroix? Just so you know... I'm just as qualified as you are, brother. We both went to top culinary schools.

As for turning the reins over… I'll be old and gray before that happens and you know it."

"That's not what I'm saying at all," Terian interjected as he scratched his beard. "You're a great chef, but it's not your life's dream. Not like it is for me."

"No, it wasn't always my dream to be a chef, but I do love it, Terian."

"Pop didn't pull you out of school to come home and work the business. I was a few months away from graduating." That was seven years ago now. He'd never told his sister that he was failing and that was the reason their father demanded he withdraw. His father told him to keep it between them—it was their private shame to bear.

"I guess he felt it was better for you to gain real experience," Torrie responded. "You're a fantastic chef so it didn't hold you back."

"I don't agree."

She shrugged off his comment. "We should just tell Dad that we intend to work together as equal partners. You can have your own restaurant and we share in the running of LaCroix."

"You know Pop's not gonna go for that. I think he enjoys watching us compete."

"Terian, I'm not interested in competing with you. LaCroix is as much ours as it is Dad's. It's our legacy."

"Unfortunately, Pop doesn't see it that way at all."

Terrance LaCroix liked to call all the shots and he valued being the best. He'd been the top student and athlete in high school, the top of his class in culinary school, and for years his restaurant was highly popular. He'd raised Terian in that same manner—to be the best. There was no second best as far as Terrance was concerned.

There were times Terian wished he'd gone to Italy with Torrie to study. But he knew his father expected him to attend the same school in Paris as he had. The pressure to do as well as his dad was hard to deal with, and he found himself struggling to keep up his marks.

His dad also didn't have to deal with a student like Aubrie DuGrandpre, who excelled in every class. She'd also captured his heart, which added a different kind of stress. In the end though, his need to have his father's blessing outweighed his feelings for Aubrie.

When his father realized that Terian was barely holding his own in school, he decided that on-the-job training would be more effective with Terian and ordered him back home. There really hadn't been a choice.

Ashamed and feeling like a complete failure,

Terian left school and the love of his life behind. He was determined never to look back.

Until his past collided with his present when Aubrie opened Manoir Rouge in New Orleans a few years later.

"How did you come to choose this island for your restaurant?" Torrie asked. "Have you been here before now?"

"No. I think Aubrie mentioned it once when we were in school," Terian responded. "I did some research and decided it was the best place to open my restaurant."

She stopped in her tracks. "I'm going to ask you again…are you sure this isn't some sort of payback?"

He glanced over at his twin. "This has nothing to do with Aubrie. It's about making money. Aubrie lives in Charleston. She used to come here for the summer with her cousins, but it's not like she owns this island." Deep down, there was a slight twinge of joy at the thought of opening a restaurant on the island Aubrie loved so much. He wanted her to know how it felt when she opened Manoir Rouge in New Orleans. But more than that, everything about the island felt right—it was the perfect place for his new beginning.

He eyed his sister. "Aubrie will just have to get used to the idea of sharing this island with me."

"Still, you don't fully know the reach of the DuGrandpre family…" Torrie's voice died as she looked past her brother. "Speaking of which…"

"What is it?" Terian asked.

"I thought that was you," a voice said behind him.

Terian turned around, coming face-to-face with someone he never expected to see today. "Phillip DuGrandpre, what are you doing here? I thought we left you in NOLA."

"My family came to Charleston to celebrate the sixtieth anniversary of the DuGrandpre Law Firm. My cousins are hosting a party at their house here on the island."

"Aubrie's parent's—they have a home on Polk Island?" Torrie inquired as she eyed Terian.

He was surprised to hear this as well. He'd had no idea that her family owned property on the island. A feeling of uneasiness snaked down his spine.

"It's a vacation home," Phillip said. "I came out here to take a stroll, but I'd better head back before I'm missed. Hey, the whole clan is at the house. Y'all should come by."

"We don't want to intrude." The prospect of running into Aubrie set Terian on edge.

"You won't be. All you need is an invitation and I just invited you."

"I'd like to go," Torrie said. "We don't have to stay long."

Phillip pointed straight ahead. "The house is right there."

Just three hundred feet away, the three-story home had floor to ceiling windows on almost every inch of wall facing the ocean and featured a beachfront Olympic-size pool behind its gate.

Terian and his sister exchanged looks before she responded, "That's no house. That's a mansion."

"My sister is easily impressed," he said calmly while trying to ignore the wave of apprehension now sweeping through him. The DuGrandpres of New Orleans were well established financially, but they didn't live as lavishly as this.

"It's an impressive estate, to be sure," Phillip said. "As you can see, my cousins have done very well with the firm. I'm actually thinking of leaving the district attorney's office to become a criminal lawyer. It pays better."

Terian chuckled. "I can't see it. Not from a man with your personal conviction and passion."

"I'm serious," Phillip responded as they walked across the warm sand toward the DuGrandpre mansion. "Aubrie's gonna be surprised to see you."

"I'm sure she will be," he responded. He was the last person in this world Aubrie would want to see.

"You didn't tell me her family was rich," Torrie said in a whisper.

"I didn't know," he whispered back. "I knew they were well-off, but nothing on this scale."

As they neared the DuGrandpre estate, Terian heard music playing, people laughing and conversations floating in the wind. "Sounds like a good time," he said.

Phillip laughed. "My family know how to throw a party."

They followed him through a wrought iron gate.

"Wow…" Torrie murmured, her eyes bouncing around, taking in their grand surroundings.

Live oak trees offered serene views of the Atlantic Ocean. On their left, an Olympic-size swimming pool complete with dressing room and shower took center stage in the sprawling garden. A white gazebo sat off to the right of the property. Colorful rose bushes dotted the well-tended lawn. Women wearing brightly covered summer dresses, men in slacks and linen trousers with short sleeve shirts moved around the elegantly decorated backyard.

"This place is really beautiful." Torrie seemed spellbound. "I can see why Phillip is consid-

ering changing careers. The Charleston Du-
Grandpre's are living large. Maybe I should've
become a lawyer."

Terian didn't respond. He scanned the crowd
and felt the tiny hairs on his body stand erect as
he met Aubrie's shocked, then hardened gaze.
She clearly wasn't happy to see him.

They stared across the yard at one another for
a tense moment before she began walking toward him and Torrie. Terian wasn't sure what to
expect, but from the expression on her face—it
wasn't good.

Phillip hurried over to meet her.

Aubrie was met halfway by her cousin. They
talked for a moment before she continued her
approach. Normally, she would take off in the
opposite direction whenever they saw each
other in New Orleans, but today was different.
He was on her turf.

"Here she comes… Are you okay?" Torrie
whispered.

"I'm fine," he responded. "We might as well
get this over with."

"I just hope Aubrie doesn't cause a scene."

"She's not like that," Terian said, hoping
what he said was true. She wasn't like that or
at least she hadn't been when he knew her. He
hoped she hadn't changed.

"Hello, Aubrie," he greeted her when they were finally face-to-face.

Judging from her expression, Terian had the sinking feeling that this face-to-face was not going to go well.

CHAPTER TWO

AUBRIE AND TERIAN stared at each other across a thick, ringing silence. She stood there eyeing him, her chin lifted slightly in defiance. Unwillingly, she took in his beautiful hazel eyes, close-cropped hair, his neatly trimmed beard and mustache, perfectly etched lips and smooth chocolate-tinted complexion. He was close enough for her to smell the aquatic citrus scent of his aftershave.

Aubrie had met Terian in culinary school. He was the first and only man to break her heart.

She had run into him a few times over the years in New Orleans, but refused to have anything to do with him.

"What brings you to Polk Island?" she asked, keeping her tone neutral and without emotion.

"Vacation," he responded. "My sister wanted to see for herself what's so special about the island, since it's a popular spot for getaways. You've met Torrie, haven't you?"

"Yes," she responded. "It's nice to see you again."

"You, too. Phillip invited us. I hope it's okay."

"It's fine, Torrie." Aubrie returned her gaze to Terian. "I hope you both will enjoy the party."

"Aubrie..." he began.

She cut him off by saying, "I have to go. I need to replenish the food."

Agitated, Aubrie walked briskly toward the house. She wanted to throttle Phillip for bringing them to the party, but he didn't know of the tension between her and Terian. She had nothing against Torrie. However, the two of them being there only made her feel uncomfortable, and she had never been able to hide her emotions.

"Sis, you okay?" her brother asked when she entered the kitchen. "You look upset."

"I'm fine, Ryker."

"Things looked a bit tense between you and that guy Phillip brought with him."

As casually as she could manage, Aubrie said, "That was Terian LaCroix. His family owns LaCroix Restaurant in New Orleans. He and his sister are visiting the island. Phillip ran into them during his walk."

"Are you all on good terms?"

Aubrie nodded. "We're not friends if that's what you mean—just cordial toward one another. Their showing up here just caught me by surprise. That's all."

Ryker eyed her for a moment before saying, "So there's nothing more?"

"Nope."

She released a short sigh when her brother left the kitchen to join the others outside. No one in the family knew anything about her former relationship with Terian.

After seeing to the meats and vegetables that needed to be replenished, Aubrie composed herself and was about to rejoin everyone when Michelle met her at the door.

She stepped aside to let her friend enter the house.

"Who is that gorgeous man out there with the hazel eyes?"

"That's *Terian*." Michelle was the only person who knew about her and Terian, so Aubrie didn't have to pretend that his presence wasn't bothering her.

"Really?" Shaking her head, Michelle added, "What a waste of all that handsomeness."

"For sure."

"The woman with him must be his sister. They have the same eyes."

Aubrie nodded. "Yes, that's Torrie. His twin."

"Are you okay with him being here? You know I don't have a problem telling them to leave."

She laughed. "I know you don't, but it's really not necessary."

"Then you need to put a smile on your face. You can't go out there looking like there's a problem. It might make him feel like he still matters to you."

"You're right. The last thing I want is for Terian to get the idea that I care anything about him."

"So, who is the cute guy that came with him?"

"That's Phillip… He's my cousin," Aubrie stated. "*He's* the one who invited Terian to the party."

"Oh, okay. Phillip is the district attorney in New Orleans."

She nodded. "Yes. I wasn't aware that they knew each other, but with them both living in New Orleans… I shouldn't be surprised."

Michelle quickly assessed her. "Okay, now walk out there and be your normal friendly self."

"I'll remind you to do the same the next time someone taps on your last nerve."

"Girl…"

They burst into laughter.

Composed once more, Aubrie saw that the food on the buffet table had been replenished. She didn't spare a glance in Terian's direction and tried to forget he was there. It wasn't as easy as she'd hoped.

After all these years, Aubrie's heart still raced and she grew weak in the knees whenever Terian was near, despite her deep-rooted anger toward him. She'd grown weary of his earlier attempts to talk to her as if he hadn't betrayed her.

The last thing Aubrie wanted was for Terian to realize how much he'd hurt her, so she'd do her best to avoid talking to him. Besides, there was nothing left to say.

TERIAN LEANED TOWARD his sister and whispered, "I'm not sure coming here was a good idea. I think I saw smoke coming out of her ears."

"Yeah, I saw the way she looked at you. What on earth did you do to that woman?"

Looking straight ahead, he answered, "Nothing."

Torrie shook her head in disbelief. "Terian, I don't believe you. Whatever it was—it must have been awful. Maybe I should go ask her."

"Look, we dated for a while, then it ended. It's been seven years, but I guess she's not over it."

"She acts like you betrayed her in some way. Were you unfaithful?"

"How long y'all planning on being in town?" Phillip returned to the table with a plate heaped with food. "Y'all should get in line. Aubrie's restaurant catered this event. Everything is delicious."

Terian was relieved by Phillip's appearance. He didn't want to discuss his past with his sister. He didn't like the person he was back then. He vowed to only have this conversation once and it would be with Aubrie.

"I'm leaving tonight," Torrie responded to his query. "But Terian will be here a few more days. What about you?"

"I leave next Sunday." Phillip glanced at her brother. "If you're still in the area on Saturday—you should come to the gala. It's going to be in Charleston."

"I appreciate the invitation," Terian said. "I'd be happy to attend. I've been thinking of staying around longer than I originally planned. I'd like to see more of the island."

They got up and navigated toward the food station, but before they reached it, Torrie drew Terian aside.

"What are you talking about?" she asked, her voice low. "You have to get back to the restaurant. Dad will have a fit."

"I'm not going back to New Orleans."

His sister's mouth dropped open in shock. "Terian, when did you decide this?"

"Just now."

"But things are up in the air with the restaurant. Your offer might not be accepted and even if it is—you still have to get approved for the financing. What are you going to do until it's yours?"

"Get settled here. Polk Island is going to be my home."

"I'm still processing that you're actually moving. When do you think you'll come home?"

"I'm not sure, but I have to go back at some point. I need to pack up and put my house on the market." He glanced in the direction of the house and saw that Aubrie had reappeared. Their eyes met, so he quickly picked up a plate and eating utensils.

Even though he'd turned away, Terian could feel the heat of Aubrie's gaze on him. He was grateful she didn't try to embarrass him—he'd known that wasn't her way. But she had found a way to hurt him. She'd opened Manoir Rouge— a new star on the rise in his city while the restaurant owned by his family was dying a slow death. When Manoir Rouge earned a Michelin Star, he was happy for her, but he also envied her success.

He considered a second attempt to talk to her but decided against it since this wasn't the right time or place. He hated this distance between them and longed to make things right. When she opened her restaurant in New Orleans, he'd tried to explain things. However, Aubrie refused to listen to him.

She didn't appear to have aged at all, although he knew seven years had passed. They met during orientation at the Ferrandi School of Culinary Arts in Paris, France. The only Americans in their class, the two instantly bonded. Their relationship eventually became a romantic one during their second year abroad. But this didn't hinder Terian's competitive nature. It was important to be the best student—only he wasn't. Aubrie was the top student in their class. Although he tried not to let it bother him—it did. And when he couldn't beat her, his father had pulled him out just like he did when Terian didn't make quarterback in high school. When he was offered a position on special teams—Terrance forced him to quit.

The problem was, Terian had left culinary school without telling Aubrie. Right before their senior project was due.

At thirty-three years old, Terian was deeply ashamed of his actions where Aubrie was concerned, and wanted to make peace with her. He'd tried emailing her and asking to meet, but they went unanswered. Terian had even called and left a couple messages at Manoir Rouge. She clearly wasn't interested in hearing anything he had to say.

"It's time we head back to Charleston," he said to Phillip after they had been there for an hour and a half. "I need to make sure my sister makes her flight."

Phillip walked them halfway to where the car was parked.

"Safe travels," Terian said to Torrie.

"What do you want me to tell Dad?"

"I'll deal with our father."

She smiled. "See you in New Orleans at some point."

He hugged her. "I'm going to miss you."

"I'll miss you, too," Torrie responded.

Terian went to the hotel after leaving his sister at the airport.

He navigated to the mahogany desk in his hotel room and stared down at his reflection in its uncluttered surface.

How am I ever going to make things right with Aubrie if she's not willing to have a real conversation with me?

Terian forced the question out of his mind. He couldn't allow any negative thoughts to take over.

In the seven years he'd known her, there wasn't much that had changed about her. She still wore her dark hair in its naturally curly state, and her golden honey complexion free of makeup. She still had that same easy smile, although it was no longer reserved for him. Aubrie was beautiful and very intelligent.

Deep down, Terian had allowed himself to believe that the reason Aubrie kept running off was because she still had feelings toward him, but now he wasn't so sure. Her brisk departure left a sudden chill hanging in the air. He just couldn't dismiss the cold remoteness he glimpsed in her gaze.

It bothered him that Aubrie might actually hate him. He swallowed the white-hot pain he felt just thinking about it.

"TERIAN SURE LOOKED uncomfortable the entire time he was here," Michelle said while helping Aubrie clean and gather up her equipment at the end of the evening.

"Good," she uttered. Aubrie was furious at her vulnerability to him. She would've preferred to have reacted as if it didn't matter that he was there, but his presence sent her running off.

Michelle picked up a tablecloth, folding it. "Phillip must not know what happened between the two of you. I can't see him inviting them if he did."

"No one knows about it," Aubrie responded. "Except you. I was too ashamed to tell my family. They weren't as supportive back then."

"Oh…"

Tossing a handful of napkins in a crate, she said, "I've run into Terian a few times in New Orleans. Each time, he's tried to bring it up—I just walk away. He's called and even emailed me, but it's seven years too late. I don't want to hear anything he has to say."

"If he's that insistent, then he probably wants to apologize, Aubrie."

She eyed her friend. "Like I said…*it's too late.*"

"Would you have listened to him when he left Paris without a word?"

Aubrie shook her head. "Probably not. I was beyond furious."

"So, when *is* a good time for Terian to apologize?"

"*Never,*" Aubrie responded, her lips thinning with anger. She couldn't believe her friend would ask her something like that. She had a right to her feelings.

"Do you really feel that way?" Michelle inquired.

"I want to," Aubrie replied after a moment. "I shouldn't be this angry with Terian. What's done is done and I've moved on."

"Doesn't sound like you have. I'm just saying…"

"I have, and then I see him," Aubrie said. "Things were fine until he showed up in my world. When he left school without telling me, Terian didn't care whether he hurt me or not. I just wish he'd leave me alone. We have nothing to talk about."

"If it were me, I'd be curious to hear what he had to say."

"That's where you and I differ, Michelle. I don't see any point in looking back."

"Sometimes you have to see where you've been before you can move forward."

"In this case…it's just best to keep my distance from Terian. Hopefully, he'll be leaving town soon."

"You probably won't see him again, since he's only visiting the island and you live in Charleston."

"True," Aubrie murmured with a smile. "Good riddance, Terian LaCroix."

CHAPTER THREE

THE FOLLOWING SATURDAY, Aubrie entered the Ballroom at the Ritz-Carlton Hotel in Charleston. She admired the decor, including the gold fabric wallcovering and the statement chandelier. Her eyes strayed to the carpet, studying the gold, teal, blue and gray pattern. She kept a mental file of color themes for future renovations or restaurants.

Aubrie fingered the diamond-white fabric covering on her chair as she watched family and friends dressed in tuxedos and jewel-toned gowns mill about the room. Musicians played classical music to accompany the various conversations whirling around her.

Her aunt Eleanor Louise DuGrandpre requested that the women in the family all wear white gowns. Aubrie glanced down at her own—a one-shoulder, column-style dress custom designed by her cousin Renee Rothchild Bowman.

It's nice having a fashion designer in the family.

Her long curly hair was pulled back and fashioned into a sophisticated bun.

She broke into a grin when Michelle walked in wearing a body-hugging gold strapless gown, which complemented her honey blonde curls.

Aubrie met her halfway. "You're certainly going to turn heads tonight," she told her.

"Thank you," her friend responded. "You look gorgeous. I'm loving that dress on you. I think I'll ask Renee to design my dress for the Heart Association Ball."

They were soon joined by Jadin, who was wearing a pleated tulle floral appliqué gown in white with rhinestone accents.

"That dress is beautiful," Michelle murmured.

Aubrie agreed. "Did Renee design your gown, too?"

"Her assistant Kayla designed it. Renee's in high demand these days."

"I guess I need to get on her calendar like now," Michelle said.

"Yes," Aubrie and Jadin agreed in unison.

They took their seats.

Not long after, Rochelle made her grand entrance in a short-sleeved, platinum-silver tulle and lace ball gown on the arm of her husband, Jacques. Her salt-and-pepper hair was fashioned into a stylish updo.

Michelle glanced over her shoulder. "Wow... look at Mama Rochelle..."

"Ooh, Michelle, you did a wonderful job with her makeup," Aubrie said. "She's a beautiful woman, but tonight, she seems to be glowing. She looks almost ethereal."

"Auntie does look really happy," Jadin responded.

Aubrie vowed to find out what was going on with her mother. There was something different about her.

When she saw Elaine, a friend of her mother's and a Realtor, walk into the ballroom, she went over to say hello.

They talked for a few minutes before Aubrie said, "I'd like to meet with you sometime this week to discuss the commercial property on Hibiscus Drive. I've been thinking about opening my next restaurant on Polk Island."

"I have to tell you that I have another person interested in doing the same thing," Elaine responded. "He's from New Orleans."

Suspicion flared.

"Are you talking about Terian LaCroix?" Aubrie asked.

"Yes, do you know him?"

"I do," she responded as casually as she could manage. Deep down, she was seething.

Terian had lied to her. She shouldn't be surprised.

When Terian entered through the ballroom doors accompanied by Phillip, Aubrie was momentarily taken aback by how handsome he looked in the black tuxedo. His hair lay in tiny waves and his mustache and beard were neatly trimmed.

Too bad he's such a liar.

She released a low sigh. Phillip was seated at the table next to the one where she sat with her family.

Her nostrils flared with fury as she gave Terian a hostile glare. She hoped it would discourage him from coming over to talk to her. She turned her attention to the family members seated with her.

Aubrie could feel him watching her, but she wouldn't give him the satisfaction of looking in his direction. After a moment, she got up to get a glass of wine. She needed something to calm her nerves.

On her way back from the bar, Terian sprang up and blocked the path to her table.

"Why do you keep doing this?" she asked. "We don't have anything to say to each other."

"Aubrie, I don't agree. At some point we need to talk about what happened."

"The time for that was before you left school.

And I know the real reason you were on the island," she stated. "You weren't just visiting on vacation. You're looking at commercial property to open a restaurant."

His eyes registered his surprise. "How did you find out?"

"The owner and the Realtor are *close* friends of my mother."

"I see." He suddenly seemed uncomfortable and started pulling at the neck of his shirt.

She hoped her eyes conveyed the fury within her. "I might as well tell you that you don't stand a chance at buying that property on Hibiscus, Terian. I'll simply outbid you. I know Elaine quite well. She'll take the highest offer. In fact, I'll outbid you on any property you're interested in. I'll make sure that you won't be able to open anything on Polk Island. Not even a fast-food franchise."

He didn't respond.

"Do everyone a favor and just go back to New Orleans."

"I know I'm not your favorite person, Aubrie, but I've never known you to be so antagonistic."

His chiding tone only served to make her angrier. "Just shows that you don't know me at all, Terian. You never did."

"Leaving school without telling you was

wrong…" Terian responded. "But I'm not that same person."

"Really? Lying about being on the island for vacation…" She shrugged nonchalantly. "It really proves that you haven't changed one bit. We used to be honest with one another… Anyway, it really doesn't matter anymore."

"Why are you so intent on ruining me?"

He dared to look wounded. Aubrie broke into a harsh chuckle. "You're doing a great job of that by yourself, Terian."

"I'd really like a chance to talk to you. I don't like all this animosity between us."

"I've said all I care to say."

Without giving Terian a chance to respond, Aubrie walked past him to her table.

"Judging from the hurt expression on his face, you just gave that poor man the business."

Aubrie turned in her seat to face Renee Rothchild Bowman. "Trust me, cousin, when I say that he deserved it."

"Can you put me on your schedule sometime next week? I want to discuss catering for the bridal fashion show."

"Sure. I'll call you tomorrow with some dates." Aubrie smiled. "I have to say that marriage certainly agrees with you."

"Greg and I are very happy," Renee responded.

"That's wonderful to hear."

Aubrie kept her back turned to Terian. She forced him out of her mind so she could enjoy the rest of her evening. She had no idea when he left, but his absence made her feel much better—at least that's what she told herself. Deep down, she felt bad for what she'd said to him. Aubrie had taken no pleasure in hurting him. Not like she thought she would. All she wanted to do was discourage him from opening his restaurant on the island. It was bad enough that she had to see him from time to time in New Orleans.

Polk Island wasn't big enough for the two of them.

"HEY, IS SOMETHING going on between you and Aubrie?" Phillip asked Terian when he caught up with him outside the hotel. "I've noticed that things seem to be really tense between you two."

"She's clearly not a fan of mine," he responded dryly. He had come outside to get some fresh air and to shake off the harshness of Aubrie's words. He had to ask himself, *Why do I keep trying?*

What shook him more was the thought of losing the building for his restaurant. It was the perfect place. He was not about to give up so easily, but he'd have to come up with another plan. Terian was barely aware that Phillip was still standing there.

"I've never seen Aubrie act like this," Phillip said. "She's always been very sweet and welcoming."

"We dated briefly when we were in France. I made some mistakes with her and it's obvious she hasn't forgotten them."

"I take it that you haven't had any luck trying to talk things out with her?"

Terian nodded. "I've tried several times, including a few minutes ago, but she's not ready to hear me out."

"Well, I hope one day you'll be able to make things right between y'all."

"Me, too," he responded. "I don't like all this tension between us."

"You must've really made her angry."

Terian remained silent. He didn't need anyone else judging him—he already felt like the worst kind of person. He wanted to make peace with Aubrie, but her attitude toward him made it a difficult task. They were once so close. Terian would give anything to renew their friendship. It was too much to expect that she'd ever allow them to be more than friends.

"You don't have to leave."

"I think it's best," Terian responded. "Besides, I have something I need to work on."

"I fly out first thing tomorrow morning. I guess I'll be seeing you around."

"Thanks for inviting me, Phillip."

"I hate that things turned out badly for you."

"I'm not giving up. I'm going to make things right."

"Between you and Aubrie?"

Terian nodded. "Yeah. I can't say any more than that. I haven't figured out exactly how I'm going to make it happen yet."

"Well, I wish you luck."

He pasted on a smile. "Thanks. I'm really going to need it."

"I SAW YOU talking to Terian earlier," Michelle said when Aubrie returned to her seat after taking some photos with her parents and brother. "What did *he* have to say?"

"I really didn't give him a chance to say too much," she stated. "I told the man to go back to New Orleans. Seeing him here in Charleston and on the island just rubs me the wrong way. It's almost like he's invading my personal space. I think Terian just brings out the worst in me."

Michelle finished off her glass of wine. "Good for you, but you know he probably felt the same way when you were in New Orleans."

"I don't care how Terian feels about anything,"

she responded. "I do feel bad for being so belligerent with him though."

"Girl, please..." Michelle uttered. "It's all right to have a petty moment. Besides, he deserved it."

"It just really ticked me off when Elaine told me that he was interested in buying that empty building on Hibiscus," Aubrie announced. "I'm going to have a conversation with Molly about this. She and her husband owned Lawson Steakhouse."

"Are you talking about the one on Polk Island?"

She nodded. "I'm pretty sure this was Terian's attempt to get back at me for opening my first restaurant two blocks from his family's. I told him that he didn't stand a chance."

"You're probably right," Michelle stated. "No point in him getting his hopes up."

"Before I forget...did Ethan ever speak to you about tee shirts for his staff? Jordin mentioned at the party last weekend that he was going to contact you."

Michelle broke into a smile. "He did. Ethan and Jordin are coming to the shop on this coming Wednesday to look at some ideas for design. I'm also meeting with your cousin Trey about shirts for the museum staff as well. Girl, your family alone will keep the doors open. I appreciate all the support from y'all."

"You do great work so it's well deserved," Aubrie said.

Michelle started to sway to the music. "I'm ready to dance. I need to find a partner."

"Phillip loves dancing. Why don't you ask him?"

Before Michelle could respond, he suddenly appeared out of nowhere and asked, "Would you like to dance?"

She winked at Aubrie, then responded, "Sure."

Aubrie saw another member of her family walking toward her and smiled. "Leon Rothchild...the firefighter who broke the hearts of all the single women on Polk Island and here in Charleston when he got married."

He laughed. "Hey to you, too, cousin. Seems like the only time I get to see you is whenever we have dinner at Manoir Bleu." He sat down in the chair temporarily vacated by Michelle.

Aubrie looked at him. "I know I need to do better when it comes to spending time with the family, but with restaurants in two different cities...it's been a bit hectic. Now that I've hired an executive chef for Manoir Rouge, things are finally settling down for me."

"I understand completely," he responded. "For the past two weeks, Misty's been pulling some long hours at the café, with her cook on medical leave. Then with my work schedule and the children's activities…we haven't been able to spend much quality time together."

"I promise I'm going to do better." Aubrie glanced around. "Where's your wife?"

"I left her and Gia near the ladies' room talking. They were waiting on Aunt Eleanor."

She smiled. "I'm heading in that direction right now."

"You'll probably find my brother somewhere nearby. Trey was talking to the mayor."

Aubrie made her way through the sea of guests in attendance. She felt so much freer now that Terian was gone. She hoped he'd take her advice and go back home to New Orleans.

Regardless, I won't have to see him again.

THE NEXT DAY, Aubrie stopped to visit her mother after leaving Manoir Bleu in the capable hands of her floor manager and her executive chef.

She found Rochelle relaxing on a lounge chair beside the large swimming pool. Aubrie stood near the patio door studying her. There was definitely something different about her mother. She was determined to find out what it was.

She walked over, asking, "Mama, what's going on with you?"

Rochelle looked up at her and smiled. "Nothing. I'm just enjoying this time in my life."

"Naw… I know you…it's more than that," Aubrie sat down in the empty chair beside her mother.

"Well, earlier this month, I had a health scare and it's prompted me to focus on what's really important."

"What kind of health scare?"

"I found a lump in my breast," Rochelle said.

Aubrie was instantly concerned. "Why didn't you tell me?" she asked over the loud thumping rhythm of her heartbeat.

"Because I didn't want to burden you or Ryker until I was sure there was something to worry about," her mother responded. "Turns out it was nothing. Thank goodness."

"I'm glad to hear that." The knot in her stomach melted away and her heart stopped racing.

"I now have a real appreciation for each day I wake up," Rochelle said. "I don't intend to waste another moment on things that don't really matter."

"I'm glad you're cancer free, Mama. But you can't keep stuff like this from your children."

"I didn't tell your father either. There was no point in everyone walking around all worried—especially since it turned out to be nothing serious."

"What's going on with your breast?"

"I have a cyst and some calcification. Non-cancerous, but I must have another mammogram in six months."

"I'm glad your doctor is on top of this."

"Me, too." Changing the subject, Rochelle said, "I'm so glad all the anniversary events are done. I'm exhausted."

"Everything was really nice, Mama. You and Aunt Eleanor Louise should be proud."

"I meant to ask you about the young man who accompanied Phillip. How do you know him?"

"That was Terian. He and I attended culinary school together. His family owns LaCroix Restaurant."

"Oh, Margo and Terrance are his parents. I went to high school with his mother. It's a small world…"

"Yes, it is," Aubrie responded.

Too small.

Back at home, Aubrie did a couple of loads of laundry. She thought about her mother's health scare and was thankful it wasn't anything serious. She thought about how fragile life can be at times.

There wasn't time to waste by living in the past or postponing dreams. More than ever, Aubrie wanted to open her third restaurant on the island. She just had to make sure she out-bid any other offers on the Hibiscus property.

Images of how handsome Terian looked at the gala kept popping up in her mind. She never thought she'd find a beard so attractive on him. She was never a big fan of facial hair until now.

"I don't want to think about you," she uttered. Terian didn't even deserve to take up space in her mind.

She placed a Cornish hen in the air fryer basket. While it cooked, she decided on mushroom rice and broccoli to accompany the meat.

After she finished eating, Aubrie called to check on things at the restaurant, then cleaned the kitchen.

She spent the rest of the evening watching television and reading. Tomorrow, she'd be back to working fifty-plus hours a week, so she fully intended to enjoy her brief reprieve.

CHAPTER FOUR

AUBRIE WAS AS dedicated to holding a grudge as she was to running the two restaurants.

He knew Aubrie might be vindictive enough to try and keep him from opening a restaurant on the island, but he wasn't ready to give up the idea just yet. Terian didn't doubt she could sabotage him because she had already established her brand in Charleston and surrounding areas, while his family business was in a financial crisis.

Shortly after he settled in bed, his cell phone rang.

"What's up, Torrie?"

"Daddy wants you to come home," she said. "I told him that you were still on vacation."

"Is that all you said?"

"I didn't mention anything else. How was the gala?"

"It was nice."

"Did you get a chance to speak to Aubrie?"

"I did briefly," Terian responded. "She basically told me to go home and that I didn't stand a chance opening a restaurant on the island. Torrie, she's related to the Rothchild family, as in Polk Rothchild—the ancestor the island is named after. I met some of the family at the gala—they're all very close. There's truth in what she said. Aubrie can block any property I attempt to buy."

"So, what is your plan now?"

"My plan?" he repeated.

"I know you, Terian. I know you're already thinking of a way to get what you want. You'll find a way to get around Aubrie."

"I don't know, but I'll figure something out."

"Terian, there's still a chance for you to come home and work things out with Dad."

"There's nothing to work out. He made me look like a fool in front of the contractors. The restaurant needs some repairs, and the appliances need to be updated. When I told Pop what I was doing—he didn't say a word. Then when the people show up—he tells them to leave. That he didn't authorize any work to be done. I've had it, Torrie. I told Pop that I quit and I meant it."

"Dad admitted he didn't handle things the right way."

"That may be what he told you, Torrie. The truth is that Pop's determined to have his own way, so that's why it's best for me to go off on my own. I'm not giving up on my dream this time."

"Then you shouldn't," she responded. "You know I'll support you in any way that I can."

"I appreciate you saying that. It means a lot to me."

After he hung up with his sister, Terian called his father.

"I hope you've had a chance to cool down some," Terrance said. "It's time for you to come home and get back to work."

"I quit, remember? Besides I'm on vacation."

"Son, it's time for you to grow up. Stop being so sensitive. Look, I apologize for the way I handled the situation, but you forced my hand."

"You don't have to worry about that anymore. I'm not coming back to the restaurant."

"Terian…"

"Pop, I need to go. I'd like to enjoy the rest of my vacation."

"This isn't over. We'll talk when you come home."

"Talk to you later," Terian said before ending the call.

He turned his attention back to his laptop and reviewed the information on the real estate website before pressing the Send button.

It was time for him to take a leap of faith.

TUESDAY AFTERNOON, Aubrie walked into the Polk Island Real Estate office with purpose. She felt good about this meeting. She was about to acquire her third restaurant. She was already playing around with what she would call it. At the moment, she was thinking of Manoir Rose.

She was directed to a conference room.

Elaine was already seated at the table when she entered.

Aubrie glanced around. "Is someone else joining us?" There were four bottles of water and notepads on the table.

"Yes. Molly should be arriving shortly. And—"

Before Elaine could finish, Terian walked in. He seemed as stunned to see her as Aubrie was to see him.

"What's going on?" they asked in unison.

"Molly will explain everything once she gets here."

Aubrie didn't have a clue what was happening, but she had a feeling she wasn't going to like it. She took a seat near the door, while Terian sat across from her. She couldn't believe Elaine would do something like this to catch her off guard.

She could feel the warmth of Terian's eyes on her, but she refused to look at him for any length of time. When she did spare him a glance—she made sure her expression was blank, lacking any emotion.

"I'm sorry I'm late," Molly Lawson said as she walked briskly into the conference room. "There was an accident on the bridge, which slowed traffic down a bit."

Elaine appeared to practically sag with relief. She was most likely glad to have the heat taken off her.

"It's great seeing you, Aubrie," Molly said. "And it's wonderful to meet you, Terian. I am familiar with your father. He's a fabulous chef. Please give him my regards. My late husband and I would always visit LaCroix whenever we were in New Orleans."

"I will," he responded, then said, "I must admit that I'm confused with what's going on right now."

"I'm sure you are," Molly said. "This concerns my building on Hibiscus—you both submitted offers to buy it. As I considered the offers, I got an idea I'd like to propose."

"And that is what?" Aubrie asked.

"What do you think about the two of you working together?"

Aubrie shifted in her chair. "Excuse me?" She couldn't have heard Molly correctly.

"It would be fabulous. Two renowned award-winning chefs working together…"

Aubrie caught herself before she uttered the words, *You've got to be kidding me!*

"Are you *serious*?" Terian said, echoing her thoughts.

"I actually think it's a great idea," Elaine interjected.

"At least give it some thought," Molly said. "I've lived on the island long enough to know that the residents and tourists alike don't want just another steakhouse, seafood or specialty restaurant." She paused a moment before saying, "Aubrie, I've heard you say this often. People want an experience when they dine out. They can eat food at home. That's a true statement."

Aubrie cleared her throat. "I'm sure Terian and I have very definite ideas…"

Smiling, Molly said, "I have faith that the two of you can find a way to marry those ideas to make this new venture one of a kind. Do you know why Larry and I were so successful? It's because we were a team. We started off as business partners and it turned into so much more."

Terian looked as shell-shocked as Aubrie felt. As far as she was concerned, Molly was still so grief-stricken over the loss of her husband that she wasn't thinking straight.

Surely, she didn't believe...

Regardless, there was no way she'd ever work with Terian.

TERIAN SAT IN DISBELIEF. His dream of his own restaurant was *this* close to becoming a reality. If he'd wanted a partner, he would've asked his sister. He wondered if Molly Lawson lacked faith in his and Aubrie's abilities to be successful in a solo venture on the island.

She lacks faith in me. Not Aubrie.

From what he'd read, Terian learned that Lawson Steakhouse had been a premier destination.

Their popularity grew out of the wine and new menu tasting events held several times a year. The food, with its innovative menu, gained rave reviews every year they had been open. The wine list was well curated and featured new wineries as well as those with a longstanding reputation for excellence. The restaurant had a Michelin Two Star rating and had won several awards before it closed.

"I'd like you both to think about what I've said." Molly rose to her feet. "I'm willing to accept an offer from the two of you as partners. If I don't hear from you within seventy-two hours, then I'll assume you decided to pass. I have a gut feeling about this. I've never been wrong about these kinds of things."

As soon as Molly left, Aubrie stood up. "I guess I'd better get back to Bleu. This was a complete waste of my time." She couldn't believe Molly would suggest something like this or that Elaine would go along with the idea.

"I really think you should consider her suggestion," Elaine said. "Both of you."

Aubrie glanced over at Terian. "Sorry, I'm not interested. There are other properties on the island I can purchase."

Elaine got up and walked over to Aubrie. "True, but not with the view of the ocean. You can't deny that the Hibiscus location is perfect."

"Not if I have to share it with Terian."

"I'll give you a call later." Aubrie left the conference room without looking back in his direction.

Elaine walked back to the table and sat down. "What exactly are your thoughts about a potential partnership?"

"It's not going to work," Terian responded. "You may have figured out that Aubrie and I have history. She isn't going to collaborate with me on anything."

"Sounds to me like you'd be willing to try."

"The idea is intriguing," he admitted. "But

I wanted to do this on my own. I didn't want to be accountable to anyone else. If I needed a partner, then I'd choose my sister."

"If you have to pass on this property, did you see anything else here on the island?"

"No. That was the perfect location…"

"Talk to Aubrie and see if you two can find a way to make this work for you both," Elaine suggested.

"You know Aubrie, so I'm sure you know how stubborn she can be," Terian said. "She isn't going to change her mind."

However, he wasn't ready to give up completely. Molly Lawson's idea was a good one. And if she was so intent on forcing a partnership upon him, then he'd just ask Torrie to be his partner.

He left the real estate office a short while later and headed to the hotel.

Inside his room, Terian sought refuge on the balcony to contemplate his next steps. It bothered him a little that Molly Lawson didn't think he could cut it on his own, but he'd prove her wrong.

Without Aubrie's help.

He made a phone call to his sister.

"Did you put in your offer?" Torrie asked as soon as she answered the phone.

"Hello to you, too," Terian responded. "I put in my offer."

"And?"

"What do you think about becoming my partner?"

"Partner?"

"Yeah. We can do this together."

"Terian, what's going on?" Torrie questioned after a moment. "You don't want a partner."

He told her about his meeting.

"I know you don't want to hear this, but partnering with Aubrie actually sounds like a great idea," Torrie said. "Think about it… You'd split the financials. You can do more with a partner than you'd be able to do on your own. That's if you can get Aubrie to agree."

"She won't."

"Talk to her about it."

"Just to have her say no to my face? She pretty much walked out of the meeting, saying she'd find another property. Aubrie isn't interested in working with me."

"Come up with a strong proposal. Make her *want* to team up with you."

Terian spent the rest of the evening trying to come up with a way to convince Aubrie to be his partner.

He knew the idea struck a painful chord with her. When they were in school, it was a shared dream. They'd planned to marry and open a restaurant together. Only he packed up and left school near the end of their senior year without a word to Aubrie.

It wasn't because he had a change of heart—it was because his father ordered him home to work under his tutelage. Ashamed and feeling like a failure, he walked away from their goals, dreams and their love.

How could he convince the woman he once abandoned physically and emotionally to trust him enough to be her business partner?

THE NEXT MORNING, Terian strode through the elaborate double doors of Manoir Bleu. He approached the Maître d's stand. "I'm here to see Aubrie."

"And you are…"

"Terian LaCroix."

"Please wait here."

Terian released a soft sigh of relief. At least she hadn't banned him from the restaurant. Not yet anyway.

He looked up to see Aubrie making her way toward him. She didn't look any happier to see him than she had the previous day. Terian felt increasingly uneasy under her scrutiny, but he had come all the way here and he couldn't turn back now.

"What are you doing here?" she asked. "I thought I'd made myself clear on where you stand with me."

Awkwardly, he cleared his throat. "Yes, you have, but I'd like a chance to speak with you privately. I'm not leaving until I do." Terian sent up a silent prayer that she wouldn't go as far as to have him thrown out.

There was a pensive shimmer in the shadow of her eyes, but after a moment, Aubrie relented. She gestured for him to follow her.

In the office, she strolled around her desk and sat down, arms folded across her chest. "Go ahead. *Talk*."

"I'm sorry, Aubrie. What I did to you in college was wrong. I never should've left the way I did. I should've trusted you enough to tell you what was going on with me. You probably won't believe it, but I felt terrible, and I've been trying to apologize to you ever since I saw you that first time in New Orleans."

Aubrie's face clouded with anger. "You left me to handle our senior project alone. I almost didn't get it done in time, Terian. But the worst of it is that you just up and left France— no goodbye…nothing. I didn't deserve to be treated that way."

Terian felt horrible. "You're right and I'm so sorry about all that. There was so much pressure on me back then to be the best in my class. My dad attended the same culinary school and was the top student. Five years later, he left France and returned to New Orleans to open his own restaurant. He expected no less of me. I wasn't like him though. Aubrie, you were arguably the best in our class… I felt like I was letting my dad down. I didn't want to disappoint him… He thought it was better for me to withdraw and come home instead of barely making it through to the end."

"You worked hard, Terian. Your grades were improving. I never understood why you didn't have enough faith in yourself."

"You have no idea what it was like to be Chef Terrance LaCroix's son."

"You're right. I don't. When you left, I realized that I never really knew you."

Seeing the hurt etched in her expression, Terian felt the full weight of what he'd done to Aubrie for the first time. Even if she accepted his apology—it would not be enough.

AUBRIE TRIED TO project an ease she didn't feel in Terian's presence. She just sat there, her eyes trained on him, watching him warily. Her hands, hidden from sight, twisted nervously in her lap. There was a time when she believed his word, trusted Terian completely. In this very moment, he seemed contrite and sincere, but did she dare believe him?

However, she couldn't ignore the glimpses of the man she used to know and love. Aubrie was suddenly tired of being angry with Terian. She believed that he spoke the truth. She read the regret etched in his eyes and sensed his disquiet. The pained expression on his face was genuine.

"I accept your apology," Aubrie said after a moment. "After the meeting yesterday, I'm sure apologizing isn't the sole reason behind your visit. Why don't you tell me why you're really here?"

"I thought about what Molly Lawson said, and I realized that she may be on to something. I also realize that I don't really stand a chance on Polk Island. *Without you*. Aubrie, I'm proposing a partnership. You and I both really want that building, so we should open the restaurant on the island as partners."

She met his idea with heavy silence. They weren't anywhere close to being able to work together. Chewing on her lower lip, Aubrie stole a look at him.

After a long pause, she said, "I accepted your apology, Terian, but I'm not interested in partnering with you. Thank you for your visit, but I really need to get back to work."

"You're not going to hear me out?"

"I've listened to everything you've said so far," she countered. "But you and I can't work together because I don't trust you."

"I'm not that same person you used to know. Just let me prove it to you."

She shook her head no.

He stood up and said, "I didn't want to hurt you."

"But you did."

"Aubrie, I need this restaurant. If it means partnering with you—I'm willing to do it. I *need* your help."

"I'm sorry."

"Would you at least look at this proposal?" Terian placed a copy in front of her. "Read it and see if you still feel the same way when you're done."

Aubrie was secure in the knowledge that she was one of the top chefs in the country, but Terian was a phenomenal chef as well—he just didn't seem to know it. She couldn't deny that together, the two of them could do great things. But outside of trust issues, a partnership between them still wouldn't work because their goals were different. He relished being the best, while Aubrie focused on the pleasure her meals brought to others. Her entrées were inspired by the romantic ambience in Paris and New Orleans, marriage proposals, wedding celebrations, anniversaries and date nights.

To get him out of her restaurant, she said, "Leave it with me. However, I'm not going to change my mind, Terian. I'll never work with you."

"After you read it, I believe you'll feel differently."

"Don't count on it," Aubrie warned him.

Terian slowed his steps as he neared the door. He paused in the doorway to say, "This is a nice restaurant. You've done well for yourself."

"Thank you."

"I've always wondered why you chose to open your first restaurant in New Orleans two blocks away from ours. I thought it was because you wanted me to watch you soar. Your star shines so brightly in my hometown—the very place I wanted to be top chef."

"You haven't changed much."

"Why do you say that?"

"You still think that everything is about *you*. My choosing to open Manoir Rouge in New Orleans had everything to do with *my* family. I guess you've forgotten that my roots run as deeply as yours in that city."

"Still… I'm sure it gave you some satisfaction to see my restaurant decline as yours rose to fame."

"Terian, do me a favor and stop measuring me by your standards or your level of *petty*. Now I really need to get back to work."

"I hope to hear from you soon."

"Don't hold your breath," she muttered after he left.

Aubrie couldn't believe Terian's audacity in suggesting a partnership. She'd meant it when she offered her forgiveness, but that didn't mean they were ever going to be friends. He was just a defining moment in her past.

Now she had to keep moving toward her future. A future that would never include Terian.

CHAPTER FIVE

TERIAN WAS TAKEN aback by Aubrie's rejection. He really didn't expect her to turn down what he believed was a solid plan, which could greatly benefit them both. It was clear that she was reacting with emotion and not a business sense. He hoped once she read the proposal, she would indeed change her mind.

If she didn't... I don't know what path to take next, especially if Molly Lawson is committed to having us work together. She couldn't force them to become partners, but she also didn't have to sell her property to either of them.

He could always eat crow and go back home to work in the family restaurant, but it would be stifling and frustrating for him. He and his father didn't agree on anything concerning the business.

I need something of my own. It's always been my dream. It also bothered him that *Aubrie was already two restaurants ahead.* It gnawed at him that he'd allowed his father to convince him to leave an executive chef position at a Michelin

Three Star restaurant in Beverly Hills three years ago to return home. But then, Terrance hadn't been happy when he'd announced he'd landed the position. He stayed home a short while after leaving school, but Terian had something to prove to himself.

He'd won several prestigious awards and his career was soaring. Then Terrance called with promises of giving Terian more responsibilities and complete run of the kitchen at LaCroix.

He shook away that last thought. This wasn't a competition between him and Aubrie. He wasn't going back down that road. He wanted to repair what was broken between them. He wanted that just as much as the restaurant.

Terian held on to his belief that she would come around after reading the proposal. He wouldn't allow himself to think any other way. He'd spent enough time living his life according to his father's dream and he'd paid a high price. Now he was determined to do things his way. It was the only path to true happiness and maybe even love.

Love might be too much to hope for, Terian decided.

He drove across the bridge that separated Charleston from Polk Island.

Beds of bright, colorful flowers adorned both

sides of the road and welcomed him back onto the island.

He headed into the parking lot of the hotel and pulled into an empty space. When he got out, he went straight to his room, but he didn't intend on staying inside. He was going to the beach. It was a much better way to pass the time than sitting inside his room waiting for the phone to ring for a call that might never come.

He chased away the disturbing thought.

AUBRIE STILL COULDN'T understand how Terian could actually believe that she'd consider taking him up on his proposal. There was just no way...

Shortly after twelve, she took a break and walked to Michelle's shop, which was in the next block. "You won't believe who showed up at the restaurant," Aubrie said when she entered the shop.

Without looking up from her work, Michelle responded, "Terian LaCroix."

Aubrie's eyebrows rose in surprise. "How did you know that?"

"I was across the street at Starbucks earlier, and I saw him walking across the parking lot. Now, you know I don't miss nothing. I figured I'd either get a phone call or a visit."

Aubrie chuckled. "All right, Detective Chapman."

"So, what did he want?" Michelle asked.

"He apologized for what happened. I could tell he was sincere, but I knew he had another reason for coming."

"Girl, say *no*."

Aubrie frowned. "Terian wants to be my business partner."

Michelle's eyebrows rose in surprise. "Huh? Oh, I thought he wanted to get back with you."

"He proposed that we do as Molly Lawson suggested and open a restaurant together. Can you believe that?"

"Yeah, I can actually see that. When you told me about the meeting last night, I said that it sounded like a good idea."

"I ignored you then and I'm ignoring you now."

"Think about it, Aubrie… You and Terian are two of the best chefs in the country. I remember you telling me how well he was doing in California. Think about the publicity alone."

"Michelle, I don't think I could ever trust him."

"You wouldn't be his competition. You'd be on the same team."

"He left a proposal with me, but I haven't looked at it."

"I think you should. You've always said that he's a great chef."

"He is," Aubrie said. "I can't take that away from him. It just makes me wonder why he isn't doing more for his family's restaurant. It shouldn't be struggling to stay afloat." She heard all the rumors whenever she traveled to New Orleans.

"All I know is if you and Terian team up— it would be like two superheroes coming together to fight evildoers," Michelle stated with a chuckle.

A mental picture of her and Terian in capes and tights prompted laughter from Aubrie. "I just had a visual pop into my mind."

"At least read the proposal."

"I'll think about it, Michelle. I honestly don't see how I could ever work with the man."

"You're a smart businesswoman, Aubrie. I know you'll make the right decision."

"Enough about that. Do you have any plans this weekend?"

"I'll be home. What's up?" Michelle asked.

"I was thinking about going to that new art gallery on Elliott. They're hosting a VIP reception on Sunday afternoon. The owner sent me a couple of tickets."

"I'll go with you."

Aubrie looked at the clock. "I need to get back to Bleu. I'll give you a call later."

As she walked back to the restaurant, she debated whether to read Terian's proposal. Aubrie didn't see the point in doing so since she'd already turned him down. It would be a complete waste of time. There was a tiny part of her that was curious, but not enough for her to act on it.

Maybe when he didn't hear from her…Terian would move on. And Aubrie hoped he'd do it as far away from Polk Island and Charleston as possible.

TERIAN COULDN'T AFFORD to just walk away empty-handed, so he returned the next day to see Aubrie.

"What are you doing back here?" she asked. "I already told you I wasn't interested in working with you. Your showing up here isn't going to make me change my mind."

"I had a feeling I'd never hear from you," he responded. "That's why I came back. Have you had a chance to look at the proposal?"

"No, I've been busy."

Terian sat down in the empty chair facing her desk. "Aubrie, please don't do this. I've come to you for help. You can't imagine how I feel— this isn't easy for me to be here, but this is my life…"

It was something in his voice that made her ask, "What's going on with you?"

"I need to make something happen for myself," Terian responded. "Someplace new, where I can rebuild my reputation. My dad... he's not interested in handing over the reins. Not anytime soon. As long as I stay there, I'm nothing more than a sous-chef."

"You're much more than that, but I'd like to know why here? Why Polk Island?"

"Because of its popularity. I didn't know your connection to it."

Aubrie looked as if she didn't really believe him. "You knew I lived in Charleston though. Why not choose Los Angeles or Dallas or even Atlanta?"

"There wouldn't be as much competition on a small island."

Aubrie nodded in understanding. "I suppose that makes sense... But I don't trust you. Without trust...there's nothing."

"You did have trust in me once and I'm asking for a chance to earn it back."

She picked up the proposal and skimmed through it. She then reviewed it with more interest.

"I'm impressed," Aubrie murmured. "When did you come up with this?"

"After the meeting."

Terian remained silent as she continued to read. He prayed that she'd be open to becoming his partner once she understood exactly what he was proposing.

When she finished, Aubrie looked at him. "You've really put a lot of thought into this, I see."

"To be honest, I've thought about us working together many times over the years—I never believed it would happen though. You're not only the best chef I know—you're also a successful businesswoman." He pointed to the framed degrees from University of Charleston on her wall. "Those degrees in business management and finance confirm that you're the right partner for me as far as I'm concerned."

She seemed to be studying him. Terian hoped that what she saw was his determination, his drive and ambition. For the first time in a long while, he felt centered, focused and goal oriented. There was a time when she admitted to admiring those qualities about him, but that was years ago. He needed to make her believe in him again. To remind her that he was hardworking and willing to give his all for this new venture.

"This proposal is solid, Terian, but as I've sa—"

He cut her off. "I know you don't trust me,

Aubrie. Still, I'm asking you to give me a chance. You and I talked about co-owning a restaurant when we were in school. I never let go of that dream. You want the building on Hibiscus and so do I. It's the best location on all of the island. Molly is willing to sell the place to *us*. Do you really want to let it go to someone else because of your pride?"

"Knowing Molly...she'd hold on to it until she gets what she wants," Aubrie said. "I have to think about it. Put your number on the proposal, and I'll give you a call to let you know my decision."

Terian wasn't sure he'd really hear from her. That must have registered on his face because she said, "You'll hear from me either way."

He smiled. "I look forward to speaking to you."

"Terian...don't come back here tomorrow or the next day. Once I've made my choice—you'll be the first to know."

Aubrie sat on the sofa and read through the proposal once more. She spent a couple of hours mentally weighing the pros and cons of working with Terian.

The idea just seemed ludicrous, but strangely enough...it was one that could work. Surprisingly, they had the same goals for the restaurant, and as partners they could accomplish so much more. There were times when two heads were better than one. Together, they had more capital available. The island didn't have a high-end restaurant. The steakhouse was very successful, but when Molly's husband unexpectedly passed away, she decided to close the business.

Like her, Terian wanted to bring the authentic flavors of France and New Orleans to the island. Her mind was already birthing ideas on ways to set this restaurant apart from her other two, which served mostly Creole and American dishes.

But Aubrie couldn't base her decision only on business—she had to consider her personal feelings about Terian. He'd broken her heart in the past, so she had some trust issues. Aubrie had yet to decide if it was more that she didn't trust him or if she didn't trust herself around Terian.

She had loved him with her entire being once. Was she afraid that she'd fall under his spell once again? It was a question Aubrie didn't want to answer. Was it the reason why she'd sabotaged his prior attempts to explain what happened? Why she'd held onto her anger for so long?

She wasn't sure she could work so closely with Terian and not be affected in some way.

But she'd never been one to shy away from a good business idea. There was a small part of her that was thrilled he'd finally stepped out on his own. He'd made a name for himself and built a solid reputation in Beverly Hills, then stepped away from it all—it seemed a repeat of his actions in culinary school.

In that moment, she was struck with the idea. The only way she'd be comfortable working with Terian was to add a failsafe—a clause giving her complete ownership if the business relationship became problematic.

As Aubrie reached for the phone, she shook her head. "I can't believe what I'm about to do..."

When he answered, she said, "Hey...can you meet me in about an hour?"

"Sure."

"I'll text you the address."

Aubrie glanced down at the baggy sweatpants and tank top she was wearing. Her hair was pulled up in a ponytail, a sloppy one.

Maybe I should change clothes or at least comb my hair.

She dismissed the thought as quickly as it had come. *Why am I worried about what he's going to think?* This was part of her normal wardrobe whenever she was lounging at home.

Aubrie purposely didn't tell Terian which

way she was leaning. She wasn't going to make it that easy for him.

This was strictly a business decision for her. Nothing more.

TERIAN SAT IN the rental car parked at the curb and stared at the three-story drive under house, with a two-car garage. It was a nice place, painted a sage green with a dark green trim. A large dogwood tree in the front yard signaled the start of spring with a wave of bright pink blooms in unbelievable color variations against the vibrant greenery.

"Aubrie, you've done quite well for yourself," he whispered.

Terian got out and walked up the front steps.

She opened the door seconds after he knocked.

"C'mon in," Aubrie said.

He was greeted by a well-appointed formal dining room and living room. Terian caught a glimpse of the large gourmet kitchen with quartz countertops.

"Your home is beautiful."

"Thank you," she said. "I've only been in here six months. The downstairs, my bedroom and the loft are all furnished but the other three bedrooms are empty."

He sat down on the sofa. "I've been in my

place for almost two years, and I still have rooms that need furniture and decorating."

She awarded him a brief smile before taking a seat on the other end as if she were afraid to get too close.

"Like I mentioned on the phone… I read your proposal. It's very well thought out. I really think the fusion of our styles will offer customers a unique dining experience."

"And?"

"It's a viable business plan," Aubrie stated. "And you've come up with some great marketing ideas for the restaurant. Terian, my only concern is working with *you*."

"I'm not the same person I used to be, Aubrie. And this works both ways. I must trust you, too."

"I've never done anything to betray your trust."

"I'm not questioning if I can trust you, but it's still a risk that you might use this as a way to get even with me."

"I believe what goes around comes around, Terian. I'd rather use my energy on important things than waste it by thinking of ways to get revenge."

"I promise I won't let you down, Aubrie. We were a great team in school and I'm sure we can be a great one now."

"I can't believe I'm saying this, but I'm willing to do this with the understanding that if this doesn't work out—I'll buy you out."

"You mean you'll take my restaurant from me."

"It will be *our* restaurant, Terian. If I see that we don't work well together, then one of us will have to leave. I'm betting that you don't have the money to buy me out, so the only other option will be to sell or I buy you out."

He hadn't considered that they wouldn't be able to work together. No point in starting now. "Okay, I'll agree to that."

Terian could tell by the stunned expression on her face that Aubrie hadn't expected him to accept her terms. He hoped it was nothing more than a bluff, but even if it wasn't, Terian really couldn't afford to turn her down.

"Are you sure about this?" she asked.

"Yes," he responded. "I don't think it'll come to you buying me out."

"I'll have the partnership contract drawn up."

He nodded. "Aubrie, you won't be disappointed."

"Only time will tell," she responded.

Terian stared down at the polished hardwood floors.

Eyeing him, Aubrie said, "Why don't you take a couple of days to think this over?"

"I don't need to," he said. "We're both super passionate about food, perfection and running a high-end establishment. That's why we'll make a good team. We'll be equal partners. Because of your business acumen, I think you should be a managing partner. I'm more suited to be a Head or Executive Chef. I'll manage all aspects of the kitchen while you take on the business administration. Especially since you have two other restaurants to run."

"I'm fine with that," Aubrie responded. "As long as you remember this is going to be *our* restaurant. Not yours or mine. I also want equal creative input as well. I'd like to help shape the theme, decor and menu items."

"That's not a problem. I agree that it's ours," he said with a grin. "Hey, just got another idea. How about we promote duo chef events at least twice a year, like Molly suggested? We can come up with a special menu. During those times, I'll work on desserts while you focus on the main dishes."

She smiled. "I love that idea. We could even do it for the grand opening."

"I was thinking we'd do something like a fifteen- or sixteen-course meal," Terian said. "Have a traditional French dinner."

"Ooooh, that would be nice," Aubrie murmured.

"We could have the servers dressed in tuxedos…first class all the way."

"I'm not sure working in a tux will be comfortable. Maybe just the pants and a tuxedo shirt or vest."

"I really like the idea of a tuxedo," he responded, lifting his chin a notch.

"It would be too much."

There was an air of defiance in her tone, but Terian decided to let the matter drop for now, especially since there wasn't any tension circling around them like before. He took this as a good sign. He was happy and relieved that she'd agreed to be his partner. Now that Aubrie was back in his life—he wasn't going to lose her a second time. Terian allowed himself to entertain the idea that given an opportunity, he could possibly win her heart once again.

ROCHELLE DUGRANDPRE WAS in New Orleans for the funeral service of a friend who'd succumbed to lung cancer. The service was a celebration of the woman's life and accomplishments. The sanctuary was filled with mourners and there didn't seem to be any dry faces in the congregation. Rochelle was overcome with grief and other emotions as she thought about her recent health scare and what could have been.

After the service, she made her way out of

the church along with the other people in attendance. The church was packed—Nancy was well-known and loved by many.

"Rochelle…"

She turned around when she heard someone call out her name. "Margo…hey, beautiful."

The two women embraced.

"How are you?" Rochelle asked.

She and Margo LaCroix used to be close when they were in high school, but they grew apart when Margo began dating Terrance.

"I'm good. And you?"

Rochelle's eyes filled with tears. "Right now, I'm in disbelief. I can't believe Nancy is gone. I had no idea she was sick. She never told me."

"She didn't want to tell a lot of people," Margo said. "You know how private Nancy was. I knew only because I ran into her at the hospital a few weeks before she died."

Rochelle nodded. "She was that. I'm really going to miss her."

"Me, too," Margo responded.

They walked outside together.

"You and Jacques must be so proud of Aubrie. The restaurants are doing great."

Rochelle smiled. "It's definitely her calling. Speaking of children, I saw Terian. I hadn't seen him since he was a teenager playing football."

Margo looked surprised. "Where?"

"He came with Phillip to our sixtieth anniversary gala."

"In South Carolina?"

Rochelle nodded. "I take it that you didn't know he was there."

"I had no idea," Margo replied. "I knew he was on vacation, but Terian didn't tell us where he was going. He and Terrance had a falling-out before he left. I'm just hoping they can sort everything out when he returns."

"They will," Rochelle assured her. "I've had a few tiffs with Aubrie and Ryker, but things eventually worked themselves out."

"How did you accomplish that?"

"Margo, to be honest, I had to learn to stay in my lane. My children prefer to solve their own problems without interference from me or their father."

"My daughter's like that. Torrie tells me all the time that she'll ask for my help if she needs it."

"A polite way to say mind your business," Rochelle said with a chuckle. She pulled out her car keys.

"Are you going to the repast?" Margo asked.

She shook her head. "I don't think so."

"How about we go somewhere and catch up?"

Rochelle smiled. "I'd like that. You and I haven't hung out in a while. We're overdue."

"We have to do better about staying in touch."

She rode with Margo to a nearby restaurant. Inside, they were seated within ten minutes.

"I had my own health crisis," Margo announced. "I was having terrible migraines. I was scared that I had a tumor or something. Turns out I had to stop with the caffeine, alcohol and skipping meals. I was trying to lose weight."

"I understand," Rochelle said. "I found out I have a cyst and calcification in my breast. Like you, I was scared. I thought it was cancer. That and losing Nancy… I look at life differently. I'm more intentional about enjoying what time I have left."

"I'm with you on that."

When the server came, they ordered their meals.

"How is Terrance doing?" Rochelle inquired.

"He's good. Just having a hard time with letting go of his control. Terian has some good ideas, but Terrance won't give him a chance. Those two are butting heads like nobody's business. I keep telling him that he's gonna run Terian off like he did before."

"They just have to find a way to communicate and work together." Rochelle took a sip of her iced water.

"My husband needs to recognize that there's more than one way to do something," Margo uttered. "I love Terrance but there are times I want to chew him up and spit him out."

Rochelle laughed. "I haven't heard that phrase in a long time. It's good to be home."

An hour later, Margo dropped her off at her car.

"I enjoyed lunch with you, Rochelle. You have my number so let's keep in touch."

"I will," she said. "I've missed our friend-ship."

Rochelle was glad to have Margo back in her life. Over the years, she'd lost several friends. She didn't want to waste another precious moment losing touch with the friends she had left.

CHAPTER SIX

SO MUCH FOR this being a simple business partnership. It frustrated Aubrie that seven years later, she still got weak at the knees around Terian; that his beautiful smile had her spellbound, and the smooth Southern charm he possessed still sent spirals of nervous energy in her belly. Until recently, she'd been too blinded by her anger to notice the effect Terian had on her.

The tingling in the pit of her stomach prompted Aubrie to doubt her decision to partner with him. She couldn't afford to lose control over her emotions. She'd worked too hard to bury them down deep. Deep enough that they'd never resurface. But it didn't take long for her heart to jolt and her pulse to pound whenever Terian came around.

I can do this. I can work with him. I just have to remain focused and not let him become a distraction. I won't let him.

Aubrie stretched out on her sofa, plopped a pillow under her head and closed her eyes. She wanted to get in a quick nap before she had to leave for the restaurant.

Her phone began vibrating.

Aubrie groaned as she sat up to check the caller ID.

She decided to let the call go to voice mail after seeing that it wasn't anyone she needed to talk to right away.

She lay back down.

Terian entered her mind just before the edges of sleep could snatch her away. He was staring at her with those beautiful hazel eyes and that gorgeous smile.

Why did he have to be so handsome?

Unfortunately, thoughts of Terian left her struggling to fall asleep and she finally gave up. Aubrie sat up and turned to the food channel.

She sat there looking at the television while she assessed each of his qualities in her mind. The idea of working with Terian no longer brought her unease—her previous reservations seemed to dissipate into nothingness.

This restaurant was a dream come true for Terian. He wouldn't risk losing it to her—that much Aubrie knew to be true. He was never going to let that happen because in his mind, that would mean she'd won.

Terian wanted to be the best in all areas of his life. Losing to Aubrie was not an option.

MIDWEEK, AUBRIE WELCOMED Terian into her office. "Thanks for coming by. We need to fill out some additional forms for the loan officer."

"No problem," he responded. "I'm happy to do whatever it takes to make this happen."

"I have to say I love your enthusiasm. As we get closer to the closing, I get more excited about our venture. I really believe it's going to be great."

"It is," Terian said. "I don't know about you, but I have so many ideas for our restaurant. And the menu... I don't know how we're going to narrow down our offerings."

She chuckled. "That was my problem when I opened Rouge. I wanted to cook everything."

"How did you select what you'd serve?" Terian signed off on the second sheet and passed it to Aubrie for her signature.

"I chose items I felt complemented each other and were favorites for romance, holidays and other special moments."

"I like that."

"I know that you wanted to serve gumbo, but I don't think it's special enough for what we're envisioning for the restaurant."

Terian settled back in the chair and asked, "So what do you suggest?"

"Why not tell our story?" Aubrie responded.

"People will wonder how we became partners—let's tell them through the foods we serve."

"I actually like that idea."

She smiled. "I thought you might."

"We seem to be getting along… Are you still worried about things becoming complicated between us?"

She shrugged. "We haven't closed on the property yet. I want to see how things go when we begin the real work."

"I have faith in us," he said.

I used to believe in us. Then you walked out of my life.

This time she was prepared if Terian did one of his disappearing acts. Aubrie had money in reserve to buy him out and take complete ownership of the restaurant.

"DAD WANTS A face-to-face," Torrie stated when Terian called her later that evening. "He really believes he can convince you to come back to work. I have to tell you that I don't like being in the middle."

He heard the frustration in her voice. "I'll fly home next weekend, Torrie. But to be honest, I'm in no real hurry to see him. I'm sure Pop's just going to threaten to disown me again. He'll tell me how striking out on my own isn't going to work, like he did when I was in California.

I'll fail…blah…blah…blah. Then he'll make promises that he has no intention of keeping. He knows how much LaCroix means to me. I promised Granddad that I would carry on our legacy. You know how he's always dreamed of six or more generations running the restaurant."

"It's all Granddad used to talk about," Torrie responded. "As for Dad…you know how he is. I can't figure out why you let him get to you like that. I told you back then to stay on the West Coast, but you wouldn't listen to me."

"I hated disappointing him. But mostly I wanted to make the LaCroix name bigger and better. Besides, Pop never believed I could make it without him despite my success in Los Angeles. There's no turning back for me this time. I intend to show him I can run a restaurant my way."

"I'll let you argue with our father about that," Torrie stated. "He's been real contrary lately."

"What's going on with him?" Terian questioned.

"I don't know. I just hope he'll get over it soon."

"Me, too."

"How are things going with the restaurant?"

"Better than I could've ever hoped," he responded. "Aubrie really knows her stuff when it comes to fine dining."

"So do you."

"Not really," Terian said. "That's what Pop wanted for ours, but we never got there—mainly because he refused to do any of the renovations I told him were needed or be more innovative. He didn't want to hire the additional staff or pay any real money. He just wants to blame Aubrie for our decline in popularity, but he's wrong."

"You have real feelings for her."

It was a statement, not a question.

Torrie knew him well.

"At the risk of sounding like a cliché—she's the one who got away."

"After all this time… I knew it was someone— the reason why you could never fully commit to anyone. Terian, why didn't you ever tell me?"

"I was going to right after graduation, but then things took a bad turn and I dropped out…" Terian paused a moment, then said, "I couldn't talk about it after that."

"Fix whatever you broke, dear brother."

"I'm trying," he said.

"You and Dad really need to talk. You need to tell him how you feel about his resistance to change and your need to have your own place."

"We will. Just not sure how much good it will do. Pop will never change."

"Remember how he couldn't stand Luke when

we first started dating. Now they're like best friends."

"Your relationship with Pop is different from mine," Terian stated. "He doesn't expect you to be like him—it's my job alone."

"You have a choice in this, brother."

"I've already made it. That's why I'm staying here in South Carolina."

"But you need to tell Dad," Torrie said.

"Next weekend…"

Terian's conversation with his sister stayed with him for the rest of the day.

He didn't become a chef because his father demanded it of him—it was of his own desire. Terian recalled the joy he felt cooking with his father and grandfather. He relished the times spent with his grandmother picking apples, pears, lemons and limes from the small grove of fruit trees his grandparents had planted on their property. He learned at a young age how to make homemade preserves and pies. He and Torrie would argue over who could bake the best apple pie and make the best lemonade. Although he'd never admit it to his sister—she won, hands down. His was good, but there was just something about Torrie's pie that made it better. She once told him that her secret ingredient was love. While he focused on winning—she didn't care about that. Torrie would say that her joy came from watching others find pleasure in her cooking.

She sounded just like Aubrie now that he thought about it. Those two would really get along great if given the chance.

AUBRIE SWITCHED HER television to the food channel. Even as a child, she loved watching cooking shows. For her sixteenth birthday, she asked for her own set of cookware. Having earned her first Michelin Star for Manoir Rouge plus numerous accolades, she wasn't focused so much on earning distinctions—they were important to her brand, but so were her customers being pleased with her food and their overall experience in her restaurants.

She picked up her cell phone to check her calendar and review her schedule for the weekend. Aubrie had almost forgotten she'd promised Michelle that she'd work the volunteer booth at the race for breast cancer on Saturday morning. She would leave there and go straight to the restaurant. On Sunday evening, they had tickets to attend a reception at the art gallery.

Helping out the cancer foundation took on a special meaning to her after her mother's scare.

Thirty minutes later, she left her home for the gym. She ran into her cousin Jordin coming out of her husband's office.

"Hey… I didn't expect to see you."

"I came by to drop off some stuff for Ethan," Jordin said. "I need to get back into my exercise routine, but I have a high-profile litigation case right now. I'm really hoping we can reach a settlement soon."

"Good luck with your case. I must tell you that I do miss my workout buddy."

"I'll be back soon." Jordin gestured toward the juice bar. "Do you have a few minutes to get something to drink?"

"Sure."

"Ethan's been raving about the cherry vanilla almond milk with honey. He drinks it after his yoga class."

"I love the citrus carrot juice with passion fruit," Aubrie said.

They ordered their juice drinks.

"How is the new restaurant coming along?" Jordin inquired.

"Things are going well," she replied. "Terian and I are very excited about this new venture and especially about it being on the island." She'd confided her decision to take on a partner to her cousin and made Jordin promise to keep it a secret for now.

"The restaurant is going to do well over there."

"I don't know why I didn't think of opening

one on the island years ago." Aubrie shook her head. "Maybe because the steakhouse was there."

Jordin took a sip of her juice. "It did really well. Do you have any idea why it closed?"

"Molly's husband died," she responded. "Molly decided to close the restaurant and move to Texas to be with her daughter. Last time I spoke with her, they were thinking of opening a place in Houston."

"I have to say that I'm surprised you decided to partner with someone this time," Jordin said. "You already have two very successful restaurants."

"It was actually at Molly's suggestion that Terian and I decided to do this venture together."

"Well, I'm excited for you."

Aubrie stole a peek at the huge clock on the wall. "No point in putting this off any longer. I need to put in my time on the elliptical and weight training."

She got off the stool and grabbed her tote. "It's good seeing you, cousin."

"You, too."

Before she headed to the equipment, Aubrie stopped by Ethan's office to say hello.

"I saw you and my wife at the juice bar. You two looked deep in conversation, so I decided not to disturb you," Ethan said. "Oh, before I forget…we have some new boot camp classes coming next month."

"I'll grab a schedule," Aubrie replied.

They talked a few minutes more, then, after securing her tote in a locker, she made her way to the area where the equipment was set up.

She put her towel and bottled water down and began performing a series of stretches.

Thoughts of Terian attempted to invade her mind, but she fought them off. For the next hour, she centered her mind on peaceful and serene images while working out.

She showered and changed into a dress and sandals, then drove to Manoir Bleu, smiling the entire drive there.

She loved her job.

CHAPTER SEVEN

On Saturday morning, Aubrie and Michelle stood side by side as they checked in the volunteers for the event. Since learning about her mother's health scare, Aubrie vowed to be more proactive in volunteering. She seized her first opportunity for sponsorship when the original caterer had to back out suddenly.

"They got Manoir Bleu all over the place," Michelle noted aloud. "That's great. You're providing all the food for the volunteers, the media and organizers. Next year, you might be the titled sponsor."

"I don't know about that."

"Please…this food isn't cheap. They're getting a lot having you as a sponsor."

"I'm happy to help in any way I can."

Their conversation came to a halt when another group of volunteers gathered around the booth to get their assignments.

Aubrie glanced upward. It was a perfect day for the race. Not a cloud in the sky. She'd always considered entering an event like this, but there didn't seem to be enough time to train for a 5K with all her other responsibilities.

She glanced over at the signage displaying her restaurant logo and smiled. She was very excited about this sponsorship opportunity and did plan to take Michelle's advice and put in a bid for event caterer for the next one.

Smiling, Aubrie handed a tote bag to a volunteer. "Everything you need is in there."

"We have a nice turnout for the event," Michelle said. "I think there are more people here this year than the last two."

"That's great," she responded. "It's growing in popularity."

Michelle pointed toward the entrance. "You might need to check for a tracking device."

"Huh…" Aubrie glanced in the direction in which she was pointing. "What is he doing here?" she asked, spacing the words evenly.

Michelle gave a slight shrug. "Must be looking for you."

"I don't think so. Terian's dressed like a runner."

"Girl, he might be trying to fit in."

"I'd like to know how he knew I'd be here."

"Ask him," Michelle said. "I'll do it if you want."

"No, I got this." Even though they were now business partners, she didn't want Terian just popping up on her. Aubrie wasn't ready to change her mind about him. He still had much to prove to her.

TERIAN REVIEWED THE map for the 5K race. This was his fourth, and the first without his sister. He hoped to do the 10K race next year.

While he walked, Terian finished off a bottle of water.

He couldn't believe his eyes when he spotted Aubrie at the volunteer booth.

"I didn't expect to see you," she blurted when he strode up to her. "Why are you here?"

Terian thought he glimpsed a bit of agitation in her eyes. Surely, Aubrie didn't assume he'd come because of her. The idea almost brought a smile to his lips.

"I'm here to run," he responded. "My grandmother lost her battle with breast cancer. I'm here for her."

It was then that she seemed to notice he was wearing a photo pin.

Aubrie peered closer. "Is that your grandmother?"

"Yes."

"She was a beautiful woman."

"Inside and out," he responded.

"I think it's a wonderful way to honor her," Aubrie said. "Do you know where you're going?"

He smiled. "Actually, no."

"There's a booth right across from the juice bar. That's where you check in."

"Thanks for your help," he told her.

He left Aubrie to pick up his race bib, timing chip and swag bag.

Terian did a warm-up to raise his heart rate and to get his muscles ready to go. He noticed a nearby sign. Manoir Bleu was a sponsor of the event.

Next year, their restaurant would also be a sponsor, he decided. Only it would be a titled sponsorship and he planned to also put in a bid to provide food.

It was time for them to line up.

Terian had no idea that Aubrie would be here, but he wasn't disappointed. Everything took on a clean brightness whenever she was around.

There was still a gulf between them, but it was getting smaller—at least he hoped this to be true. The more they spent time together, the clearer it would become to Aubrie that he'd changed. He hadn't always been patient, but he couldn't afford to be anything but when it came to her.

AUBRIE WATCHED TERIAN walk away.

When she turned around, she found Michelle standing there with a huge grin on her face.

"Don't even say it. I already know what you're thinking."

"That man is some kinda fine."

She sent a sharp glare in her friend's direction. "What did I just tell you?"

Michelle picked up a bottle of water and took a sip. She swallowed, then said, "Now, you know I tell the truth as I see it."

Aubrie exited the booth. "I'm going to check on lunch for the volunteers. I want to make sure my staff brought everything. If not, they'll have to go back to Bleu to get it." It was still early, so they had time to do damage control if any issues came up. Aubrie never liked waiting to the last minute.

"We sure appreciate the box lunches. I wasn't crazy about having cold pizza. That's what we had last year."

"It's the least I can do," she responded. "By the way, nice job on the tee shirts for the volunteers."

Michelle broke into a grin. "Thank you, girl. The committee told me that they're thinking of special shirts for the participants next year."

"That's wonderful," Aubrie said.

She left the booth to help when her staff arrived with the food.

Aubrie wondered briefly how Terian was

doing. After the volunteers were fed, she could leave the booth and catch the last of the race.

He's my partner, so I have to cheer him on.

At least that's what she told herself. Aubrie wasn't sure that was the only reason she wanted to see Terian run, but no way was she going to explore the impulse further.

CHAPTER EIGHT

MONDAY MORNING, Aubrie turned off the alarm inside the restaurant.

She walked briskly toward her office, her heart beating just a little bit faster than usual, because she would soon be meeting with Terian. She wasn't thrilled to be in such close quarters with him. Aubrie knew she'd have to find a way to overcome that feeling because they were going to be working together. She wasn't ready to admit her attraction to him.

They sat in her office going over additional specifics of their partnership agreement. She would be meeting with her brother soon to ask that he write up the legal document. The only person in her family who knew about her partnership with Terian was her cousin Jordin and her friend Michelle. Well… Molly and Elaine knew about it, but she'd requested that they not say anything to her parents—Aubrie wanted to be the one to share this news with her family.

When they finished, the subject turned to food and the menu.

"I always say that every menu should tell a story," she said while reviewing Terian's menu wish list. "So, food selection is important. You have some really good ideas listed here, but they don't stand out. We want our food to stand out."

Terian sat in one of the visitor chairs with his iPad. "I agree," he responded. "One thing I noticed about your entrées, you definitely bring the elegance and romance of New Orleans."

"I've always loved the authentic Cajun flavor in your cooking," Aubrie said. "We want to bring that along with the rich flavors of French cuisine. I was thinking we could find a way to marry the two styles while introducing something new."

"We can do that," he said. "That's easy."

"It may not be as easy as you think. There are some differences in our styles. Terian, you tend to cook more traditional meals. Don't get me wrong—There's nothing wrong with the shrimp etouffee or seafood gumbo. I have great respect for them, but I'm more modern…more molecular, I'd say."

"I dined at Manoir Rouge, and all the plates were elegant, even the classics, yet there was a modern look about them. However, my vision for the food is that it shouldn't look like a piece of art. For example your crawfish etouffee…

You make the rice your centerpiece with the crawfish and vegetables all around it. Then you top the rice with a whole crawfish—head and all. But then, you've always had a flair for the dramatic."

"Customers come for an experience," Aubrie said with a shrug. "It's about the wine, food, service and *presentation*—the whole experience. And speaking of wine, we should hire a Sommelier. It's always nice to have a wine expert on hand to educate and advise our guests."

"We can decide on that later," Terian stated. "What do you think about a black and gold color theme?"

"It's overdone. We need to come up with something else."

"What do you have in mind?" he asked.

"I haven't thought that far," Aubrie stated. "I have too many other things on my brain right now."

"Yeah, I suppose you do with two other restaurants to manage."

She folded her arms across her chest. "Does that bother you?"

"What?"

"My owning two other restaurants. Are you worried that I'm not going to give this one my full attention?"

"No, not at all," Terian replied. "I didn't

mean anything by what I said. Honestly, I don't know how you do it. I'm in awe."

"I'm sorry… I guess I'm just tired."

"We're good, Aubrie. Better than good."

The flame Aubrie saw in his eyes brought long-buried emotions to life. His nearness made her senses spin, prompting her to say, "Terian, we are business partners. *Nothing more.*"

"I know that."

"Make sure you don't forget it," Aubrie stated.

"I can control my emotions. You have nothing to worry about."

"Great," she said. "We'll get along fine as long as you remember that our past relationship is just that. It's history."

Aubrie didn't mean to sound harsh, but she didn't want there to be any doubt that what once existed between them was over. She wasn't looking to repeat the same mistake.

TERIAN WAS EXCITED to be working with Aubrie. He hoped she felt the same way about him. She was planning to have her brother, Ryker, draw up the formal agreement and file all the required paperwork to make their partnership legal and binding. They had a conference call earlier with Elaine to update her.

Although Aubrie accepted his apology, Terian was well aware that there was still a wide fissure in their relationship—one he would work hard to fill.

The more time he spent around her, the more Terian realized that she wasn't the same girl he once knew. Aubrie was now an assertive, confident and self-assured woman—all the qualities he admired. Now that they were going to be partners, he was determined more than ever to tear down the wall she'd erected around herself when it came to him. It would take time to regain her trust, but Terian didn't care.

He would wait.

Now he had to talk to his parents. His mother would be fine with his decision, but his dad… he was going to be furious.

Terian couldn't put his life on hold any longer. When he left Los Angeles at his father's request it had been a mistake. This time he intended to stand his ground. It was important for him to build his own brand in the restaurant industry. He wanted this new restaurant to be recognized not just for the food and drinks, but also for its design.

LaCroix Restaurant was once an award-winning eatery, but it was tired now. The decor was dated, the kitchen was visible but the appliances and equipment desperately needed replacing. The chandelier lights and leather banquettes had long ago lost their wow-factor. And the menu needed revamping. Terian couldn't get his father to understand the importance of structural designs and traffic flow to the success of a restaurant. He couldn't get him to realize that in an age of social media, people thrived on uniqueness.

Terian wanted to revive LaCroix to its former glory. It could be New Orleans' latest hot spot once again—the restaurant had a lot of potential, but it seemed that only he cared.

He shrugged. It was no longer his concern.

AUBRIE INVITED HER parents to lunch, along with Ryker and his wife, to tell them that she'd taken on a partner. She had one of the private dining rooms set up for them.

Ryker and Garland were the first ones to arrive.

"What's going on?" her brother asked. "Are we celebrating something?"

"In a way," Aubrie responded with a grin. "You'll have to wait until Mom and Dad arrive before I say anything more."

"Does this have anything to do with a Michelin Star?"

She laughed. "No, it's nothing like that, Ryker. Not yet anyway."

"The girls told me to remind you that you owe them a movie date," Garland said.

"I do," Aubrie confessed. "Tell Amya and Kai that we will do it soon. I miss my nieces."

She noted the look Ryker gave his wife; it was the look of pure love. Some people were just lucky to find the right person for them. Aubrie imagined it was a wonderful feeling.

Her parents arrived.

"I have some news," Aubrie stated after her parents sat down at the table.

"You're opening up another restaurant," Rochelle interjected.

"I am, but this time I'll have a partner. Terian LaCroix. He came with Phillip to the party and the gala."

"How long have you known him?" her father inquired.

"Seven years," Aubrie responded. "We attended culinary school together."

"Really? You never mentioned this before," Rochelle said. "I just saw his mother when I was in New Orleans. Does she know?"

"I don't think so. We had to talk things through before we told anyone."

Ryker met her gaze. "I must admit that I'm surprised by all this. Seemed like there was some tension between you two the night of the gala."

"We had an issue some years ago, but that's all been resolved."

"Are you sure about this?" Rochelle asked.

"Yes," Aubrie responded. "Mama, I'm very sure. We've found a property on Polk Island that's perfect. Remember the place on Hibiscus?"

"It should do very well there," Jacques stated. "I have been missing the steakhouse that used to be there."

"Thanks, Daddy. We're still working out many of the details." Looking at her brother, she said, "Ryker, I'd like for you to draw up the partnership agreement and file the necessary paperwork."

"Why don't you and Terian come by the office later this afternoon and we'll get the official paperwork started."

She smiled in gratitude. "We meet with the owner at three. We'll come see you after that."

A server came to the table to take food selections.

"We hardly see much of you now," Ryker said. "Three restaurants are going to keep you busier than before."

"I'm going to be handling the administrative stuff. Terian will be the executive chef."

Later that afternoon she and Terian met with Elaine to do a final walk-through of the space.

"How did your family take the news?" Terian

asked as they navigated around the dining and bar area.

"They were fine with it," she responded. "In fact, you and I have a meeting with my brother to get the paperwork started after we leave the restaurant."

"Great. The place is really going to work out perfectly," Terian said. "It's going to be something totally unique to Polk Island."

Aubrie agreed. "We're going to need all new appliances in the kitchen."

They each made notes on their tablets.

"When do you plan to tell your family?" she asked after they walked outside.

"I'm going home next weekend for a few days. I'll tell them while I'm there."

"I hope it goes well."

"Me, too, but even if it doesn't—I'm not changing my mind. The reason I'm going home is so that I can put my house up for sale and pack."

"Do you plan on living in Charleston?"

Terian shook his head. "I found a rental on the island. I'll buy something after I sell my house. It's actually a couple of blocks from the restaurant."

As she drove back across the bridge to Charleston, she turned to glance at Terian. "Do you need anything before we get to the law firm?"

He shook his head. "I'm good. I don't think anything could get any better than this."

Aubrie hoped he was right.

MOLLY WALKED INTO the restaurant fifteen minutes before they were about to leave. "I was hoping I'd catch you two."

"Hey, Molly," Aubrie greeted. "Terian and I just finished our walk-through."

"Great. Did y'all get the report from the appraiser?"

"We did," Terian responded. "We found a box of photos in one of the drawers. We left them on the counter in the kitchen for Elaine to give to you."

"I've been looking for them," Molly said. "They were taken during the first year the restaurant opened."

They were joined by Elaine, who'd just finished a phone conversation in the office. "Molly, you made it."

"Seems like I'm always running these days." Molly eyed Aubrie and Terian. "I can see that I was right about you two. You make a great team."

"What makes you so sure about us?" Terian asked.

"You and Aubrie have that look—the same one Larry and I had. You both have a fiery pas-

sion for good food and a deep desire to succeed."

"I can't deny that," Aubrie said.

"Neither can I," Terian added.

Molly glanced around, her eyes bright with
water. "I'm going to miss this place. Larry and
I had some great times here. It's my prayer that
you and Terian will create wonderful memories
that will sustain you for a lifetime."

"Thank you," Aubrie responded. "You and
Larry set the bar really high, but Terian and I
are up to the challenge." She glanced over at
him. "Right?"

"For sure," Terian said. "We hope you'll
come back for the grand opening."

"I'll definitely be back. I have to see what
you and Aubrie do to this place. I have no doubt
it's going to be fabulous."

"It will be the talk of Polk Island," he said.

Aubrie smiled. Terian appeared so confident
and self-assured in this moment. She hoped he
would remain that way, especially after Terrance LaCroix found out about their partnership. Aubrie had a feeling that he was going
to be livid.

CHAPTER NINE

TERIAN WALKED OUT of the New Orleans airport, his gaze searching for his sister's vehicle. As soon as he smelled the air, he knew he'd come home. He couldn't wait to walk once more around the Garden District and the French Quarter. Terian loved growing up in New Orleans and felt a shiver of sadness that he would no longer live here.

I can always come back for a visit. The thought soothed him some.

Torrie pulled up to the curb.

He stuck his luggage in the trunk, then climbed inside the SUV.

"I told Daddy we were coming by the house," she said as she drove toward the airport exit.

He nodded.

"Are you sure about all this?" Torrie asked when they pulled into the driveway of his parent's house, a ranch-style brick home. The lawn was always neat and flowers in bloom.

He nodded. "I am. It has to be done."

Terian wasn't as calm as he led his sister to

believe. He wasn't looking forward to what was sure to be a confrontation, but it couldn't be avoided.

He walked into the house behind Torrie.

An exasperated male voice drifted into the foyer, the tone containing a strong suggestion of reproach. "It's about time you decided to come home. I hope you won't be looking to take any more time off this year." Terrance La-Croix wasn't the type of man to keep his opinion to himself.

"Hello to you, too." Terian strolled into the living room and gave his mother a hug.

"I'm glad you came home," Margo whispered. "We missed you."

"I haven't been gone that long," he said with a chuckle.

"I hope you and your father will talk and hear each other out. You two are just so much alike."

"I'm willing, Mom. I don't know about him."

"You just do your part."

"I will," Terian replied.

He entered the living room and made himself comfortable on the sofa before saying, "Pop, there's something I need to tell you."

"What is it?" Terrance's mellow baritone bristled with his attempt at control.

Terian sat down on the loveseat. "I wasn't

just on vacation. I was looking for a commercial property on Polk Island."

His father's expression was one of shock, then transformed to a look of confusion. "What? *Why* are you looking at commercial property?"

"I'm going to open my own restaurant."

Terrance released a harsh chuckle. "With what money?" His tone turned chilly.

"I have some cash saved. I also have a partner," Terian said. "Aubrie DuGrandpre. It'll be an equal partnership. We had the papers drawn up before I left Charleston."

Frowning, Terrance asked, "Why would you do a fool thing like that? That woman is our competition. Son, why do you want to put more money in her pocket?"

"Pop...you need to stop trying to blame Aubrie for what happened to us."

"Why not? She's the reason our restaurant isn't doing as well as it used to do."

"That's not true," Terian said, grinding the words out between his teeth. He had to get his father to see the truth.

"So, you're on her side, I see."

"Pop, I'd like for you to hear me out."

Terrance shook his head. "I don't want to hear nothing you got to say right now."

"You're acting like I'm betraying you."

"You are."

"My decision to go into business on my own doesn't have anything to do with you," Terian said. "Polk Island is a popular tourist location. It makes good business sense to open a restaurant there."

"What about LaCroix?"

"Pop, I don't work there anymore. Besides, you've always known that I wanted something for myself. What's wrong with that?"

"You're not in this alone, Terian. You have a partner. But what you need to remember is that you're a LaCroix. My father and granddaddy saved up every penny they could to open that restaurant. Your mother and I took it over and made it better. We worked our fingers to the bone…"

"I know that. And I'm still willing to help with the restaurant—that's if you want me involved."

"You quit, remember? We don't need you." Terrance's tone had turned nasty.

"Yes, we do need him," Torrie interjected. "Dad, you're not listening to Terian. He's not working against you."

"He's not working *with* me either."

"I've tried, but my hands are tied when it comes to LaCroix," Terian stated. "The restaurant needs renovations and a revamped menu, but you keep refusing to do anything about it. You second-guess everything I do when it comes to that place and I'm tired of it."

Torrie nodded in agreement. "He's right, Dad."

"If y'all feel that way, maybe we don't need to keep tossing money in a sinking ship. I guess folks want all that glitz and glam like they have over at Manoir Rouge... Well, I ain't doing all that."

He got up and left the room.

"I don't understand him," Terian said.

"Don't be so hard on your father," Margo said as she emerged from down the hall. "You've given him a lot to think about. He just needs some time."

"What I don't understand is why Dad was so willing to invest all that money into building tiny homes for the homeless, but he doesn't want to spend a penny doing any of the necessary renovations in the restaurant," Torrie said.

"He did what?" Terian asked. "I mean it's a nice gesture, but we don't have the money for that. He needs to put everything into keeping the restaurant going. This is so frustrating..."

"I'm beginning to think that he's not interested in doing that," his sister said. "Not anymore. At least that's the way it sounded to me. He doesn't even come in as much as he used to. All of the employees are looking to me for direction."

Terian eyed his mother. "Is that true?"

"No, he loves the restaurant. I think he just feels like giving up, but we can't let that happen. Son, your leaving… He's disappointed." Margo paused a moment before saying, "I'll talk to him and try to get him to understand your side of things."

"I didn't do this to hurt Pop."

"I know that. And your father will come around."

Terian didn't agree. Once his father made up his mind about something…that was it. This was not the way he wanted to leave things.

All he wanted was his father's blessing. Unfortunately, he would have to accept that it may never come.

"ALL RIGHT, TEAM… I'll see y'all tomorrow," Aubrie said on her way out. She'd been at the restaurant since 8:00 a.m. for inventory and was tired. It was almost 8:00 p.m., and she was looking forward to going home.

Shortly after she arrived home, Aubrie dropped a load of clothes into the washing machine, then stood there glancing around. She'd purchased the house with the hopes of one day having a family. She was thirty-three years old.

Her biological clock was ticking louder by the minute.

Aubrie hadn't had much luck in the romance department, but she was partly to blame for that as well. She'd spent the last few years focused on building her brand. While her hopes for marriage had dwindled some, there was still hope for children—even if she had to go the adoption route. There were so many children in the world who needed a loving home.

When the laundry was finished, Aubrie settled in the family room, watching television as she folded the clothing.

She turned off the TV and carried the basket to her bedroom when she was done.

After a quick shower, she got into bed with her laptop.

She looked up Terian's profile on Facebook. Her eyes landed on a photograph of him.

Tall and muscular, he looked handsome in the gray suit he wore. His smile lit his beautiful hazel-colored eyes.

What am I doing? I can't seriously be thinking about Terian like this. What we had ended a long time ago.

Nervous tension jumped in her veins as she realized that the feelings she thought were long dead and buried were begging to be resurrected. Every time Terian smiled at her, Aubrie felt the warmth of it deep down in the pit of her stomach.

She quickly turned off her computer to avoid spending the rest of the evening staring at photographs of him. It wasn't just his physical attributes that drew her. Terian was a bit self-absorbed at times, but that wasn't the whole of him. He was sensitive and caring. He never liked making anyone angry. It bothered him to his core, and he would try just about anything to keep the peace. This seemed to be much of his relationship with his father.

She knew he admired and respected his father—so much that he often sacrificed his own dreams to please the man. He'd even pushed Aubrie off to the side for him. Because of that, she couldn't trust him outside of their business arrangement.

Aubrie vowed that she'd never allow Terian room to break her heart a second time. It wouldn't be too hard to keep him away, she decided. They both agreed their only relationship would be a professional one, based on business.

GOING HOME HAD been necessary, but the gulf was even wider now. Terian made several attempts to talk to his father before he left, but he couldn't get Terrance to see things his way. He felt an acute sense of loss with the way things were between the two of them.

Despite the long trip from New Orleans to Charleston, Terian stopped at Manoir Bleu to see Aubrie before crossing the bridge to Polk Island.

She was in the dining area straightening a tablecloth when he arrived.

"Hey… I didn't know you were back," Aubrie said.

"I just got here," he responded. "I drove my car."

"That's almost a twelve-hour drive. Did you stop and sleep?"

He nodded. "I spent the night just outside of Atlanta. Got up early and headed here."

Terian was touched that Aubrie seemed concerned about him. It meant that she still cared even if she never admitted it.

"How did your visit go?"

"My dad didn't take the news well. I kinda figured he wouldn't."

She made sure the clear vase with a floating candle was perfectly centered. "I'm sorry to hear this."

Terian gave a slight shrug. "It's fine. He acted exactly as I figured he would."

He recounted the conversation with his parents. "My mom said she understood why I made this move. She also told me that my father would eventually understand—I'm just not entirely convinced of that."

"Give it some time," Aubrie stated.

"Before I forget...my sister's getting married in a few months. Torrie asked me to invite you to the wedding. It would be a huge favor because I need a plus one."

"Why would she do that?" Aubrie asked. "She doesn't really know me."

"My sister would like to remedy that."

"And *Torrie* invited me?"

He nodded. "Yeah. She's going to send you a formal invite closer to the date."

Aubrie smiled. "I'll think about it, okay? I need to see how things go with us working together."

"Do you have doubts about us?"

"No, I don't," she responded. "At least not right now."

"I guess I'll head over to the island. I packed up my house and put it up for sale. I need to get busy looking for a permanent place to live. I found an apartment but it's only a short-term lease."

"Do you need a Realtor?"

"No, I think I'm good. I prefer to look on my own first."

It took Terian forty-five minutes to get everything from the back of his SUV into the apartment he would temporarily call home.

MICHELLE DROPPED HER shopping bags on the sofa and rummaged through her designer purse to retrieve her ringing cell phone. She didn't want to miss this call.

"Hello."

"Hey, beautiful lady. How was your day?"

Grinning at the sound of Phillip's voice, she dropped down in a nearby chair. "Busy, but I'm not complaining. It keeps my business going."

"I'm coming to town this weekend if you're not busy."

She got up and did a little dance, then said, "I don't have anything planned."

"Great. I'll text you after I make flight arrangements."

Her smile broadened. "I can't wait to see you."

"I feel the same way," he responded.

They talked for a few minutes more before hanging up.

Her phone rang again fifteen minutes later.

"Aubrie…what's up?" Michelle said when she answered it.

"Hey, I just found out that there's a jazz festival this weekend in Savannah. Do you want to go with me?"

"Not this time. I already made plans."

"Okay. No problem. I'll see if Ryker and Garland want to join me."

"If not, you can always ask Terian."

"I'd rather not. It might give him the wrong idea."

Michelle loved that Aubrie wasn't the type to question her every move. They were great friends because they respected one another's boundaries. It wasn't that she wanted to keep her budding relationship with Phillip a secret, but it was too soon to talk about it. She didn't want to say anything until it was a viable courtship. She knew Aubrie would understand because she was the same way when it came to dating.

"You'd just have to make it clear that it's not a date—you're only going as friends."

"I think it's best to just keep it professional between us for right now," Aubrie stated.

"Good luck with that…"

"Why did you say that?"

"Girl, Terian's still into you. I can see it all over his face whenever he looks at you."

"Whatever…"

DEEP DOWN, Aubrie felt she was acting like a teen crushing on the most popular boy in school. But it was because of the tension Terian's very presence wrought inside her. She had to look past the fact that he was the first man she ever loved when she needed to look at him objectively as her partner. But it was hard to be objective when Terian gazed at her with those beautiful hazel eyes; when he smelled so good and when his energy seemed to fill all the corners of a room. He'd always had that effect on her as much as she wanted to deny it.

She spent the remainder of the evening watching television until she got up to prepare for bed.

A short time later, she lay in bed thinking about how much it had thrilled her to see Terian earlier. But she'd never let him know this.

Aubrie thought about the invitation to attend Torrie's wedding as Terian's date. She couldn't help but wonder at the real reason for the invite.

Was Torrie trying to help her brother win her over in some way?

A sudden thought popped into her head. Aubrie sprang up, propping her back against the pillows. She hadn't considered that he might eventually meet someone. She wondered how she'd respond to seeing him with another woman. A man like Terian wouldn't stay single for long.

It's not your business, a little voice whispered in her brain. *Terian has a life of his own and it has nothing to do with you.*

She didn't fall asleep until well past midnight, but Aubrie was up at sunrise. She and Terian were meeting at the closing attorney's office. Thirty days since their partnership began. It was really happening.

Terian must have felt the same way because he said, "I can't believe this day is finally here. We finally get the keys to our new restaurant. It's official and now the real work begins."

She smiled at seeing him so happy.

"I've had this dream for such a long time..."

"I know exactly how you feel," Aubrie said. "I felt the same way with both my restaurants."

They left the lawyer's an hour later with the keys.

"I think we should celebrate," Terian said.

"I don't have time. I have to get back to Bleu." Aubrie felt bad about disappointing him. She knew how much this meant to Terian, but she couldn't abandon her own restaurant.

"Can you meet me at our restaurant tomorrow morning?" he asked. "I'd like for us to go back over the renovation plans."

She could tell by Terian's cool tone that he wasn't happy with her at this moment, but it honestly couldn't be helped. Aubrie wasn't about to back down just to spare his feelings. She had her own responsibilities. That hadn't changed with the opening of their new restaurant. "Sure... I'll see you then."

She stopped and turned to look at him. "Congratulations, Chef."

He gave her a brief nod. "Same to you."

On the way to work, Aubrie came up with a way to salvage the day and make it special for Terian.

THAT AFTERNOON, Terian sat in his living room with a flute of Champagne in his hand, the bottle on the cocktail table. This wasn't what he'd had in mind for such a signature day. Apparently, Aubrie thought of it as any other day. Maybe when a person already had two successful restaurants—it felt like more of the same.

He shook his head at the thought. She probably wasn't as enthused because he was her partner. That felt more like the reality to him.

It was his first restaurant and a dream that had finally come true. Terian wished Torrie could've been here with him—they'd have a real celebration.

He glanced around the condo. The movers had delivered his furniture two weeks ago and there were only a few boxes he had yet to unpack. He wanted to get settled before the closing so that afterward he could focus solely on the restaurant.

He put the flute on the table, then settled back on his couch with his eyes closed, listening as soft jazz played in the background. The music echoed what he was feeling deep in his soul. In his mind, Terian could see the notes floating around in vivid color.

The beautiful medley was rudely interrupted when a smiling image of Aubrie popped into his head.

"I don't want to think about you," he uttered. "You ruined this day for me. All you really care about is your own two restaurants."

He heard what sounded like a knock.

Terian got up to answer the door.

"Chef Terian LaCroix…"

"Yeah, that's me."

"These are for you," the young man said.

He handed a bouquet of yellow roses to Terian.

"I also have Champagne and a food delivery for you."

He smiled. "Torrie…"

His smile vanished when he saw that the food had come from Manoir Bleu until he read the note.

Terian,
I know how important this day is to you. I'd hoped to spend it with you. I'm short-staffed this week, but we will celebrate this

milestone together. However, I wanted to send you something special. Enjoy tonight because it only gets busier from this point forward.

To our success!

He opened the package to find a beautiful assemblage of meat, cheese, spreads, artisan bread, olives and nuts on a wood plank. Aubrie had thoughtfully put together a traditional French meat and cheese board. She even included another little note which read:

To make sure you eat something with all that Champagne.

Terian felt a small thread of guilt for thinking Aubrie would dismiss this day so easily.

Later that evening, she called him.

"What are you doing?"

"Just sitting here listening to music."

"How much Champagne have you drunk?" Aubrie asked.

"Just a couple of glasses."

"Did you eat something?"

"I did. I ate some of the delicious cheeses and meats you sent over. Thanks for that."

"I hate that I couldn't be there…however, if you're up for some company, I can drop by."

Terian sat up straight in his seat. "Sure. You can have a glass of Champagne with me."

"I was thinking the same thing. I'll see you shortly."

He should've known Aubrie wouldn't disappoint him. She cared about people—she knew how much closing on the restaurant today had meant to him. He felt bad for judging her too harshly earlier.

He realized that he had to trust her motives when it came to being his partner. Aubrie was just as invested as he was—he had to believe it.

When she arrived, Terian handed her a flute. "Are you hungry?"

"Oh no, I'm fine," she responded. She held up her Champagne and said, "Congratulations, Terian. You've been dreaming about this for as long as I've known you. This isn't quite the way I envisioned our celebrating, but it will do. I'm extremely happy for you and I'm excited about our partnership. Thank you for including me on this journey. To our success."

"To our success," he responded. "Thank you for trusting me, Aubrie. Because of you, my dream is now a reality."

"Because of *us*," she said. "I guess we should also toast Molly because it was her idea for us to team up."

"To Molly," Terian toasted.

His phone rang.

"It's Torrie."

He answered saying, "I have you on speaker, sis. Aubrie and I are having a glass of Champagne."

"Congratulations to you both," she said. "I wish I was there to celebrate with you."

After his conversation with Torrie ended, Terian and Aubrie sat in the living room discussing their plans for the restaurant.

He was thrilled that what started as a solitary celebration was no longer the case. Terian broke into a smile. His evening suddenly seemed so much better with Aubrie's presence. He realized in that moment that he was tired of being alone.

CHAPTER TEN

THEY SPENT THE next morning at the Hibiscus property with a contractor to go over the renovations for the restaurant. Afterward, they left the island and headed to Manoir Bleu. Until the other property was ready, they planned to work out of her office there. They spent the first hour or so looking at employee uniforms online. Terian sat with his iPad in hand while Aubrie was on her computer.

"I like the silver swirl brocade vest on the second page," she said. "It's a nice look for the waitstaff."

He grinned. "Since you completely tossed out my idea for tuxedos, that would be my first choice. I'd also like for the staff to wear the same type shoe if they don't require special ones."

"Make sure they're affordable."

"I will." Terian looked up. "Aubrie, thank you for last night. I have a confession to make."

"About what?" she asked.

"I felt like maybe you didn't feel the same way

I felt about the closing. I know you've done this twice before, but this is my first time."

"That's why I sent the flowers, Champagne and the food. It's also why I came to the island last night after work."

"I realized this now."

"Terian, I know how much this means to you—it means a lot to me as well. I wanted to celebrate with you."

"You did," he responded. "Last night was perfect when you arrived, Aubrie. I appreciate everything you did, especially the unexpected delivery." Terian smiled. "You surprised me again this morning when you had a special breakfast prepared. I appreciate meeting your staff here at Manoir Bleu. You have a good group of employees."

"Thank you," she responded. "It was my pleasure."

"In school, we always figured we'd be married with a family by the time we turned thirty," Terian said.

"We were young," Aubrie said with a small laugh. "We thought we knew everything about life. Turns out we were wrong—we still had a lot to learn."

Terian nodded. "Yeah, we did. Who knows... If I hadn't screwed things up, maybe we would have gotten married."

"Things ended up the way they were supposed to happen," Aubrie responded.

Terian took in her beautiful features. He thought he would never get tired of looking at her oval face, her high cheekbones and perfect nose. Aubrie possessed lips that just begged to be kissed. For just a moment as he gazed at her, Terian glimpsed a hint of vulnerability in the depths of her warm brown eyes, and an unexpected surge of emotion welled up inside him.

"I think we should call it a day," she suggested, putting an end to his thoughts.

"That sounds good," he responded while studying her blank expression. It made him wonder if that moment of vulnerability he'd witnessed earlier was really there or had it been a figment of his imagination.

"Terian… I really hope you won't walk away this time like you did seven years ago."

"I'm not going anywhere, Aubrie."

It wasn't until Terian was in the car and heading to Polk Island that he wondered if he'd made a mistake in partnering with Aubrie. Maybe the truth of the matter was that she wasn't ready to leave that dark period in his life behind. Maybe she hadn't really forgiven him.

Not completely.

How are we supposed to work together with this cloud hanging over us?

THE NEXT DAY, Aubrie was glad Terian wasn't going to be at Bleu this afternoon. Especially since she woke up wondering if she'd made a mistake in bringing up the past to Terian yesterday. She knew it was born out of a moment of doubt in becoming Terian's business partner.

No, this was the right move to make, she decided. *I just have to gain control of my emotions. I can't let his past betrayal keep me from giving Terian a real chance.*

She glanced up at the clock on the wall behind the bar, then went back to her office to reconcile the orders from the night before.

Her floor manager appeared in the doorway.

"Do you need something, Rachel?" Aubrie inquired.

"Andrew just called. His wife is in labor, so he won't be coming in tonight. I told him that I'll step in as Maître d' this evening. I just wanted to let you know."

"Oh wow," she murmured. "The twins aren't due for another month. I'll be praying for a safe delivery."

"That's what I told him. It's a good thing I keep a black dress in my locker."

Smiling, Aubrie said, "Rachel, thank you. I'll be here if you need any help."

Andrew had told her that he would be taking

time off after the babies were born. It appeared that would be happening sooner than later.

Looking down at her To Do list, she would have to make changes to the staffing schedule.

It was going to be a long night, she decided. But things like this were bound to happen.

TERIAN FOUND AUBRIE'S nearness so unsettling that he'd kept his distance the day before. He felt they both needed time away from one another. However, they had a meeting with a vendor at Bleu this afternoon.

She arrived a few minutes behind him.

"You look tired," he said when Aubrie removed her sunglasses.

"That's because I am tired. It was crazy busy at Bleu last night."

"That's a good thing, right?"

"It is, but it's also exhausting. One of my employees just had twins, so he's going to be out for the next six weeks."

"Do you need any help?" Terian asked. "It might be a good idea for me to shadow you. And you don't have to pay me."

"You managed your father's restaurant, didn't you?"

"Torrie took care of the administrative stuff in addition to being the pastry chef. I was more of a sous-chef. My dad had trouble handing over the reins completely."

"Oh, I didn't know," Aubrie said.

Shrugging, Terian responded, "I guess he didn't think I was ready."

"If you do this, then you will need to work in every area. I had to do it before I had my own restaurants, and it was a good experience for me."

"Sure. I can do that," Terian said. "I started as a dishwasher, then runner, server and then finally, a cook."

"That's good. You won't need as much training as I initially thought," she teased. "It's hard to believe you were ever a dishwasher. When we were in school, I always ended up with kitchen duty."

He laughed. "The way I remember it…you always volunteered to wash dishes."

"I see you and I remember things differently."

They chatted a few minutes more about their time in France.

Before Terian stood up to leave, he asked, "Can I start tonight?"

Aubrie grinned. "Sure. Be back here at four o'clock."

"See you then."

Terian felt like he'd made some inroads with

Aubrie because she seemed more relaxed and welcoming than she had in their previous meetings. He had no idea what to attribute the change to—he was thrilled that it happened. The gap was finally closing.

CHAPTER ELEVEN

TERIAN SPENT THE first night working as a Maître d'. Although he wasn't going to complain, he was bored with greeting the customers and escorting them to their table. He yearned to be in the kitchen, where the excitement took place.

Aubrie appeared by his side. "How's it going?"

"Great," Terian responded.

She chuckled. "You're miserable. It's written all over your face."

"It's not hard to seat people at a table. I should be in the kitchen. I told you I already know how to be a host, a runner and a server. Seating people is nothing."

Aubrie was careful to keep her voice low enough for just him to hear what she was saying. "You're not just *seating* people, Terian. Their dining experience starts with *you*. Your job is to anticipate their needs and make this a memorable evening for them. Stop focusing on what you want. Focus on the guests."

He felt a wave of indignation flow through him. He wasn't her employee, yet she was treating him like one. Swallowing his feelings, Terian muttered, "Yes, ma'am. Treat each guest as a VIP. *Got it*."

He felt his annoyance with her melt away at the genuine smile she awarded him. She was right and he knew it. He needed to work on his temper and lack of patience. Terian realized that it was time to start thinking of someone other than himself.

From that moment on, Terian took his cues from each guest and inquired about special occasions. If celebrating, he sent over special menu items or drinks to make their experience more memorable.

He noted the way Aubrie walked around the dining area, briefly pausing at each table to acknowledge her customers.

At one point, she caught him watching her and gestured for him to join her. Rachel took his place as Maître d'.

"This is Terian LaCroix," Aubrie said, formally introducing him to a couple he had seated and who were now almost ready to leave. "He and I are opening a new restaurant together on Polk Island." She glanced up at him. "This is Dr. John Reynolds and his wife Mildred."

"Thank you for sending over a bottle of Champagne and the chocolate-covered strawberries," Mildred said. "John and I appreciate the gesture. You made this dinner that much more special."

"There was a note attached to your reservation that you were celebrating your twentieth wedding anniversary," Terian said. "Congratulations once again."

Aubrie introduced him to a few other guests.

"Thank you for that," he said after the Bleu closed. "They all sounded excited about the new restaurant."

She agreed. "You should get to know the regulars. Dr. Reynolds and his wife love Polk Island so we can count on them dining with us."

At the end of the night, Terian volunteered to help with the cleaning.

"You did a fantastic job," Aubrie told him. "Tomorrow, I'll need you here by ten at the latest."

"That's fine."

She walked him to the door. "I'll see you tomorrow."

Terian was bone weary by the time he made it home, but he felt it had been a good day. He felt a thread of shame for his actions earlier. He realized how he must have looked to Aubrie. He vowed to adjust his attitude going forward. He respected Aubrie and looked forward to learning from her.

AUBRIE WASN'T QUITE sure what to expect, but Terian had surprised her. For a moment there, she thought they were going to have a disagreement, but he backed down—something he wouldn't have done seven years ago.

Several of her female guests had inquired whether he was single. Aubrie didn't blame them. Terian looked handsome in his black suit, his short hair long enough to make soft curls, and those hazel eyes… He never had a problem when it came to turning a woman's head in his direction.

Her phone rang.

"Hey, Michelle."

"How did it go?"

Aubrie grinned. "Terian did a wonderful job. He's worked in his family's restaurant since he was old enough to hold down a job."

"But didn't you say that one was more of a casual dining spot?"

"I did, but remember I told you that Terian spent a few years working in Beverly Hills as an executive chef. I just want to make sure he can manage this new restaurant in the event something happens to me."

"You're not going anywhere."

"No, I don't have any plans, but things happen, Michelle. This is Terian's dream, and I want him to succeed, even if it's on his own."

"You really believe in him."

"I do," she responded. "Maybe more than Terian believes in himself."

"Sounds to me like you two are working out well," Michelle stated.

Aubrie laughed. "Girl…it was one night… He's shadowing me tomorrow. Let's see how that goes."

"You sound like you're expecting there to be a problem. You just said you believe in this man."

"Terian likes to have his own way. He's never been one to take anyone's advice about anything." She paused a moment before saying, "I must admit that he's great with the customers. Charming actually."

They talked for almost an hour.

Aubrie stretched and yawned.

After making sure the house was locked and the alarm turned on, she made her way upstairs to her bedroom for a shower. She was exhausted, both physically and emotionally. She hoped a shower would revive her.

Half an hour later, Aubrie lay in bed and stared up at the bedroom ceiling, her lips turned upward into a smile. She was happy that the tension between her and Terian was starting to ease. She could admit now that she'd really missed their friendship.

She shifted her position in bed, then glanced over at the clock on the nightstand.

I need to get some sleep. I have a long day tomorrow.

She changed positions once more and consciously willed away thoughts of Terian. She squeezed her eyes tightly closed while seeking the sweet oblivion of sleep.

It didn't take long because she was exhausted.

Six hours later, the glaring light of morning sunshine streamed through the window, snatching Aubrie from blissful dreams into reality.

With the sun getting brighter and the clock reading almost seven, she sat up and eased out of bed, then padded barefoot to the bathroom.

It was seven thirty when she emerged out of her bedroom, dressed in a pair of light blue jeans and a white tee shirt. She carried a hanger containing the clothes she planned to change into once the restaurant opened.

Terian would be shadowing her today. Aubrie couldn't figure out why the mere thought of him following her every move ignited a wave of nervousness within. Even now, her stomach quivered like jelly.

Get it together. I can do this. I have to forget my attraction to this man. He is my partner. Nothing more.

Terian arrived a full fifteen minutes early.

"If you're hoping to impress me—it won't work," Aubrie said without taking her eyes off her computer monitor. "You never liked being late anywhere."

"I wasn't sure you'd remember."

He smiled at her and she felt the warmth of it deep in the pit of her stomach. "I remember everything."

Aubrie pondered if it was because she hadn't dated anyone in the past six months that Terian touched such a vibrant chord inside her.

She cleared her throat softly, then said, "The first thing we're going to do is make a bank run. We need to deposit last night's receipts."

His eyebrows rose a fraction. "You leave the money here overnight?"

"I put it in the safe and deposit it the next day."

"I guess I can see your point," he responded.

She cast her gaze outside the window, where a breeze stirred the trees, playfully tugging at some of the leaves. Aubrie watched for a moment, then rose to her feet and walked around the desk. "We'll be back before the lunch crowd comes in."

When they returned, she reviewed the paperwork with him.

It was almost a struggle for Terian to stay awake.

"You look bored."

"I'm sorry," he said. "I've never cared for the administrative part of the business."

"What were you going to do if I'd turned you down?"

"I don't know."

"Why didn't you ask Torrie to be your partner?"

"I did," Terian responded with a wry smile. "She turned me down. She wants to focus on being a wife and eventually a mother."

"Oh."

"She's very excited about getting married."

To avoid getting lost in his gaze, Aubrie refocused on the business side of owning a restaurant. "It's important that you know everything it takes to manage not just a restaurant but a fine dining establishment. You have to know how to run it from top to bottom."

"I don't have a problem learning how to do everything. I just prefer running a kitchen over doing a stack of paperwork." He grinned. "I guess that's why we make a great team."

Aubrie knew when she agreed to become Terian's partner that her life was about to change; she just wasn't sure if it would change for the good or the bad.

TERIAN HOPED AUBRIE didn't get the wrong idea about him. He was indeed interested in learning the ins and outs of restaurant ownership—something he'd asked his father to do, but there were certain aspects of it that just didn't excite him.

"Are you ready for what's next?" Aubrie asked when she returned to the office.

"I am."

"Follow me."

Terian got up and did as he was instructed.

"I think you'll like this part," she said as they walked into the kitchen. "We're going to prep for tonight."

He grinned. "Yeah, I like being in the kitchen. Has the inventory already been done?"

"Yes. I took care of it when I got here this morning," she responded. "And I've already placed orders with our suppliers."

Terian washed his hands, then donned the apron Aubrie handed him.

She quickly introduced him to her kitchen staff.

"This is Lance. I think you met him last night. He's my executive chef…"

"Yes, I did," Terian said. "You kept this kitchen moving."

"Hey, congratulations on the new restaurant," Lance responded. "I can't wait to check it out."

Terian knew his way around the kitchen and

felt instantly at home. He glanced over at Aubrie and grinned.

The kitchen was where he belonged. They both knew it.

"YOU DON'T NEED to use garlic in rouille," Aubrie heard Terian saying when she entered the kitchen.

"Terian… I need to speak with you," she said before things could potentially get out of control.

He followed her into the office.

Aubrie closed the door behind him, then said, "I shouldn't have to tell you this, but I will. My chefs know what they're doing."

"Then they should know that you don't need to use garlic in rouille, just saffron. Or maybe they don't know the difference between aioli and rouille."

"Our rouille is made using potato," she responded. "We use potato, garlic and jalapeño as opposed to the cayenne pepper, along with saffron and water. So, trust me…they know the difference." She swallowed her irritation before saying, "It's my recipe."

"I've never put garlic in my rouille," Terian insisted. "It's the way I've made it for years and it's gotten rave reviews."

"You're not here to critique our ingredients,

Terian. You're here to learn how to run your own kitchen."

"I just thought you'd want it done right. And since when do you put herbes de Provence in bouillabaisse? It goes better with meats…"

"Terian, this is my kitchen. In this restaurant, things will be done my way."

The room was enveloped in tense silence.

"I was trying to help," he said after a moment.

"Tonight, I'd like for you to check the quality of the food and garnish before it goes out with the servers," Aubrie stated. "That's all you're to do. I have enough chefs in the kitchen."

Terian gave a stiff nod. "Fine. I can do that."

"One thing you need to remember," Aubrie said. "You're not the only chef around here. My brand has been established. You're still trying to build yours."

"I hear you loud and clear."

"Good," she uttered.

Aubrie couldn't believe Terian had the gall to come into her restaurant and tell her what to put in one of her recipes.

She stayed in her office a bit longer than she'd planned because she didn't want to face Terian. She was angry with him.

They had been getting along so well. But his attitude reminded her of their time at culinary school. She hadn't liked this side of him then and she didn't now.

FUMING, TERIAN WALKED out of the office. He paused outside of the kitchen to get his emotions under control.

How dare she talk to me this way. I'm not one of her employees.

He released a cleansing breath. The truth was that he'd had no right to interfere. He knew he'd be furious if she'd done that to him. She was a renowned chef… If she wanted to add or take away certain ingredients—it was her right.

This was not the way he wanted things between them. He spent the rest of the evening regretting his actions and questioning why he'd responded in that way. Maybe there was a part of him that was jealous. He wasn't able to finish culinary school. Terian couldn't deny that it bothered him.

His insecurities were his problem and something he alone would have to deal with.

At the end of the night, he and Lance inventoried the supplies.

"Here's what's needed for the next day," Terian told Aubrie, who was in her office.

She looked at him and smiled. "Thanks for stepping in to help when things got busy."

"I have to admit that this was different from what we do at home, but a good experience."

Aubrie eyed him.

"Look, I'm sorry about earlier," Terian said as he sat down in the chair facing her. "I should've kept my mouth closed. You have every right to use whatever ingredients you like. I was wrong."

"Thank you for your apology," she responded. "One of the first things we learned in school was that we should never disrespect the kitchen of another chef."

"You're right," he said. "I promise it won't happen again."

Aubrie settled back in her chair. "Please see that it doesn't."

He could tell that he'd lost ground with her. The invisible shield around her was up again.

"Why don't you go on home," she suggested. "We'll start fresh tomorrow."

Terian rose to his feet. "How much longer are you planning to be here?"

"Not too long. The staff should be done soon." Aubrie pushed away from her desk and stood up. "I'll walk you to the door."

"I meant it. I'm sorry."

"Terian, we're good."

"I hope so. I don't want any friction between us."

"I'll see you tomorrow," Aubrie stated.

Her cool reserve was back. Terian wanted to kick himself for being such a jerk.

"MARGO, IT'S GOOD to hear from you," Rochelle said. "I was planning to call you, but I've been preparing to go to court on a difficult case."

"I'm sure you know that our children have decided to go into business together. They're partners."

"Yes. How do you feel about it and how is Terrance taking this?"

"Rochelle…that stubborn man of mine is getting on my last nerve," Margo uttered. "He's upset that Terian's moving on without him but doesn't want to accept that he is the reason why our son is leaving."

"Have you tried talking to him?" Rochelle asked.

"I'm letting Terrance work through his emotions before I sit him down and smack him with the truth."

"Handle it, girl…"

Margo laughed. "I'm not gonna let my man or my children work my nerves. I have to protect my peace."

"I'm with you on that," Rochelle said. "Life is too short to let drama take over."

"You didn't say how you felt about Aubrie and Terian."

"I think they make a great team and an even cuter couple."

"I feel the same way," Margo gushed. "I look forward to getting to know Aubrie."

"I have a feeling this partnership is going to get quite interesting," Rochelle said.

"Hopefully, we'll have a front-row seat."

"We just can't interfere. I tried that when my son was dating the woman he married. Margo, I made a mess of things. He almost lost Garland. I learned my lesson, so now I just sit on the sidelines."

"I just want to see Terian happy. He deserves it."

They talked for a few more minutes before hanging up.

Aubrie appeared in the doorway of Rochelle's office at the law firm. "Hey, Mom…"

"What brings you here?" Rochelle asked. She hadn't expected a visit from her daughter. "I'm happy to see you though."

She walked into the corner office and sat down. "I wanted to visit. That's all."

"How are things between you and Terian?"

"Mom, we're just partners."

"That's what I meant," Rochelle said. She couldn't stop grinning because she'd had a feeling that there was more going on with her daughter and Terian.

"We've had a few hiccups, but things are going well." Aubrie eyed her mother. "Since when are you so interested in my restaurant openings?"

"I saw Margo LaCroix at Nancy's funeral. She told me about Terrance and Terian's relationship. It made me realize that I don't want to kill your dreams. I'm sorry I wasn't supportive in the beginning."

"That's in the past…"

"I intend to make sure it stays there," Rochelle said. "I'm going be supportive of all your dreams, my love. The same with Ryker and even the grandchildren."

"I'm loving this new you…"

"Me, too." Rochelle looked at Aubrie. "I am so very proud of you."

"I didn't come here to get all emotional, Mom. I appreciate what you said. It means a lot to me."

Aubrie stood up. "I guess I'd better let you get back to work. I need to check on the restaurant."

Rochelle smiled. "I'm glad you came by to see me."

"I am, too."

"Don't forget to stop by your father's office. I don't want him to be jealous."

Aubrie chuckled. "I'll do that. Love you."

"I love you, too."

Rochelle watched her daughter walk across the hall to her father's office with pride. She hoped Terian would find the strength he needed to stand up to Terrance the way Aubrie had stood up to them.

She remembered the day Aubrie had announced she had no intention of becoming a lawyer. She declared that she was going to attend culinary school because she wanted to be a chef. It was at her college graduation party.

Ryker had gifted her with study guides to help prepare Aubrie for the LSAT.

The party ended abruptly as she and Jacques tried to convince Aubrie that being an attorney was her family's legacy—her calling.

Her daughter had refused to listen to what she believed wasn't true. Aubrie stormed off to her room.

Rochelle and Jacques decided to use what they believed to be tough love. They told Aubrie if she intended to go to culinary school in Paris, she would have to pay for it herself. They would only pay for her to go to law school.

Aubrie went to her aunt Eleanor on Polk Island and worked at the café and bakery. Rochelle was pretty sure Aunt Eleanor had paid some of Aubrie's school expenses, although she denied it.

It had taken some time, but Rochelle had come to gradually respect and accept Aubrie's decision. She'd realized that she couldn't live her daughter's life.

CHAPTER TWELVE

WHILE THE NEW restaurant was being renovated, Terian and Aubrie worked out of Manoir Bleu. Over the next month, they focused on creating the menus and hiring staff. She was glad there hadn't been any other issues between them. Terian was careful to keep his opinions to himself. He stayed out of anything that had to do with Bleu or Rouge.

"We still need to settle on a name," he stated.

"What were you planning to call it before we became partners?" Aubrie inquired.

"Terian's. What else?" he replied with a grin.

She shook her head. "I don't know why I asked. I should've known that."

"We can still go that route…"

She shook her head. "No, we can't."

"Okay, have you come up with any ideas?" Terian asked.

"Affinité?"

"It's nice, but no."

"Why not?" she asked.

"It means affinity. That doesn't represent our restaurant."

"Okay, what about La Truffe Noire?" Aubrie questioned.

"The Black Truffle. What's with you and colors? Red, blue and now black."

"Just say you don't like it," she uttered with an eye roll. "Leave it at that."

"I've heard people call Polk Island a little paradise," Terian said. "When we were in school, we talked about naming our restaurant—"

"Paradis," Aubrie interjected. "That's it, Terian…that's the name. It's perfect."

He nodded in agreement. "I think so, too."

Aubrie sank back against the cushion of her chair. "I'm glad we were able to agree on the name."

Later, when Rachel came into the office for a meeting with her, Terian disappeared with a wave. Aubrie had a feeling he was headed for the kitchen. It's where he seemed to feel most comfortable.

"He's so handsome," her floor manager whispered. "I heard that you and Terian went to culinary school together."

"We did."

"How did you convince him to open a restaurant on the island?" Rachel inquired.

"It was actually Terian's idea. He presented it to me, and we decided to become partners."

"It seems like you two are a great team."

"I think so," Aubrie murmured. "It's a dream we had when we were in school. We're finally making it happen. It feels almost surreal."

She returned her attention to her work when Rachel left the office.

Aubrie leaned back in her chair and closed her eyes. For the next five minutes, she indulged in a mental staycation.

She wouldn't allow thoughts of Terian to enter her mind. But that was almost impossible, given that most of her thoughts were focused on their partnership and plans for the restaurant. Terian took center stage.

"What's this?" Aubrie asked when he walked into her office an hour later carrying two bowls.

He handed one to her.

She glanced down. "I see there's crawfish… potatoes, chopped onion… I see red and green peppers."

"It's a crawfish boil soup," Terian stated.

"So, this is what you've been doing." She sampled it. "This is *delicious*, and I'm not a huge fan of crawfish even though it's a popular item here at Bleu."

He sat down in the empty chair facing her. "My maternal grandmother used to make it.

My parents don't eat crawfish. The only time I'd have this was when Torrie and I spent the summers with Grandma."

"Are you thinking of putting it on the menu?" Aubrie asked. "Because I think you should. We can make it a seasonal offering."

Terian gave her one of his devastating grins. "I'm glad you like it."

"I really do. It's *sooo* good."

"I know it's early, but what do you think about a menu tasting for our future employees during one of their training sessions."

"That's actually a great idea," she responded. "Let me know what I can do to help when the time comes."

"I'd like for you to help me prepare the food."

Aubrie was stunned. She figured the last thing Terian wanted was to share his kitchen with her. "You're inviting me in your kitchen? To cook?"

"Yes. It's partly your kitchen, too. What do you say?"

"Sure. I'd love it, but let's get something straight right now. Am I free to cook with my choice of ingredients?"

"Let's discuss it," Terian responded with a grin.

They enjoyed an easy conversation while they ate.

When they finished, Terian rose to his feet. "I'd better get these back to the kitchen. I promised Lance I'd clean up my mess."

Aubrie smiled. "He is very particular about his kitchen."

"He said the same thing about you." Terian walked briskly toward the door but paused a moment. "Thanks, Aubrie...for taking this chance with me. It was a good decision. I'm glad to have you as a partner."

Aubrie was stunned. No way would she rekindle those feelings...the heartache.

She had to set him straight...and now.

"We're business partners, Terian. That's all. You need to accept that."

The look he sent her as he walked away made it clear that he had other ideas.

"How did Aubrie like the soup?" Lance asked when Terian strode into the kitchen.

He nodded. "She thinks we should put it on a seasonal menu for our new place."

"I agree. It was delicious."

"Thanks so much for letting me use your kitchen," Terian said.

"No problem. I appreciate your help with prepping and picking up some of the items we needed."

Terian placed the bowls in the sink. "After I wash the dishes, I'm ready for whatever is next on the To Do list."

"I'll get you to prep ingredients for the sous-chefs."

After he finished, Terian studied each recipe Lance gave him for that night's menu and gathered all the necessary ingredients while the kitchen staff made sure each station was ready with the required utensils and equipment. He was careful to keep his thoughts and opinions to himself.

"There's a fish market on the island," Lance said. "That's where you should buy all your seafood. But your meats...you have to come to Charleston for that."

"I know Aubrie has her own suppliers, but if you don't mind, I wondered if you could put together a list of them."

"I'd be glad to," he responded. "Hey, I'll be going to market tomorrow. Why don't you come with me? I can introduce you to folks."

Terian smiled. "I'd like that."

Although he had moments of doubt, he was truly happy with the way things were working out with Aubrie.

If only he could focus on something other than her beautiful smile and look of confidence. The scent of her perfume lingered in the room long after she left. Terian spent the rest of the day fighting against his feelings for Aubrie. After all these years, he still felt the same about her.

Until he'd come to Polk Island, he had done nothing but look inward. For a while he felt sorry for himself, that he'd abandoned his dreams.

Paradis would be opening in a few months. If only his father could understand just how much this meant to him.

"TERIAN MADE LUNCH for you... That's so sweet," Michelle murmured.

"He wanted me to taste a soup that he wants on the menu. Try not to read too much into it." Aubrie needed a break, so she had walked down to her friend's shop for a chat.

"I think it was more than that. I've seen how he looks at you." Michelle turned her computer screen around. "What do you think of this design? It's for a book club."

"Michelle, what are you talking about? Terian and I are becoming friends again. That's all." She paused a moment to look at the monitor, then said, "That's nice. I like it."

"That's how *you* feel, Aubrie. You can't speak

for Terian. I can look and tell that he wants more from you."

She shrugged. "Well, he's going to have to settle for a platonic friendship. It's all I have to offer him."

"Honey, that will change. I know what I'm talking about."

Aubrie eyed her friend. "By the way, what's been going on with you? Normally on the weekends, you want to go shopping. I know I've been busy with the Paradis opening, but don't think I haven't noticed how you've been missing in action lately."

"I've just been staying out of the way," Michelle said. "I know how focused you are when you're opening a restaurant. Besides, you and Terian need time to bond."

"Girl…whatever…" Aubrie said with a chuckle.

A woman walked into the shop.

She waited while Michelle took care of her customer.

"Aubrie, when are you gonna admit that you still have feelings for Terian?" Michelle asked when they were alone.

"I have no idea what you're talking about." Aubrie glanced down at her watch. "I need to head back to the restaurant. Talk to you later."

"Uh-huh… I know what you're doing right now."

"Nothing gets past you," Aubrie said as she headed to the door.

"And you know it," Michelle yelled in response.

CHAPTER THIRTEEN

"TODAY'S THE BIG DAY," Aubrie said as she set up the utensils and necessary equipment at her station. They were finally starting staff training after completing the hiring process. "We'll see what the staff thinks of our menu."

"Being here in this kitchen makes it all the more real," Terian responded. "I feel like a kid on Christmas Day."

She laughed. "I know that feeling well. It was like that for me when I opened both Rouge and Bleu. And now with Paradis, so you're not alone."

"I don't know why I feel some apprehension. I keep telling myself that this is just an employee training session."

"It's normal, Terian," Aubrie said. "I'd be worried if you didn't feel nervous at all."

"I'm really glad you're here."

"I wouldn't be anywhere else. We're in this together."

Aubrie's words and the look she gave him made Terian's stomach do a somersault.

He cautioned himself to rein in his emotions.

He checked the clock, noting it was almost time for the employee training. "I guess I'd better get changed."

"Two of my people from Bleu will be helping in the kitchen."

Terian let out a soft sigh of relief. "Thank you. Especially since we haven't hired a pastry chef and fish cook."

"We're all good," she responded. "Go change and try to relax."

A myriad of emotions whirled through him as he changed into his uniform.

He exited the men's bathroom just as Aubrie strode out of her office.

"Everyone's here. Are you ready?" she asked with an encouraging smile.

"About as ready as I'm going to get," he replied. "I do have to tell you that you've developed one heck of an onboarding manual."

"Thanks. I can't take the credit for it. I had a lot of help from my parents."

An hour later, they stood in front of their employees.

"All of you have gone through the basic training and now it's time to increase your menu knowledge," Terian said.

"There are times when a diner will read through the menu and have questions," Aubrie said. "The questions can range from how something is prepared to what's in this dish or what do you recommend? We can't prepare you for every question that may come up, but Terian and I can ensure that you know the answers to the most common questions."

"Aubrie's right," Terian interjected. "Allergy knowledge is a very important part of understanding the menu. It's imperative that you learn about any possible allergens on the menu, anything from seeds and fish to nuts and eggs. There are so many allergens, but we'll keep a list posted."

When servers brought out the food, he said, "On the table before you are our appetizers. From left to right: shrimp and andouille sausage gumbo dip, green chili hush puppies with garlic aioli, Creole crostini, cranberry jalapeño dip, Creole seafood potato wedges and buffalo chicken lollipops."

"Feel free to take notes while sampling them," Aubrie stated. "And write down your initial impressions. We know some selections may not resonate with you, and that's okay. However, try to think of something positive to say about each of them. We want you to share those thoughts with our dining guests—it's about making connections through the love of good food."

While they were eating, she slipped into the kitchen to check on the soups and salads.

Terian joined her a short time later. "How's it going?" he asked while trying to still the nerves whirling in the pit of his stomach.

"The buffalo chicken and grilled steak salads are ready to go out," Aubrie responded. "We need to start preparing the entrées. Everything is prepped and ready."

Terian walked briskly to his station and began working while Aubrie did the same.

When the entrées were carried out, she went out to talk to the employees. He walked over to the door and listened from the kitchen.

"The first dish contains marinated duck breasts with Creole peach pepper jelly," Aubrie said. "Next is the Creole spiced sirloin, and the Cajun shrimp and bacon pasta. We will also have a pan-roasted lobster with brandy cream. We made a couple of them and cut them into pieces for you to taste. You won't get your own lobster."

"I already know the pasta will be one of my favorites," said a young woman. "I love shrimp and bacon, too."

"It's definitely mine," Aubrie responded. "Keep in mind that these are only a few of our offerings on the menu. We will be doing one more of these trainings because I want everyone to become familiar with every item we serve."

Terian moved away from the door when she finished her presentation. He didn't want Aubrie to catch him eavesdropping. He didn't want her to get the idea that he didn't trust her because it wasn't true. He enjoyed listening to her because she had such a special way of teaching about food.

It was clearly her passion.

AUBRIE WAS PLEASED with the way the training had gone. All their new employees seemed to enjoy the food. When it came down to the desserts, the Creole bread pudding with Bourbon sauce was voted staff favorite.

At the end of the night, she and Terian sat in the office. They lingered over cups of hazelnut-flavored coffee and conversation.

"I think everything went extremely well," Aubrie stated before taking a sip from her mug. "We had a few minor hiccups in the kitchen, but nothing serious."

"I must confess that I was a bit concerned about Raul's salary, but he's worth it. He proved that he deserves to be the sous-chef."

"Humph… I knew it the moment I read his résumé," she responded.

"People can put anything on a sheet of paper.

The sample he prepared was decent, but seeing how he handled himself tonight… I'm convinced."

"I remember how you pitched a complete fit when I told you I'd hired Raul. You really lost it when I mentioned how much we were going to pay him."

"Well, you were right once again, Aubrie."

"You do know it's not about my being right, Terian. I'm just as invested in the success of Paradis as you are. We both want the same thing. When it comes to the kitchen, I try to stay in my lane. You've already said that you don't really like the administrative part—I happen to enjoy it." Aubrie wanted to reach across the desk and take his hand in hers, but she fought the yearning. She didn't want to feel anything for him except friendship.

"I realize that I have to relinquish some of my control."

"Terian, you're more like your father than you care to admit," Aubrie said.

"You really believe that?"

"I do."

"Wow…" he uttered.

"I don't mean it as an insult."

"C'mon… I'll walk you to your car."

In the moonlight, Aubrie thought she saw a

whisper of longing in his gaze. She needed to shut that down for both their sakes.

Clearing her throat softly, she said, "I'll see you tomorrow morning."

"Drive safe," Terian said. "Text me when you get home."

It touched her that he cared for her well-being. It was a glimpse of the man she fell in love with.

Aubrie gave herself a mental shake. She couldn't afford to think like that. She had to keep her emotions under wraps.

THE RENOVATIONS DONE and the opening looming, they hired a wine expert for Paradis. Aubrie sat on a bar stool while Terian paced the floor.

Shaking his head, he said, "I can't believe I let you talk me into hiring a Sommelier." He was worried about the finances and didn't want to end up being in the red.

"He's going to work part-time," she said. "I'm thinking we can also hold special events like wine tastings."

"Can we really afford him? I trust you, so if you say we're good, then I'll be fine." To his way of thinking, they were spending too much money. There was still so much left to be done.

"Yes," Aubrie responded. "We're good, Terian."

He released the breath he'd been holding.

"If you're not busy tomorrow, I'd like to take you someplace," Aubrie said. "Frogmore Village and Hilton Head. You have to experience the area and the food. I always find inspiration whenever I visit those places."

"Sure. I'd love to go. I still enjoy visiting new places and trying different foods."

"Great… We'll have a good time, Terian."

"I don't doubt that for a minute," he responded. "I always have a good time with you."

"It's been a long time since we last hung out together."

"I know, but I don't think you've changed that much."

"I guess you'll see for yourself," she said with a smile.

Aubrie didn't seem so guarded now, which pleased Terian. They were good friends once and he wanted to renew that friendship.

Maybe this trip to Frogmore would do the trick.

One could only hope.

CHAPTER FOURTEEN

TERIAN SAT IN the front passenger seat of Aubrie's SUV. He was excited about spending the day with her.

They made small talk as she drove down Route 21 to the tiny village of Frogmore on St. Helena Island.

"The people living here are part of a distinct group of African Americans who were able to trace their roots to the villages of the Sierra Leone territory in West Africa," Aubrie said as she drove.

Glancing around, he said, "I've never heard of Frogmore or St. Helena. Just Hilton Head."

Aubrie took him to Penn Center. "This was the first school established in the South to educate the freed slaves."

"Really?"

She nodded.

"That's the Dr. York Bailey House," Aubrie said, pointing to a two-story, American Foursquare–style home. "He was St. Helena's first African American doctor."

Terian continued to look around, taking in the surroundings. "There's a lot of history on these islands, I'm learning."

"I wanted you to see all this because we need to incorporate the culture and history into the menu."

"That's a good idea," Terian responded. "That's what I've always wanted to do with LaCroix, but my dad insisted on sticking with our staples. He didn't think much on adding new items—he'd agree to maybe one or two new entrées a year."

"I am always adding a new dish to both my menus," Aubrie said. "And I remove the ones that don't seem to sell."

"I like that," he responded. "We should do the same with Paradis."

"Agreed. You should have my cousin Trey take you on a tour of Polk Island," Aubrie said. "Polk Rothchild and his brother Hoss founded the island—Polk is Trey's four greats grandfather."

"Did Polk or his brother ever leave the island?" he asked.

"Hoss ended up moving up north. Polk left once, and that was to find a mother for his ten children," Aubrie explained. "His new wife's family came with her. I think it's now eight generations of the Rothchild family living on the island."

"Wow…your roots run deep in New Orleans, Charleston and Polk Island."

She smiled. "I'd like to take you to see some of the other islands along the coast. There's Jekyll, St. Simons and Sapelo in Georgia."

"I'm all-in," Terian responded. "Just tell me when we're going. I'm already getting some ideas for the menu."

"Great. That's the reason I brought you here—for inspiration."

"I'm inspired by everything I see around me…the sights, smells…"

"We can't leave here without having some Frogmore Stew."

"That's the low country boil, right?"

"Some also call it the Beaufort Stew," Aubrie said. "I'm taking you to my favorite eatery. It's called Fishcamp on 11th."

Smiling, Terian responded, "I trust your judgment when it comes to food."

The seafood restaurant was located on the Port Royal shrimp docks and Aubrie asked for a table on the covered verandah with a view of the boats.

For starters, Aubrie ordered the Prince Edward Island mussels. "I recall how much you love mussels. You must try these."

"I'm game. I told you that I trust *you*."

She wished she could respond in kind, but Aubrie couldn't—Terian still had a ways to go in that department.

Terian sampled the appetizer. "Calabrian chiles…cream, white wine, garlic…parmesan and leeks. Looking at this, I just got an idea. What do you think of spaghetti with mussels and these peppers? They have the right amount of heat without being overpowering."

"You have to cook it for me," Aubrie responded. "It sounds delicious."

Terian glanced around the restaurant. "I like this place."

She smiled. "I thought you would."

When they finished eating, Aubrie drove to Flemings Farm in St. Helena.

"This is where I come to pick veggies and strawberries," she said as she offered him a basket.

His eyes widened in surprise. "You actually do the picking?"

Aubrie nodded as she retrieved a straw hat from the back of her SUV and put it on her head. "My diners are always fascinated when I tell them the cucumbers, the zucchini, cantaloupe or the eggplant they're eating was picked by me or my head chef."

They walked around the farm.

Terian noted there were quite a few people in the fields picking corn and other vegetables. The last time he'd done anything like this was when he was in his teens. He used to help his grandfather during harvest times. However, his farm wasn't nearly as big as this one. Being here brought back wonderful memories of him and Big Daddy.

"Would you like to get a few items?"

He nodded. "I would."

Terian knew enough about corn to avoid husks that were starting to yellow or feel dry. He stood beside Aubrie and worked.

Conversation was kept to a minimum as they wanted to pay attention to the vegetables. When it came to the okra, Terian looked for brightly colored pods, discarding those that were dull or blemished.

"You look like you know what you're doing," Aubrie said.

"My grandfather grew his own vegetables, so he taught me enough to help him whenever I visited."

"I can't believe I didn't know that about you."

"I hate to disappoint you, but I didn't tell you everything."

"Fair enough," she said with a chuckle.

When they walked back to the car an hour

later, their baskets were filled with corn, cucumbers and okra.

"That was an experience," Terian said when they were in the car.

"Did you enjoy it?"

"I did," he responded with a grin. "I'll be coming back here often."

Her presence gave him a bottomless peace and satisfaction. Terian stole a peek at Aubrie and smiled. He never tired of looking at her. Even with no makeup, she was stunning.

Terian relished every moment they spent together. He felt as if his dormant emotions had renewed themselves. He cautioned himself not to rush the pacing of their relationship. Things were good between them, and he didn't want to make Aubrie uncomfortable.

He knew he still had a long way to go to win her trust. Then he could concentrate on regaining her love.

THE FOLLOWING WEEKEND, Aubrie invited Terian over. She found herself enjoying his company more and more. It thrilled her to see that he wasn't the same self-absorbed man he used to be when they were in school.

"I love your kitchen," he said. "I like the way you paired the cream-colored cabinets with the dark walnut wood on your island." He ran his fingers across the black and beige marble granite countertop.

"What I love most is this large refrigerator and six-burner stove top." Terian walked over to the separate wine cooler and peered inside. "Nice… I want a kitchen island with a prep sink like this."

"Then you'll need to buy a newer house," Aubrie said.

He nodded in agreement. "I don't know about you, but being in this kitchen sure makes me hungry."

She laughed. "I took out some shrimp. The seasonings are in that cabinet. Pull some out and I'll look in the pantry and refrigerator. Why don't we see what we can come up with?"

He broke into a huge grin. "I'm game…"

Minutes later, Aubrie placed lemons, garlic cloves, Worcestershire sauce and a couple sticks of butter on the counter.

Terian held up the Cajun spices he'd found.

They looked at each other and burst into laughter.

"Great minds think alike," he said after a moment. "I had barbecue shrimp on the brain the moment you said the word *shrimp*."

Aubrie reached for a loaf of French bread. "We're going to need this, too."

She pulled out a large cast-iron pan.

"We need more than one stick of butter," Terian said.

"There's another one over there."

Aubrie had enjoyed cooking with Terian at school. In the kitchen they were always in sync.

When the shrimp was ready, he tossed lemon wedges into the pan.

They sat down at the table in the breakfast area.

"This reminds me of Cafe Pontalba," Aubrie said. "Whenever we were in New Orleans, my mom and I would go there for their barbecue shrimp. I don't think we used near as much melted butter and spices, but ours smells delicious."

"Laissez les bons temps rouler..." Terian said.

"Yesss," she murmured as she ripped off a piece of bread and dipped it into the sauce. "Let the good times roll."

As the evening wore on, Aubrie's chest filled with the anticipation of an unspoken promise of a kiss. Realization dawned on her that she *wanted* Terian to kiss her. It had been a long time since she'd felt his lips on her own.

She gave herself a mental shake. It would be foolish to allow a kiss to take place between them.

Why did she have to keep reminding herself

that they were business partners? A personal relationship would put that at risk.

"I have an extremely long day tomorrow," Aubrie said, surprised to find her voice lower, deeper than usual. "We should probably call it a night."

Terian stood up. "I should be heading back across the bridge."

With a look of disappointment he opened the front door and headed to his car.

Aubrie picked up a throw pillow and tossed it across the room.

TERIAN WANTED TO kiss Aubrie so badly that it ached in his bones. They'd had a wonderful day together that stretched into the evening, cooking together and then watching movies on Netflix… It reminded him of their time in France. But suddenly, Aubrie planted a wall between them.

He wasn't giving up though. He was attracted to her like he'd never been attracted to any other woman.

In the three months that he'd worked with Aubrie, he admired the woman she'd become more and more each day. But his feelings for her were intensifying. He had to keep them reined in; he had to shut out any awareness of her as anything other than his business partner. He couldn't risk making her uncomfortable. He couldn't risk losing Paradis. They were the only two things in his life that truly meant something to him.

His relationship with Aubrie was too fragile to make the wrong move, and sometimes he wasn't even sure what that was. Terian felt like he was walking on eggshells around her, but he'd do whatever he had to do to keep their partnership intact. He didn't want his father to be right about him failing. Paradis was going to be a success. Terian would accept nothing less.

THEIR NEXT ROAD trip was to visit several islands along the coast of Georgia.

"St. Simons is known for its salt marshes and sandy beaches," Aubrie said as they strolled along the shoreline. "The lighthouse was rebuilt somewhere around 1871 or '72 after it was destroyed in the Civil War."

"It's beautiful," he responded. "Reminds me a little of Polk Island."

"Polk Rothchild grew up in Darien, Georgia. He and Hoss decided to go up north—that's where they were headed when Polk's wife became ill and died. He couldn't bear to leave her behind, so he settled on what was to become Polk Island. Tomorrow, we'll be near Darien in a town called Meridian. That's where we'll take a ferry to Sapelo Island."

"I'm loving all this history."

Aubrie smiled. "Wait until you taste the food…" She loved coming to this area to visit and wished she were able to do it more often.

"Where are we staying?"

"On St. Simons Island. My brother owns a condo here."

They headed back to the car.

"I think Phillip mentioned coming here once," Terian said. "He came to play golf or something."

"He did," Aubrie responded. "He and my brother come here at least twice a year to play golf."

Terian stared out the window of the SUV, taking in the picturesque view. "I looked up this island and found out that it's considered one of the most romantic destinations in the South."

"I didn't know that," Aubrie said. "But I can see why. It's a beautiful island."

They went to the pier.

"That's Jekyll Island over there," she said, pointing.

When they stopped to get fuel, Terian got out the vehicle. He stood there, looking around.

While he was admiring the view, Aubrie was doing the same and fought to regain her senses.

She shouldn't have noticed how good he looked in those light blue jeans and the white polo shirt. She also had no business feeling that little flutter in her stomach.

She reminded herself that this wasn't a romantic getaway, but a working weekend. She'd never had trouble distinguishing between the two before.

Why now?

As THEY DROVE through the gated entrance, Terian fully appreciated the beautifully landscaped grounds, stately oaks and tropical foliage that embellished the courtyard and beachfront lawn.

"Is this where we're staying?" he asked.

"Yes."

"Looks expensive."

Aubrie gave a short laugh. "C'mon…"

They took the elevator to the fourth floor.

"Nice condo," Terian said, his eyes traveling around the open areas of the three-bedroom, three-bath unit. The living room featured a large television and video game console. The fully equipped kitchen was inviting, but he doubted they would stay in and prepare meals.

"You can take that room over there," Aubrie stated.

He walked the short distance to the bedroom,

put his weekender bag inside, then navigated to the huge private balcony. He stared out at the trees dripping with Spanish moss and smiled. St. Simons was just as beautiful and tranquil as Polk Island.

"We will go to Barbara Jean's for lunch," she announced. "It's a staple on the island. I love the She Crab soup, the crab cakes and there's a dessert they called Chocolate Stuff."

"What's in it?"

Aubrie smiled. "It's kind of a gooey brownie, but just go with it."

He laughed. "I'm game."

Terian felt a surge of excitement. He knew this weekend was to be all business, but he wanted to have some fun as well. He had a feeling Aubrie felt the same way. Back when they were in school, they often took weekend trips to discover new places and try new foods. Being here felt no different than those trips. He knew better than to say this to Aubrie. He didn't want to make things awkward between them.

After they unpacked, they left the condo in search of food.

The restaurant was nestled in the heart of Pier Village.

Once they were seated, Terian took in their surroundings. The subdued tones and fantastic old photos of the island on the walls. He could tell by the steady flow of customers that it was popular among the locals and tourists.

Looking at the menu, he saw that they specialized in both seafood and homestyle cooking.

"You have to try either the She Crab soup or the crab cakes," Aubrie suggested.

"I want to try them both."

She smiled. "You can do that, too. I'm going to get the shrimp and grits. I've never tried them here."

"It reminds me of LaCroix in a way."

"I knew you'd say that," Aubrie said. "I thought the same thing. It has the same family atmosphere."

When their food came, they sampled the jalapeño bread first.

"This is good," Terian stated. "Just the right amount of kick."

"Try some of the shrimp and grits," Aubrie encouraged. "It's delicious."

He stuck a forkful in his mouth and nodded his approval. "I like yours better."

"That's because you love bacon."

"I like that you add bacon in yours and the creamy texture." He took another forkful. "This is good though."

After lunch they walked around the area.

"You seem to know a lot about this island," he told her.

"That's because we used to come here often. At least once a year. We'll have dinner on Jekyll at The Wharf."

"Sounds good."

His mind wasn't really on eating. Terian was worried about being alone in the condo with Aubrie for a night.

AUBRIE'S THOUGHTS CENTERED on the fact that she wouldn't be able to get a wink of sleep with Terian sleeping in the room down the hall.

He would be a perfect gentleman—this much Aubrie knew without a doubt. However, she wasn't sure that either of them could fight the attraction they felt while being alone in such close quarters. And in such romantic, tropical surroundings.

Maybe I'm making too much of this, she thought.

Aubrie pushed away the thought and focused on enjoying her meal.

"When is the Paradis staff supposed to work at Bleu? I didn't put it on my calendar," Terian said.

"We can start scheduling them for next week," she responded.

"I like the idea of them getting some real-life experience. Only three of them had prior restaurant experience. I wasn't sure about hiring staff this soon before the opening, but I get it—you want to make sure they have extensive training."

"Most of my waitstaff at Bleu went to New Orleans for training."

"Isn't that expensive?" Terian asked.

"Yes, but I consider it an investment. And it's been worth it. And all of the staff except for one cook have been with me from the beginning."

"That's great."

She and Terian continued their conversation as they finished their meals, then headed back to the condo.

In the back of Aubrie's mind was the pact they'd made to keep their relationship a professional one.

TERIAN WATCHED AUBRIE fight sleep, her eyes fluttering open, then closing until they finally shut tight. He sat there debating whether to wake her or just let her sleep. He was fighting his own battle to stay awake as well, but he didn't want to leave her in the living room alone.

He could admit now that he'd had doubts about his partnership with Aubrie, but things were going well. He had learned to ignore the conflicting emotions she ignited within him.

His father had doubts about her, but he didn't know Aubrie the way Terian did. He didn't know that she was a hard worker but always put people first.

Terian stretched and yawned. He was going down fast.

He got up and walked over to the couch where Aubrie was asleep. He tried to wake her.

"Hey, Aubrie…"

She released a soft moan and turned away from him.

Terian grabbed a nearby throw and covered her with it.

"I guess we're sleeping out here," he whispered.

Terian made himself comfortable on the floor and closed his eyes.

The next thing he remembered was someone gently shaking him.

He sat up, trying to assess the unfamiliar surroundings.

"We should go to our rooms," Aubrie said.

"I tried to wake you."

She gave him a tiny smile. "I was tired."

His gaze strayed to the mass of spiral curls framing Aubrie's face. Terian noticed she was watching him intently.

"What is it?" he asked, his voice low.

Aubrie looked away. "It's late. We should try to get back to sleep. We have to be up early, and we have a long day tomorrow. The ferry leaves at eight thirty in the morning."

They walked to their rooms.

She looked back at him. "I'll see you in a few hours."

Terian nodded. "Goodnight, Aubrie."

Hopefully, this weekend would be the beginning of a new friendship between them.

CHAPTER FIFTEEN

THE NEXT MORNING, they got up early to drive to Meridian, which was north of Darien, GA, to catch the ferry. They were going to spend the day on Sapelo Island. It had been a while since Aubrie last visited. She was sure much had changed over the years.

Aubrie was grateful that she had been able to sleep—in fact, she'd fallen asleep in the middle of the movie they were watching. Once she made it to the bedroom, she fell asleep before her head had hit the pillow.

She felt refreshed after a good night's sleep, and her body relaxed. It was something about Sapelo that always put her at ease the moment they boarded the *Katie Underwood*, the main ferry to the island.

Terian pointed and said, "I just saw a dolphin."

"I was looking at the seagulls," Aubrie said. "They have always fascinated me."

"Are all these people tourists, you think?"

"Some of these people live on the island. That

group of children we saw getting off the boat were going to school on the mainland."

Pointing near the ocean dunes, Terian said, "I don't think I've ever seen purple grass."

"They use it in basketmaking," Aubrie explained. "You are going to be amazed at the skill of the basket makers. Talk about gifted…"

"I'm going to have to buy some for my mom and Torrie."

When they stepped off the ferry twenty minutes later, he said, "It's hard to describe, but I feel like I've stepped into the past."

Aubrie smiled. "It does take you back to a place where life was simpler." She enjoyed showing Terian the island and sharing bits of history with him. She just had to keep reminding herself that this was a working trip, not a holiday. They were business partners, not a couple enjoying a weekend away.

They took a guided tour of the island that included the lighthouse that once led ships in and out of Doboy Sound, tabby slave cabins and Hog Hammock community.

"Descendants of slaves live here," she said as they passed the General Store.

Along the way, the guide explained which African traditions had survived since the Middle Passage.

Terian took pictures.

"Is he serious?" he asked when the guide mentioned that Charles Lindbergh landed his *Spirit of St. Louis* on the island.

"Yes," she responded.

After the tour, they rented bikes and took off on their own.

Aubrie led him to an area where a man stood working a grill.

"Is that mullet?" Terian asked.

"Yes. They smoke it over live oak. It's a tradition here on the island. You have to try the mullet and gravy. It's yummy. Actually, catching mullet dates back to West Africa. It's been passed down from generation to generation here on Sapelo."

They walked a few yards.

Terian stopped in his tracks. "Looks like they're roasting oysters over there."

"Smells good," she said. "Maybe we can consider a mullet dish for one of our special events."

"It's certainly something to consider... I love this place."

"It used to be one of my favorite places to visit. I always felt a sense of peace here. I think I'm going to start coming back."

Terian eyed her. "I hope you'll invite me back on one of those trips."

Aubrie looked away to avoid getting lost in those hazel depths.

"I get my red peas here on the island," she said.

"How do you cook them?"

"I add bacon and onion to them and serve with roasted garlic and Jack cheese polenta," Aubrie responded. "I always buy them here because it helps the island economically. Think about the stories you can share with diners about red beans and rice…"

"That's pretty cool," he responded.

Aubrie was close enough to drink in the woodsy scent of his cologne. She turned her attention back to their surroundings. She hadn't expected to enjoy being with Terian this much. Her emotions were all over the place, and she was powerless to do anything about it.

IDEAS FOR NEW recipes battered Terian's brain as he walked with Aubrie back to the bikes they'd rented.

"What are you thinking about?" Aubrie asked.

"How I'd like to incorporate the foods we've tried into the menu. Like the mullet… I'm glad you suggested it. What do you think of blackened mullet?"

"Sounds delicious. I was just thinking about smoked mullet, saltines and lemon wedges."

Terian chuckled. "It would make a delicious

snack for sure. We could always make a mullet stew."

Nodding, Aubrie said, "Glad we're on the same page with this."

He smiled. It was always a good thing whenever they agreed. However, when they didn't, it also made life more interesting. Aubrie wasn't the type of woman who was afraid to speak her mind. She had no problem with that at all.

Terian hoped Aubrie sincerely saw him as someone she could go on this journey with—the way she once did in culinary school. If this venture was going to be a successful one, he would need Aubrie's help. His deepest fear was his father being right about his failure. Terian wanted nothing more than to prove Terrance wrong.

He kept telling himself that he'd attained success once and could do it again. Still, Aubrie had built two restaurants on her own and had a Michelin Star. Terian reminded himself that this wasn't a competition. He swallowed his feelings of insecurity. Right now, he wanted to enjoy this moment.

Terian observed his surroundings, the people, the sights, smells—everything. He wanted to carry the memories of this place with him and translate it into the culture of the new restaurant.

Aubrie was nearby talking with one of the older residents.

He smiled when she offered to help the woman take her purchases to a parked car.

"That was nice of you," Terian said when she joined him.

"She had a lot of stuff."

"So, what's next?"

"We return the bikes and head to the ferry unless you'd like to stay a little longer. The last ferry leaves at five thirty."

"We can head back. I'd actually like to see some of Polk Rothchild's birthplace. Dorian?"

"Darien," Aubrie responded.

Once they were back in Meridian, they climbed into her SUV and headed to Darien.

Terian loved the climate, the panoramic views and clean air of the small town.

"This is a great place to rent a boat and just hang out in the ocean," he said. "I'm not a fisherman, but I could see myself deep sea fishing at least once."

Aubrie laughed. "You? Pleeze…you'd do better with bird-watching."

He had to admit she was right.

"You could go biking."

Terian chuckled. "I think you've already established that I wouldn't be good with fishing."

He stopped walking. "Wait, do you catch your own fish?"

"What if I did?"

"Then I'd have to at least give it a try," he replied.

"Feeling competitive?" Aubrie asked.

"Naw… Yeah, I was."

"You can put your mind at ease, Terian. I don't fish."

"Thank goodness."

Aubrie took him on a self-guided tour of some of the historic sites like Fort King George, the Butler Island Plantation and rice fields.

Terian immersed himself in his surroundings; the majestic evergreen oaks with hanging moss, an array of colorful blooming flowers and bright blue skies. "I never thought I'd see anything that comes close to the beauty of New Orleans. There are some really gorgeous places along the coast of the Carolinas and Georgia. Hidden gems. I'm inspired by everything I've seen this weekend."

"I'm glad you came with me," she said. "It's always nice when you can share something like this with a friend…or a partner."

CHAPTER SIXTEEN

A WEEK HAD passed since Terian's trip with Aubrie to coastal Georgia.

He was glad to have his sister visiting for the weekend. He couldn't wait to show her the restaurant—his pride and joy.

Terian realized that he had to stop thinking of Paradis as his own—he had a partner. It was time to stop putting himself first in every situation.

After picking Torrie up from the airport, he drove straight to Paradis.

"This place is coming together quite nicely," she said as they toured the building. "I really love the sapphire blue and silver color theme."

"I can't take credit for any of the decor—that's all Aubrie," Terian stated with a grin.

"Oh, I knew that. Decorating has never been your gift."

He threw an arm around her. "Torrie, I'm glad you're here. We can go shopping for a more permanent home."

"Why didn't you ask Aubrie?"

"I thought it might be a bit too personal or intimate for her. I didn't want to make things awkward between us."

"I can see your point."

"Yeah," he responded.

Leaning against the counter, Torrie asked, "How are things between you and Aubrie?"

"Very professional," Terian replied. "Our relationship is purely business."

"Doesn't sound like you want it this way."

"I was hoping we could rebuild our friendship. There are times when it feels like we're moving back to how we used to be—then all of a sudden, Aubrie's guard is back up."

"Tell me what happened between y'all at school," Torrie said. "What did you do that was so terrible?"

"I betrayed Aubrie and broke her heart. Outside of our partnership she's very cautious. I can't blame her for feeling that way, but I was hoping she could see that I've matured and am a better man than I was back then."

"Maybe this will change the more you work with her. The two of you have to learn each other all over again."

"I hope so," Terian said. "Because I have real feelings for Aubrie. I always have."

"Sounds like it's up to you to convince her of them."

He nodded. "I just need an opportunity."

After a quick lunch at home, Terian walked out on the balcony to enjoy the warm September weather. The days were still bright and sunny, the temperature just right. He stood out there, enjoying the picturesque view of the ocean.

"I'm falling in love with this island," he said when his sister joined him outside.

Torrie smiled. "I can see why you'd feel that way. It is truly beautiful here. I'm telling you now that Luke and I will be visiting often. He would've come with me, but he just started a new position."

She hesitated a moment. "Mama and Daddy should come to see all this. I think our father would better understand why you chose this island."

Terian shrugged, trying to appear nonchalant. "I don't think it'd matter much to him. He will still believe that I chose the enemy over him. I can't get him to see that Aubrie's not against us. She's a businesswoman."

"You said yourself that she opened Manoir Rouge two blocks from us to get back at you."

"That's what I thought at one time, but I was wrong."

Torrie eyed him. "I really hope you're right about her. Don't get me wrong... I like Aubrie, but she was very angry with you not too long ago. Most people don't get over stuff that easily."

"Aubrie's nothing like me. That's a move I would've made, but not her. You know for yourself that the DuGrandpres have roots in New Orleans—just like we do. She loves everything about the history, the food, the culture… It makes sense why she'd choose to open a restaurant there."

"Oh…" she murmured. "I suppose you could be right. Maybe I've been listening to Dad for too long."

They walked back into the apartment.

Terian decided to change the subject. He didn't want to lapse into a discussion of their parents. "You're a couple of months away from the wedding. Do you have everything in place?"

"For the most part," Torrie said. "I can hardly wait for November to get here. I'm so ready to be a wife to Luke… We've been talking about starting a family immediately. After all, I'm in my thirties."

"I'm looking forward to being an uncle."

She looked at him. "Are you really?"

Terian nodded. "I love kids. I'd like to settle down one day and have a family myself."

"I think you'd be a wonderful father, but I know I'll be a phenomenal auntie."

He laughed.

"I want to see Aubrie," Torrie stated. "Alone."

"Why?"

"I'd like to get to know her on my own. You know I've always admired her. I want my relationship with her to be independent of yours."

"I don't have a problem with that," Terian said. "I'll drop you off tomorrow while I'm in Charleston running a couple of errands."

"Thank you."

Terian leaned back in his chair and said, "You know… I've been craving your Bananas Foster pancakes. I bought the ingredients—I just need you to make them. Mine never taste like yours."

"That's because mine are made with *love*."

"You always say that. So did Grandma."

"It's true, Terian."

"What does that even mean?"

"Cooking not only provides sustenance for the body, but it's also nourishment for the soul. It's been proven that our emotional perception of taste can be enhanced by the amount of love and care that goes into preparing meals."

He nodded in understanding.

They changed into swimsuits and spent the late afternoon at the beach.

Terian watched as his sister spread her towel on the sand. She'd always loved the ocean. Anytime her parents planned a vacation—Torrie opted for someplace near the water.

She glanced over at him and grinned. "You know I'm in heaven, right?"

"I know," he responded.

"It's so peaceful."

Terian agreed as he stretched out beside her in a lounge chair. "Sometimes I come out here after working and just walk. In the mornings, I run if I don't go to the gym."

Torrie glanced at her phone and chuckled. "I texted a couple of pictures to Luke. He's so jealous…"

"Hey, don't be cruel," he teased.

Terian lay back, closed his eyes and relaxed. Since moving to Polk Island, he felt a bottomless sense of peace. He didn't feel an ounce of stress. Even the minor issues they had at Paradis didn't upset him to the point of distraction.

He wanted to enjoy times like this with Aubrie. Terian fantasized about bringing her to the beach for a day of fun and relaxation. He thought of the times they spent at the Parc Balnéaire du Prado in Marseille. He and Aubrie used to sit and relax along the beaches there. Another spot they loved to frequent was Deauville Beach in Normandy.

Terian wanted to make new memories with

Aubrie, even if the only thing they had was friendship. It was better than nothing.

"Torrie LaCroix is here to see you," her floor manager announced from the doorway of the office. "Should I bring her back here?"

Aubrie was surprised by Torrie's visit, especially since they weren't friends or even associates. She decided to keep an open mind about the visit, however. "Yes, that's fine. Thank you, Rachel."

"I hope you don't mind my stopping by," Torrie said when she entered the office.

"Not at all," Aubrie responded. "Your brother mentioned you were coming for a visit. How are you enjoying yourself?"

"I'm really falling in love with Polk Island."

"I can understand why. It's beautiful, romantic and a whole lot of other adjectives," she said with a smile. "Until recent years, it's always been one of South Carolina's hidden jewels."

"Did Terian tell you about my wedding?" Torrie asked. "I'll be sending you a formal invitation closer to the date."

"He did," Aubrie said. "Congratulations."

"Thank you. I'm excited." She paused a heartbeat, then said, "I came to see you because I wanted to tell you how much I appreciate you giving my brother a chance. What happened between you is not my business. I'm just thrilled he's finally following his dream."

"It was a great opportunity for both of us."

"My brother…he's always tried to please our father. Dad was much harder on him…"

"I understand," Aubrie responded.

"Terian's a good person."

"I wouldn't be his partner if I believed otherwise, Torrie. I understand that you're also an excellent chef."

"Cooking is one of my passions, too. I studied in Italy because I love all foods Italian. My father was a bit disappointed because he wanted me to go to France with Terian."

"I remember he visited you a few times during our breaks. Did you ever come to France?"

Torrie nodded. "I did once. I think you'd left to spend your break with your family."

"That's very possible," Aubrie said. "I was a bit homesick for the first year and a half."

"So was I. I would call Terian crying, and he'd have to talk me down. It helped knowing that he was only a two-hour flight away."

During their conversation, Aubrie discovered that she and Torrie had a lot in common.

"I'm really glad you came by," she said. "I've enjoyed talking to you."

"I've always wanted to get to know you, but

I knew there was some tension between you and my brother. I'm glad that's all over with."

"I understand, but for the record—we could've developed our own relationship independent of your brother."

"That's the other reason I came here," Torrie stated. "Because I'd like to do that. I've always felt that you and I could be good friends."

Smiling, Aubrie said, "I'm open to it. Why don't we start by having lunch? I had my chef prepare a Caesar salad with blackened salmon."

"Sounds delicious."

Although they didn't discuss Terian while they ate, he wasn't far from Aubrie's mind. The close relationship between Torrie and her brother mirrored the one she had with Ryker.

"I really want you to come to the wedding," Torrie said. "We're going to have so much fun."

"I'm giving it serious thought."

Terian arrived to pick up his sister not long after she and Aubrie finished lunch.

"Thanks for taking time out to spend time with Torrie."

"We've had a wonderful time together," she responded.

Aubrie noticed Terian was watching her intently. His gaze traveled over her face and seemed to search her eyes. It was as if he were trying to read deep into her soul.

She turned away from him, wanting to escape his penetrating stare. "Torrie, I hope to see you again before you leave town."

"We will make that happen," she said.

When they left, Aubrie sank down in a nearby booth.

This has to stop. She had to find a way to keep some emotional distance between her and Terian.

She had to protect her heart at all costs.

THE NEXT AFTERNOON, Aubrie stopped by the Polk Island Bakery & Café before heading back to Charleston.

Inside, she saw her cousin Leon seated in the booth closest to the kitchen. "Hey, you…" she greeted as she joined him. "I thought you'd be working."

"I got off this morning," he responded. Leon worked as a firefighter and pulled long shifts. "Just came here to get a glimpse of my wife and have something to eat."

As if on cue, Misty walked out of the kitchen and eased into the booth beside Leon. "I drove by your new restaurant yesterday. The outside renovations are beautiful. I'm glad you're opening a restaurant here on the island."

"Thank you. Terian and I are very excited," she responded.

"You're going to be a very busy woman with three restaurants."

"I'm a managing partner with Paradis and will mostly handle the administrative stuff. Terian will have complete run of the kitchen. I have my hands full at Manoir Bleu, so I hired a wonderful executive chef for Rouge. I have a great general manager there as well."

"I hope we'll be seeing you more on the island now with the opening of Paradis," Leon said.

"You will," Aubrie responded. "At least for the first six months or so, but I meant what I said to you at the gala. I'm going to be intentional about making the family gatherings."

"That's great," Misty said.

She took a sip of her iced water, then asked, "How is Aunt Eleanor doing?"

"About the same," Leon answered. "The medication she's on seems to be slowing down the progression of Alzheimer's. She's still writing in her journal and that helps to keep her on track some."

"That's good to hear. I need to stop by and visit with her."

"She'd love that," Misty enthused.

Smiling, Aubrie said, "I'll give Aunt Eleanor and Rusty a call tomorrow to see if they're free one day this week."

"So, what kind of cuisine can we expect with Paradis?" Leon inquired.

"Authentic French, Cajun and even a couple of Gullah made-to-order dishes. Of course, seafood items will be featured prominently on the menu."

"Sounds absolutely divine and mouthwatering," Misty said. "I can't wait for the grand opening."

"Terian and I have something special planned for that. We will both be cooking that evening."

"Wow...two award-winning chefs..." Leon grinned. "We need to go ahead and line up a babysitter for that night. And I have to go on a diet just to prepare for that day."

Aubrie laughed. "You'll definitely need to bring your appetite—that's for sure."

"Well, look who's just walked in..." Misty said. "Your partner."

"Hey, Terian," Aubrie moved over, making space for him. "We were just talking about the grand opening. I told them that you and I will be cooking."

He smiled. "Yeah, I'm really looking forward to teaming up with Aubrie for that special evening."

"Same here," she responded. "It's going to be epic."

"Now you've really got us excited about it."

Leon took the napkin and placed it in his lap. "Honey, just bring me a salad."

Aubrie laughed. "Oh, you were serious about the diet."

He nodded. "I want to experience everything Paradis has to offer. I want to make sure I can afford to gain a few pounds."

Terian looked confused, so she said, "My cousin is cutting back on the calories only to put them back on at Paradis."

Terian chuckled "I like that plan."

Misty shook her head. "Trust me, it'll only last for about a day. My husband loves food. The kind that will put pounds on if you don't eat in moderation."

"I thought you'd gone back to Charleston," he said to Aubrie.

"I stopped in to see Misty and found Leon here."

"I think I'll take that salad to go," Leon said to his wife. "That way I can try to catch a nap before I have to pick up the children."

Misty slid out of the booth. "I better get back to work. Come on over to the counter and I'll send out that salad."

Leon planted a quick kiss on his wife's cheek. "I'll see you in a couple of hours."

"Get some sleep."

Misty left and Leon followed once he saw

his order was ready. Aubrie glanced at Terian. "They are a really sweet couple."

"I can tell," he responded. "Since you're here, why don't you stay and have a bite with me?"

Aubrie looked down at her watch. "I can stay for a little while longer, then I need to get back across the bridge."

Terian picked up the menu. "I'm going to have a hamburger. I can't remember the last time I had one."

"I think I'll have one, too."

"You know how it is when you cook all the time—at least for me. I sample and by the time I'm done, I don't have an appetite. Whenever I'm at home, I normally grab a salad, toss some form of protein on top and keep it moving."

"I do the same thing," Aubrie responded with a chuckle.

"So, tell me more about your visit with my sister yesterday."

"It was nice. I'd seen her a couple of times in New Orleans, but kept my distance because of the tension between us. She basically said that was her reason as well."

"She likes you, too," Terian said. "In fact, I believe Torrie admires you. *We both do.*"

"What does she do when you're not there? You didn't just leave her sitting in the condo all day?"

"She's decorating the place for me."

Aubrie chuckled.

"Why you laughing?" he asked.

"Because you do need help in that department."

"All right…"

"I'm sorry, but Terian…you know you don't even try. You just throw stuff together."

"I'm eclectic."

"Uh-huh…"

"I'm glad Torrie's helping you."

He grinned. "Me, too. You know I was thinking that we should have her join us at one of our premiere events as a guest chef."

"That's a great idea," Aubrie responded enthusiastically.

If she kept ignoring Terian's good looks and contagious smile…she could continue to fight off old feelings that threatened to rise. The more time they spent together, the harder it was to keep her guard up around him.

CHAPTER SEVENTEEN

WHEN THEIR ENTRÉES ARRIVED, conversation was cut to a minimum.

Every now and then Terian would steal a peek at her. He still couldn't get over how beautiful she was, even with her hair pulled back into a messy bun, no makeup and the clothes... a black tank top and jeans.

He bit into his hamburger and chewed thoughtfully.

Aubrie stopped eating. "There you go again...drifting off into heavy thinking. What's going on in that brain of yours?"

"Actually, I was just focusing on how much I'm enjoying this meal with you."

She broke into a grin. "I'm having a great time myself."

"I hope we'll be able to do this again. Have lunch like this."

"I don't see why not." Aubrie picked up a sweet potato fry. "We don't have to act like strangers, you know."

"There are times when I feel like that's exactly what we are. Strangers." His gaze met hers. "But I'm hoping we can get back to being friends."

She awarded him a tender smile. "I'm open to it, Terian. We were young and we couldn't stop competing against one another. Now we're on the same team. It's different this time."

"Tell me the truth, Aubrie. Are we going to be able to move past what happened back then?"

She met his gaze. "If things keep going in the right direction, like they are now—I don't see why we can't."

"I hope you don't mind me saying this, but I'm glad to have you back in my life."

"Why is that?" Aubrie questioned.

"Because you make me want to be a better man. You believe in me...more than my father ever did. Paradis is going to be better than La-Croix ever was," Terian said. "I'll finally get the respect and recognition I deserve."

His words gave her pause.

"Terian, you do realize that you're not in competition with your father?"

"I know that," he responded. "I just want to be better than him. I want Paradis to be a Michelin-Starred restaurant. I want it to be one of the best restaurants in South Carolina."

"I have to say that I don't like whenever you

talk this way," Aubrie said. "It reminds me of how you used to be."

"Why? Because I want to succeed?"

She wiped her mouth on the edge of her napkin. "There's nothing wrong with wanting to succeed, Terian. But you must examine the motives behind it. When you're wanting to be the best above all else…you can end up putting yourself first. It's all about you."

"I don't agree."

Aubrie shrugged. "You should focus more on doing your best as your goal and not outperforming others. Instead of competing with others—you should be setting your own benchmarks for success."

"That's what I'm doing."

"Do you feel excited or anxious whenever you think about Paradis?"

"I have anxious moments," Terian admitted. "Why do you ask?"

"I bet your heart beats faster than normal during those times."

"Yeah, but I'm sure yours does, too."

"I'm not in a race," Aubrie responded. "My heartbeat and breathing are normal and there's no tension in my body. Right now, you look stiff as a board. Take a few cleansing breaths and relax your body."

"Working for my father was stressful."

"Now you're working for yourself. You don't have to prove anything to him."

"He's sitting back waiting on me to fail, Aubrie. I know the man. If you're not number one…well, nothing else matters."

"Terian, you don't have to think like your dad. Terrance LaCroix was very successful for a couple of decades, and he could be still if he'd allow himself to be more open-minded when it comes to making upgrades."

"He can do as he pleases," Terian stated. "I'm determined to make my own way."

"Maybe he'll be more open to your suggestions after Paradis opens and he sees what a great job you're doing," Aubrie suggested.

"I don't know…"

"Just try, Terian. Don't try to beat him. Help your father."

He closed his eyes for a long moment as he considered her words, allowing them to sink in. When he opened them and looked at Aubrie, her eyes were warm pools of brown and her lips were full and inviting. Once again, his need to kiss her hit him full force all the way to the pit of his stomach, nearly robbing him of his breath.

"I hear you, Aubrie. I'll give it some thought."

"I hope you're not just saying that."

"I'm serious," Terian said. "I heard everything you said. I do want Paradis to succeed. I want the same for LaCroix, but it's out of my hands now."

Terian thought about all the years he'd yearned for his father's approval but received only criticism instead. Why was it wrong for him to want to end up the better man? Why was it wrong to build his own legacy?

AUBRIE HOPED SHE'D been able to reach Terian earlier. It was important he realized that whenever he became so focused on winning or being the best, his actions were destructive. She wanted Terian to understand that she was not about to let him ruin what they were building together.

Just before she was about to leave the café, he came to her, saying, "I've been thinking about what you said and you're right. I need to help my dad—not try to best him. He just makes it so hard sometimes."

"Terian, you must never give up on him. If you think about it—we wouldn't be here if I'd given up on you."

"This is true."

"I know how much you love your father. I know that you've always admired him. There's nothing wrong with that. Terrance LaCroix is highly respected in New Orleans and in France."

"Sometimes I think I have so much respect for him because he demanded it of me. I wasn't ever given a choice."

"It's not so different with my parents," Aubrie stated. "They demanded respect from their children. We gave it to them. The only real issue we ever had was that I didn't want to follow in their footsteps."

"My dad refuses to understand that I just want to be a chef in my own right. Make a name for myself. I don't want to be known as Chef Terrance LaCroix's son. I want the world to know me as Terian LaCroix."

"Chef Extraordinaire…"

Terian looked at her. "Aubrie, I've seen the articles written about you and your restaurants. You've made a real name for yourself. The only time I'm ever mentioned in articles since leaving Los Angeles is as Terrance's son. And that's been some years ago."

"Paradis is going to change all that for you."

"I know. I feel like I'm so close, Aubrie."

"Why don't you work out with me tomorrow morning?" she suggested. "You need to de-stress."

"It's a date."

Aubrie chewed on her bottom lip because she didn't have a response for him. A *date*…

"To exercise the stress away, I mean," he stated with a chuckle.

"You're something else…"

"What?" he asked, a look of mock innocence on his face.

"C'mon, friend…let's get out of here," Aubrie said with a smile. "I have to get back across the bridge."

They walked outside.

"What time should I meet you at the gym?"

"Seven o'clock."

"Not a problem," Terian stated. "I'm usually up and running on the beach."

Thirty minutes later, Aubrie was on her way back to Charleston. She felt a thread of sadness upon leaving him.

She gave herself a mental shake. *I can't think about Terian this way. We're just friends.*

TERIAN GLANCED AROUND the gym. "This is nice."

Aubrie nodded. "It's owned by Jordin's husband, Ethan Holbrooke. There's a chain of them."

"It's obvious that the people who come here are serious about working out. The training looks rigorous."

He picked up a brochure. "The total body circuit training looks interesting."

"I hear it's very intense," she said. "Those

bags over there are called ground and pound bags. They are hundred-pound bags."

"I might try out this suspension training machine."

"Have fun with that," Aubrie responded. "I'll stick to the elliptical, treadmill and my cycling class. Terian, you might like the martial arts and circuit training classes. All the programs are designed to push you to your limits."

He bit back a smile while listening to Aubrie. She had such a warm, loving spirit. Terian loved her sense of humor and the sense of freedom she seemed to possess. Not only was Aubrie beautiful, but she was intelligent as well.

There had been an undeniable magnetism between them, and he had missed her greatly over the years.

His gaze landed on her briefly, taking in the purple leggings and matching sports bra she was wearing. He exhaled a long sigh of contentment. He was glad to have her back in his life. But if he wasn't careful, Aubrie would be his undoing.

AUBRIE WENT THROUGH a series of warm-ups. She kept her back turned away from Terian to avoid staring at the firm muscles bulging beneath his tank top. She didn't want to be distracted.

As strong as her attraction was to him, she vowed to never act on those feelings. A relationship other than friendship between them could never work because of their history. Besides, she was focused on her restaurants and didn't have the time or the inclination to deviate from the driving force that had been guiding her since college.

She got on the elliptical to work the tension out of her body.

Forty-five minutes later, Aubrie took several sips of water and swallowed to clear the dryness in her throat. She wiped away beads of perspiration with her towel.

Across the room, Terian was working with weights.

She did a series of stretches, then navigated to the juice bar while he finished working out.

"I feel like a new man," Terian said when he joined her.

Aubrie chuckled. "Really?"

He nodded.

They exited the building fifteen minutes later and Terian walked her to her vehicle.

"I like this gym," he said. "Would it bother you if I joined? I don't want you to think I'm stalking you."

"It's not a problem for me."

Their gazes met and held.

"But it may be for me," Terian said, before he leaned forward and pressed his lips to hers.

Aubrie stiffened.

He backed away, believing he'd misread the signals, and that he'd have to plead for forgiveness. "I couldn't help myself."

She surprised him by closing the space between them.

This time when his lips touched hers, Aubrie's lips softened and welcomed his kiss.

She responded by leaning forward as the kiss grew deeper.

It wasn't until he wrapped his arms around her, that she backed away.

Her cheeks were flushed, and she looked as if she couldn't believe what she'd just done. "Now that we've gotten that out of our system, we can go back to being normal. We can forget what just happened and make sure it doesn't happen again."

"Is that what you really want?" Terian asked.

She stiffened. "I need to get ready for work."

It was an obvious dismissal. He hesitated a moment, wanting to say something, but in the end, Terian nodded and left.

When he got into his car, it hit him that Aubrie never answered his question.

In a small way, her lack of response gave him hope.

CHAPTER EIGHTEEN

THE MEMORY OF that kiss stayed with Aubrie for the next two days. It would've been so easy to keep kissing Terian, but thankfully, she had the presence of mind to stop before things could spiral out of control.

He stirred something in her—something that hadn't been stirred in a long time. Terian prompted thoughts of loving and being loved. Thoughts of marriage and children. But the fact remained that she couldn't trust him with her heart.

Since that fateful kiss, any time they were in the same room together, the mood suddenly turned to one of painful politeness. Most times, Terian would retreat to the kitchen while she stayed in the office at Paradis.

Aubrie glanced up at the clock. She couldn't wait until it was time to leave. She still had work to do at her own restaurant.

Terian appeared in the doorway. "I brought in some egg salad sandwiches for lunch. Would you like to join me?"

"Sure," she responded. It was the polite thing to do.

Aubrie pushed away from the desk, rose to her feet and walked around it.

Together, they made their way to the dining area.

When they sat down in a booth, a touch of humor lit Terian's eyes. "Can you believe we actually survived on this and tuna in school?"

Her mood lightened. "They tasted better than the hot dogs from those street vendors."

"You mean *haute* dogs. They weren't too bad from what I remember," he responded.

She gave a mock groan. "I didn't care to eat my dog on a demi-baguette."

Terian chuckled. "I lived for the days we'd try new recipes and ingredients. Those were good eating days."

Aubrie nodded in agreement. "We had some good times in France. I miss Paris."

"We should go back there."

"I haven't been back since I graduated."

"Me either."

Aubrie looked at him. "Why haven't you gone back?"

"Memories of the way I left—it just didn't feel right. I assume that's the same reason you haven't returned."

"Yes." She bit into her sandwich.

"I'd like for us to go back to Paris together. Maybe creating new memories will take away the sting of the hurt I caused you."

"If we go, it will be on *your* dime," Aubrie said.

"Agreed."

He sat across from her looking so handsome, he almost stole her breath away.

For the next hour, they hustled around the restaurant with an easy camaraderie, which chased away the earlier tension Aubrie felt.

They shared the same sense of humor. Terian understood her and she understood him. Once again, she reminded herself that there could never be anything more between them. It wasn't helping that she couldn't stop thinking about the kiss they shared.

AUBRIE TOOK THE evening off from Manoir Bleu to finalize the Paradis menu with Terian.

"I'm sorry you had to take time off to do this."

"I needed a night away from the restaurant," she responded. "Besides, we need to get this done as well as the recipe book for the cooks. This gives us time to proof and make any corrections after we get everything back from the printing company."

"To show my appreciation for everything

you've done, I bought you something." Terian handed her a gift bag.

Aubrie looked inside, then pulled out the pair of tickets. "How in the world did you get these? They won't go on sale until Friday."

He loved seeing the look of surprise on her face. "A friend of mine is an artist and he grabbed them for me during the presale."

"I can't believe you remembered how much I love old-school R&B."

"How could I not remember?" Terian asked. "You played their music over and over—all the time…"

"I can't believe this. The seats are center stage."

"First row," he pointed out.

"Terian, thank you. This is so sweet of you." Aubrie glanced down at the tickets. "And of course, you're coming with me. Food is on me before the concert. I'm thinking we can start the evening off with oysters on a bed of salt and herbs, paired with Champagne."

"I like that."

"I'll also make marinated mushrooms, stuffed olives, salami and artisanal cheeses…"

"I can hardly wait for the main course."

"You'll have to because it's going to be a surprise," Aubrie stated with a grin.

Terian chuckled. "You have no idea what it is, do you?"

"Actually, I know exactly what I'm going to make."

AUBRIE DECIDED SHE was going to make the meal that was to be their senior project…the one she'd had to handle on her own when he'd left school so abruptly. She felt this was the only way she could finally bury the past because it still stood between her and Terian. He never knew why or how she'd come up with her menu. It wasn't random.

She knew she could never fully move on until there were no more shadows across her heart. Until now, she'd never been able to cook the items on the menu—it hurt too much.

But now it was time to lay the past to rest.

None of this would've happened if Terian hadn't been persistent in convincing her to give him a second chance.

"Look at you," Aubrie murmured when she opened the front door the evening of the show. "You're definitely concert ready."

Terian glanced down at his light green tee shirt and dark jeans, then chuckled. "You don't know what I went through to find one of these fan shirts. I had to order it online and wasn't sure it would get here in time."

Aubrie wore a similar shirt but in a peach color. She paired it with black jeans.

"Well, you look good in it, so I'd say it was worth everything you went through." Aubrie led him into the dining room. "Have a seat and I'll bring out the appetizers."

"I'm looking forward to this," Terian said.

After the appetizer, Aubrie disappeared into the kitchen and returned a few minutes later with two plates of food. She placed one in front of him.

He glanced up at her, his smile evaporating. "Why did you cook this?" He couldn't help but wonder if this was some terrible joke on him.

"I had to," she said as she took her seat across from him. "This menu was inspired by you."

"I'm not sure I understand." Terian resisted the urge to get up and leave. Just when he thought they were moving past what happened…she'd prepared the menu that was their senior project. He'd never helped her complete it.

"I guess I thought it was obvious back then that the idea for this menu was inspired by *you*. Terian, you were my best friend…the first man I ever loved. I chose the oysters because of the time we spent in Cancale."

"The oyster capital of Brittany," he said almost to himself.

"The antipasto because of that tiny little place we would go to once a month…"

"Bella Italia."

Aubrie nodded. "We would treat ourselves to a nice dinner for doing well in our classes."

He searched her eyes but found nothing but sincerity in them. She wasn't trying to be malicious like he'd originally assumed.

"I suppose you chose the short ribs because they're my favorite." Terian glanced down at the braised short ribs, carrots, pearl onions, mushrooms and marble potatoes.

"Of course," she responded. "Don't you see that I had to make this dinner. I needed to prove to myself that I've truly buried the past. Just so you know… I'd planned on making this very meal again for you the night before we were supposed to graduate."

His heart felt tight from the guilt he felt. "I'm so sorry, Aubrie."

"I don't want you to feel bad any longer," she quickly interjected. "This meal was meant to be enjoyed. Tonight, we're creating a new memory. With this meal."

"That's all I want."

"Then eat… Your food's getting cold, and we have a concert to attend." She smiled.

"This is the first time I've had short ribs

since before I left school. I couldn't bring my-self to go near them after what I'd done to you."

"Then I hope you really enjoy mine."

When they finished eating, Terian said, "Everything was delicious, Aubrie."

She smiled. "I hope you left room for dessert."

"You made dessert?" he asked in surprise.

"Of course, I did. Remember the shortbread they served at that one restaurant... I can't think of the name right now."

"The one on Avenue Montaigne?"

Aubrie nodded.

"Is that what we're having for dessert?"

"My variation of it, anyway. I made a peanut butter shortbread with caramel, nougat mousse and milk chocolate."

"Sounds delicious."

They sat across from one another, eating and talking, reliving the happy memories of their time in France.

Aubrie appeared more relaxed than he'd seen her in a long time. Terian thoroughly enjoyed the sound of her laughter as the evening progressed. He wanted nothing more than to have a good time with Aubrie.

Their lighthearted conversation continued as he helped her clean the kitchen.

He glanced down at his watch when they were done. "I guess we should get going. There will be a lot of traffic."

In the car, he said, "It's been a long time since I went to a concert. For the past three years, I missed the jazz festival."

"I'm surprised, because you love jazz."

"I didn't have anyone to enjoy the music with," he responded. "I decided to wait until I have someone special to take with me. You can't just take anyone."

Aubrie grinned. "No, you can't."

The concert was packed. Terian took Aubrie by the hand as they swayed to the music. It thrilled him that she didn't pull away from him. He cautioned himself not to read too much into it. He would just enjoy this moment with her.

Every time Aubrie looked his way, his heart did a little flip in response. After all these years, she still had a strong effect on him.

Aubrie danced and sang along as she enjoyed the live performance of her favorite band. He was enjoying himself more than he ever anticipated and was disappointed when the concert came to an end. He ushered Aubrie through the crowds and toward the exit doors.

They made it to the car and were soon on their way back to Aubrie's house.

"I had a great time with you," she said. "It was a perfect evening."

He smiled. "Yes, it was."

Terian made sure Aubrie was safe inside her home before driving away.

At home thirty minutes later, he headed straight to his bedroom.

As he showered, he tried to focus on the restaurant instead of Aubrie. She'd been open and fun—the evening was perfect, but he didn't want to overanalyze things. Aubrie could easily put up that invisible wall between them once more.

His feelings for her were deepening every minute they spent together... *One day at a time*, he told himself.

One day at a time.

CHAPTER NINETEEN

ON WEDNESDAY MORNING, Terian was already at the gym when Aubrie arrived.

"Seems like you come here more than I do," she said.

"I've been working out four days a week. It really does help with relieving stress."

"I'm sticking to my three days," Aubrie said. "It's all I can handle right now."

Terian patted his neck with a towel. "I take a kickboxing class—that's the only reason I'm coming here four times a week."

As she performed a series of stretches, Aubrie asked, "Who's teaching the class?"

"Ethan."

She burst into laughter. "Yeah, that's why I don't take that particular class. You know he's married to my cousin Jordin. She told me about his classes. More like warned."

"It's challenging but I'm enjoying it." He took a swig of Gatorade.

Aubrie started out walking on the treadmill

for about fifteen minutes. On the machine next to hers, Terian began jogging.

Even when she was working out, Aubrie still possessed that same sunny cheerfulness as she did whenever she was at Manoir Bleu. Her disposition didn't really change for the most part.

Suddenly, she gave him a look that seemed to issue a silent challenge. "You in the mood for a cycling class?"

"Yeah, I'm down."

"Are you sure you can hang?" Aubrie asked as she redid her ponytail. "I know how competitive you get."

"You said that to say what?"

"I don't want you in a bad mood when I make it to the end, and you can't."

"Now who's being competitive?"

She gave him an innocent smile before heading to the cycling room.

Aubrie failed to tell him that it was a high-intensity class. At the end of the fifty minutes, Terian was proud of himself for not quitting. He wasn't going to give her that satisfaction.

She sat down on a nearby bench.

"Are you okay?" he asked.

Aubrie patted her face and neck with a towel. "I'm sore, but other than that I'm good."

They navigated over to the juice bar.

Over smoothies, they discussed their plans for Paradis.

Terian had always loved how Aubrie's expression became animated whenever she discussed a topic she was passionate about, like different foods or preparing meals in general. It made him feel good to see her happy. Terian never wanted to be the source of her pain ever again.

"I guess we'd better get going," Aubrie said. "I'll see you in a couple of hours."

They got up and headed to the door.

Outside, Terian said, "I'll see you at Paradis."

They left the parking lot driving in opposite directions.

At home, he made a quick breakfast, showered and then dressed in a pair of jeans and a polo shirt. Terian looked forward to going to work—something that had changed when he worked with his father. He used to love working with Terrance...not anymore. He was glad that part of his life was over.

AT THE RESTAURANT LATER, Aubrie didn't waste time talking; instead they each went about their separate tasks. She had to work later at Manoir Bleu, so she was careful to balance her time between the two restaurants. That was another thing they had in common—they were both organized, but Aubrie was more organized than Terian.

She went to the post office.

"Guess what came in the mail…" Aubrie said upon her return. She placed her purse on top of the bar.

"Have the bills started coming in?" Terian asked without looking up from his task.

"No, I got a wedding invitation."

"From Torrie?"

"Yes."

Terian smiled. His gaze didn't leave her face. "Are you going to attend?"

"I don't know."

"I'd still like for you to be my plus one."

She smiled. "Let me think about it. I'll give you an answer tomorrow."

Aubrie wasn't sure going with Terian to New Orleans was a good idea. Then again, it made sense. They were attending the same event, so why not go together?

I can handle this, she told herself.

If only she believed it.

WHEN AUBRIE LEFT for the day, the empty restaurant suddenly felt cold and lonely without her. Terian stayed for a couple hours longer, then decided to go home. Paradis didn't feel the same without her.

When his cell rang, Terian was surprised to see his father's name on the Caller ID.

"Hello…"

"You sound strange."

"I'm just surprised to hear from you," he responded. "You've been too busy to talk to me the last couple of times I called."

"I'm a busy man, son," Terrance said. "It wasn't personal."

Terian believed otherwise. In the past, his father had never been too busy to take his calls.

"You there?"

"Yeah, I'm here."

"I called to see how things are going. I know how you tend to hop from one thing to the other. You still trying to open a restaurant?"

"Paradis is opening in December," he responded. "Sorry to disappoint you, Pop."

"No need to take that attitude with me," Terrance uttered. "I'm simply speaking on what I know to be true. How many times have you tried to go your own way? And how has it worked out?"

Terian winced at his father's words. "This time is different."

"So, you say… The way I see it—you'll end up losing your restaurant to that girl. I'm telling you the truth… Aubrie DuGrandpre will take it from you like she took our customers."

His heart sank at the hurt he heard beneath his father's criticisms. "Pop, I don't want to argue with you."

"Then don't," his father responded. "I'm only speaking the truth."

"Why do you want to see me fail?"

"That's not what I want for you, Terian. I just know you."

"Pop, I left because I was tired of you embarrassing me. You obviously don't think I'm ready to run LaCroix. To make matters worse, you kept pitting me against Torrie. That wasn't right and you know it."

"Looks like she will be the one to run it now."

"You aren't ever going to give it to either one of us. You love being in control, Pop."

"Well, I reckon you don't have to worry about it now."

"You're right. I don't," Terian uttered. "Look, I have to go. I'll call you later in the week."

His conversation with his father put a damper on his mood.

Terrance LaCroix didn't like to lose; he didn't like to fail. Neither did Terian, so they would be at odds for a while, and this saddened him. But it wouldn't stop his determination to succeed. His father would not be able to gloat this time.

This time I'll win.

AUBRIE WALKED INTO the restaurant the next afternoon. "The wine cooler we ordered is on back order. Right now, they can't give us a delivery date."

"That's not acceptable," Terian said.

She shrugged. "We'll be fine. Things like this happen all the time."

"I don't have to like it," he snapped. "I can't afford to have things mess up now. Everything must be perfect. I thought you understood this."

"I do understand," Aubrie stated. "You need to realize that nothing is ever perfect. Life just doesn't work that way. Things happen—we must be flexible, Terian."

"That's easy for you to say."

"And why is that?" she asked. Aubrie held back her growing frustration. She didn't want things to blow up—it wasn't that serious.

"You don't have the pressure I have on me."

"That's of your doing."

"What are you saying?"

"Terian, you need to chill. Go to a spa…get a massage…"

He looked at her, his gaze intense.

"You can stare at me all you like," Aubrie told him. "I said it and I meant it. Get out of here. You're no good to me when you're like this."

Before he could reply, she retreated into the

office to let things cool down for a bit. She wished Terian would take her advice or at least just go for a walk on the beach. She hadn't seen this side of him since they were back in school and she didn't like it.

An hour later, Aubrie walked into the bar area. She tried to assess his features but they were unreadable. "Terian, are you in a better mood?"

"I'm fine," he responded.

"I can clearly see otherwise. What happened to set you off? It wasn't just the wine cooler. What's up?"

"Yesterday after you left, my dad called to tell me how I'm going to fail and will end up losing my share of the restaurant to you."

She folded her arms across her chest. "And you believe him?"

"No, not really. I just wish he could support me for once."

"I understand how you're feeling," Aubrie said. "I went through something similar when I told my parents I wanted to be a chef. They acted as if I'd announced I was going to commit a felony. It wasn't easy growing up as a DuGrandpre in a family of attorneys. My father went as far as to threaten to disown me. It took a while, but my parents eventually got over their disappointment. I'm sure your father will eventually come to accept your decision."

"I hope you're right."

"I am. I know how gifted you are, Terian." Changing the subject, Aubrie said, "I told you that I'd let you know about the wedding."

"What did you decide?"

"I'm going with you."

Terian's mood seemed to shift. "That's great. I really needed some good news. Aubrie, we're going to have a fun time."

"I'm looking forward to it."

Aubrie decided to let Terian spend more time by himself. She left the restaurant and strolled along the sidewalk on Main Street, enjoying the feel of the sun on her face and arms. She stopped every now and then to window shop at a couple of the shops.

The blaring sound of a siren blasting caught Aubrie's attention. Her immediate thought was of Leon.

She turned in time to see a red fire engine rushing down the street in the opposite direction. Aubrie wasn't close enough to tell if Leon was riding in it, but she prayed that no harm would come to anyone.

She checked her watch and picked up her pace. She needed to get back to the restaurant.

"How was your walk?" Terian asked when she returned.

"Relaxing," she responded. "How are you doing?" He seemed to be in a much better mood. Aubrie hoped their talk had helped some.

"I'm fine. I'm looking forward to our trip to New Orleans next weekend," Terian said.

"I have to be honest and tell you that I do have some mixed emotions," Aubrie responded. "I'm not sure how comfortable I'll be around your parents."

"All will be fine. I promise."

"I'm pretty sure your dad doesn't like me."

"He doesn't really know you, Aubrie. I'm sure that once he spends some time with you—he'll feel differently."

She wasn't so sure but kept her thoughts to herself.

On Thursday night, Aubrie pulled out a suitcase and began packing for her trip. She was looking forward to going to New Orleans. She wanted to check on her restaurant there and see her family.

Torrie's wedding celebration would begin Friday night with the wedding on Saturday.

They had the entire weekend planned for their guests. Terian was part of the wedding party—he had to participate, but she was only a guest. Aubrie intended to attend the wedding ceremony and reception only.

Terian wanted her by his side for all the festivities. She promised to think about it.

While she packed, Aubrie called her friend.

"Michelle, what are you doing?"

"I just finished some new tee shirt designs. Are you still at the restaurant?"

"No, I'm home."

"Everything okay?"

"I'm having second thoughts about this trip with Terian."

"Why?"

"It's a wedding. You know…romance and all that. I had deep feelings for Terian once, and with all that love in the air… We went to a concert over the weekend and before I realized— it was like old times. I got a little caught up in the memories."

"You're afraid you're going to let your guard down."

"Michelle, I can't let him back into my heart."

"You still have feelings for Terian," Michelle stated.

"Why do you say that?"

"You wouldn't be worried about it if you didn't. You'd just see this as a trip to a place you love."

"I think I'll always care for Terian," she confessed. "But all we can ever be is business partners and no more than friends."

"Things still working out for y'all?"

"It's great so far," Aubrie responded. "For the most part, we agree, but there are times when he's resistant to the way I do things. Eventually, he comes around to my way of thinking." She released a chuckle. "I believe he'd probably say the same of me."

"So, you're confident in his ability to run the kitchen at Paradis?"

"I am. Terian's in his element whenever he's in a kitchen."

"I can't wait to taste this man's cooking from the way you talk about him."

"That's why we get along so well. We both love food."

"*Good* food."

Aubrie chuckled. "Definitely."

They talked for another fifteen minutes.

She put her phone on the nightstand, then walked into her closet to retrieve a couple of dresses. She was still trying to decide which one to wear for the wedding.

She held one up as she stood in front of the mirror, staring at her reflection.

After she laid the dress on the bed, she held up the second one.

She decided to pack them both.

By the time she finished, Aubrie was back to feeling excited and looking forward to her trip with Terian.

CHAPTER TWENTY

AFTER RETRIEVING THEIR LUGGAGE, Aubrie and Terian picked up a rental car, then left the airport.

"How do you feel about being back in New Orleans?" Aubrie asked.

"I always enjoy coming home. I'm just hoping my dad will let me enjoy this weekend. I don't want anything to put a damper on my sister's wedding celebration." Terian glanced over at her. "I hope you've changed your mind about going to the rehearsal dinner."

"I don't think that I should. It's for your family and close friends."

"If you're worried about my dad…he won't mistreat you. He's too much of a gentleman to do that."

"Don't worry about me," Aubrie said. "I can spend the evening with my family."

"You're my plus one," Terian insisted. "You can't leave me without a date for this romantic occasion."

Aubrie chuckled. "It's just a dinner."

"And everyone will have a companion."

"Are you worried they might think you can't get a date?"

His eyebrows rose a fraction. "No, that doesn't have anything to do with it. I just want my partner by my side."

"You want to show your father that we're really a team. That what you have is a partnership that's cohesive," Aubrie said. "Is that it?"

"That's part of it, but mostly I just want to spend this entire weekend with you. My sister's getting married, and I'm here to celebrate." His eyes met hers. "With *you*."

"Okay. I'll go with you to the rehearsal dinner."

Terian broke into a grin. "Thank you."

"I'm expecting you to show me a real good time here in New Orleans."

"Yes, ma'am."

Even though this city was a second home to Aubrie, Terian planned to show her New Orleans from his perspective.

After picking up the rental car, he said, "Let's get something to eat before I drive you to the hotel," he said. "After that there's something I want to show you."

Once they had eaten, Terian drove to the hotel so Aubrie could check in and then headed to Audubon Park.

Aubrie glanced around. "Where are we going?"

"Have you seen the walking maze near the stables?" he asked.

She shook her head. "I haven't. I didn't know anything about it."

He parked the car near the entrance on Laurel Street. "I figured we'd walk off our lunch."

Aubrie put a hand to her stomach. "I need to exercise after eating all that food."

"You only had yogurt for breakfast."

"I never eat anything very heavy when I'm traveling."

They walked through a wrought iron trellis at the entrance.

"Looks like there are two labyrinths," Aubrie said.

"There are," Terian responded. "As you can see, the first one is smaller. That particular pattern dates to 2000 B.C. They were designed to symbolize and facilitate healing for the residents of New Orleans after Hurricane Katrina. I would walk the path to meditate and get centered."

Aubrie was drawn to the intricate design of the redbrick walkway. "It's beautiful," she murmured. "And very serene."

"I spent a lot of time here."

"I can understand why." She knew why Terian

wanted to bring her to this place. He needed to get into a calm and peaceful state of mind before seeing his father.

"Torrie and I like to take nature walks in Couturie Forest."

"I've heard of it, but I've never been there," Aubrie stated. "Phillip has mentioned it."

"He's joined us a couple of times," Terian responded. "I'll have to take you there the next time we come here. This weekend is going to be a busy one."

"I'd like that."

They left the park and headed back to the hotel where Terian dropped her off. "I'll pick you up at seven o'clock."

"I'll be ready," she assured him. "Have fun at the rehearsal."

He chuckled. "Yeah."

TERIAN MADE HIS WAY to his parents' house. He would have liked to bring Aubrie to spend some time with his mother, but he wasn't sure how his father was going to react. Terrance wouldn't be rude to Aubrie, but he'd have no problem humiliating his son in front of her.

He parked in the driveway of the four-bedroom brick home.

Terian was surprised to see Torrie there. "I

didn't know you were here. I didn't see your car outside."

She embraced him. "Luke dropped me off. He took my car for a wash and detail."

"He's getting a head start on his husband duties, I see."

She laughed. "Actually, my car was really dirty. I've been so busy with the wedding, I neglected it."

They were joined by their mother, Margo.

Torrie embraced him, then said, "I'll see you later. I have a few more errands to run before the rehearsal." She grabbed her purse and headed out the front door.

"I'm so happy that you're home," Margo said before giving him a hug. "Did you just come to town for the wedding?"

"I did," Terian responded, hating to disappoint his mother. "Just until Sunday, but I promise I'll be back for another visit, Mom. Aubrie and I have to get back to the island."

Margo's eyes widened in surprise. "She came with you?"

"She did. Before you get any ideas, Torrie invited her to the wedding."

"So, things are going well between you two then."

"Everything is great," Terian responded.

"I'm really happy to hear this," Margo responded.

He glanced around. "Where's Pop?"

"He went to the restaurant to make sure everything is ready for tonight. Your father wants the rehearsal dinner to be perfect for Torrie."

"I'm sure it will be. Even if it's not—I doubt she'll notice. She's floating around on a cloud."

Margo laughed. "Yes, she is…"

They sat down in the den to talk.

"How is Pop dealing with everything?" Terian asked.

"He's adjusting."

"Did he tell you that he called to tell me that Paradis is going to fail? And that Aubrie is going to take the restaurant from me."

"That's just hurt talking, son. He doesn't mean nothing by it."

"His words hurt me."

"I know. I told him as much. All I can say is that you can't take what your daddy says to heart. It just takes him a minute to get used to the way things are."

"Mom, I really don't need to hear any negativity. I'm putting my all into Paradis—I'm not going to quit."

"I don't want you to think on this anymore. Your sister's getting married on Saturday—this weekend is about her, and we're gonna put everything else aside for Torrie and Luke."

"I don't have a problem with that," Terian said.

"Neither do I."

He looked over his shoulder at his father. "Hey, Pop. I didn't know you were back."

"I just got here. I caught the tail end of your conversation and I agree with your mama. We have something to celebrate—that's what we're gonna focus on."

"Aubrie came with me," he announced.

"Why?"

"Our daughter invited her to the wedding," his mother interjected. "She'll be treated as any other guest."

"Why you felt the need to say that?" Terrance questioned. "I know how to carry myself. I don't have nothing against Aubrie DuGrand-pre except she stole our customers. Our business was good until she opened that restaurant two blocks from ours. She knows good business though. Got a head for it—that much is clear." He looked at his son. "Guess that's why you decided to partner with her."

"That was only a part of it, Pop."

"It's time for y'all to get ready for the rehearsal."

Carrying a leather weekender, Terian walked up the stairs to his room.

He was tired of his father blaming Aubrie for ruining their business when it simply wasn't true. Terrance wasn't willing to accept the truth.

One day he would have to face reality.

AUBRIE OPENED THE door to her hotel room wearing a strapless teal dress that fell just below her knees. She bit back a chuckle when Terian did a double take and said, "*Wow.* You look amazing."

She smiled. "Thank you."

"Every man in the restaurant will be looking at you."

"I doubt that. But I'm sure you'll be catching the attention of all the women."

They laughed.

She picked up her purse and a lightweight sweater in a pale teal color. "Here we go…"

"I saw Torrie when I got to my parents' house. She looked so happy, Aubrie. She's looking forward to being a wife and mother. I don't think anything could make her any happier."

"I'm very happy for your sister."

"I am, too."

"How did it go with your dad?" Aubrie asked.

"We agreed to focus on Torrie this weekend."

When they arrived at the restaurant, there was a sign posted that it was closed to the public.

Aubrie hadn't been there in years, but everything still looked the same. The decor was dated and in desperate need of a makeover, in her opinion. She kept her thoughts to herself, however.

Torrie greeted them, then introduced her to Luke. "Aubrie, I'm so glad you decided to come to the wedding. We're going to have so much fun."

"Terian's right," she said. "You're absolutely glowing."

"I'm so excited I can barely stand myself."

Aubrie gave a short laugh. "I'm sure I would be the same way, Torrie. And you're right... we're going to have a lot of fun."

"It's nice to finally meet you, Aubrie," Margo said when she joined them. "Your mother is a dear friend of mine."

"She told me," she responded.

"I've heard great things about you and your restaurants. Manoir Rouge is very popular here in New Orleans."

"It's wonderful to meet you as well. LaCroix is a staple in this city. A piece of its history."

"Miss DuGrandpre, it's good to see you,"

Terrance stated. "This weekend is a celebration, LaCroix style."

"I'm looking forward to it all," Aubrie said. "It was kind of Torrie to include me."

"You're my son's partner," Terrance responded. "Practically part of the family." He took his wife by the hand, then said, "Excuse us. I see some people we need to say hello to…"

"I'm not sure what your father meant by that comment 'by LaCroix style'," she said when she and Terian were alone.

"Don't worry about it. I'm pretty sure it was directed toward me. He wasn't being unkind, however. I think it was his way of saying that you are welcome here."

She smiled at that.

Terian escorted Aubrie to their table.

Terrance and Margo welcomed everyone before taking their seats.

Servers brought out the food.

After they finished the main course and while dessert was being served, Luke stood up to toast Torrie and her family. Torrie went next and gave a toast to his family.

"This is really beautiful," Aubrie whispered. She really enjoyed witnessing this special moment between two families that would be united in marriage in less than twenty-four hours. It had also touched her the way Terrance and Margo had welcomed her.

Smiling, Terian nodded in agreement.

Aubrie started to feel that now familiar unease about enjoying his company so much. She didn't want to get caught up in his web a second time, so she vowed to keep some emotional distance between them.

After the dinner was over, Terian escorted Aubrie to her hotel room.

"Would you like to come in?" she asked. She wasn't ready for him to leave despite her misgivings.

"Sure."

"Your sister gave a really nice toast to her future in-laws. It was very sweet."

"Yeah, it was," he responded. "I don't think I've ever seen her happier than she's been with Luke. It's obvious that he loves Torrie as much as she loves him."

"That's good because she's getting married in less than twenty-four hours." Aubrie leaned forward, reaching for the television remote. "If you're not too tired, we can watch a movie."

"I'd like that," Terian responded.

Aubrie felt herself becoming drowsy halfway through the movie, but she tried to fight against it. She craved Terian's nearness.

When it ended two hours and fifteen minutes later, Terian rose to his feet. "I guess I better get out of here. If you're up early enough, we're having a family breakfast tomorrow at the restaurant."

"Isn't it just for your family?"

"You're my date, Aubrie. The invitation includes you, too."

"What time should I be ready?"

"How about eight thirty? The breakfast is at nine."

"I'll see you then," Aubrie said while wondering if the air between them was pulsing. Or was it just her heartbeat running rampant? Either way, the emotions coursing through her were ones she hadn't felt in a long time.

TERIAN WAS CAREFUL to not make any noise as he made his way to his bedroom. He didn't want to disturb his parents. As he neared their room, he saw a sliver of light escaping from beneath the door.

They're still up.

He held his breath as he crept past their room to the one where he would sleep.

It didn't take him long to prepare for bed.

He lay beneath the covers, his mind centered on Aubrie. Terian wanted to find the kind of happiness his sister had found with Luke. *I had that once and lost it, but now I have a chance to have it again.*

He'd searched his heart many times, wondering if what he felt for Aubrie was the kind of love that would last a lifetime. Even when he thought she opened Manoir Rouge to hurt him, when he thought she'd never speak to him again...the answer was always the same.

Yes.

His feelings for Aubrie had nothing to do with reason. In the weeks and months ahead, Terian looked forward to seeing what the future held for them together and separate.

He shifted his position in the queen-size bed.

Images of Aubrie continued to dance across his mind. Whenever he was around her, he couldn't help the spark of awareness that ran through his body. At the same time, the feeling was always followed with a sense of guilt. He didn't deserve someone like Aubrie. She had no problem going after what she wanted. She was willing to take risks to make her dreams come true.

Paradis wouldn't exist without Aubrie's help. There was no point in denying the truth of it. He liked having her as a partner, but there was a tiny part of him that wished he could've done it on his own. After all, she had two restaurants of her own.

Terian knew what Aubrie would tell him right now. She'd accuse him of making everything about himself.

He frowned. He hated to admit it, but maybe she was right.

CHAPTER TWENTY-ONE

TERIAN WALKED WITH his mother around the New Orleans Board of Trade, the wedding venue. Torrie wanted candles and flowers everywhere to complement the ivory and gold color palette. As far as Terian was concerned, the event planners had done a fantastic job with the decorations.

"Your sister should be pleased with the way everything looks. They did a fantastic job on the decor," Margo said. "Did you see the dance floor? It's emblazoned with Torrie and Luke's monogram just like their invitation."

"It's real nice," Terian stated.

"When I married your father—we just had the preacher marry us one Sunday after service. I never imagined doing something elaborate like this. Torrie did tell me that she was only going to marry once, and she intended to do it big."

"She's been saving forever," Terian responded. "Torrie will have a beautiful ceremony just like she wanted."

Margo glanced at her watch. "Son, shouldn't you be getting dressed?"

"I wanted to talk to you a moment."

"Are you okay?" she asked.

"I'm fine. I just don't like this space I'm in with Dad. It's uncomfortable."

"Terian, don't worry about your father. He'll come around. This is Torrie's day. Put everything else out of your mind for now. Let's celebrate your sister and Luke."

When they headed back to where the dressings rooms were located, Margo asked, "Where's Aubrie?"

"She's probably still at Manoir Rouge. I know she scheduled a meeting with her staff. She'll be here soon." He kissed his mother's cheek. "I'll see you at the ceremony."

Terian returned to the men's dressing room.

As the other men in the room continued to talk, Terian found his thoughts drifting back to Aubrie. He slipped on the vest, buttoning it closed.

He was getting in too deep with Aubrie. He knew she wasn't ready for a relationship with him—they were still getting to know one another all over again—but the more he spent time with her old feelings resurfaced…feelings that never went away.

He was grateful she'd come to New Orleans

with him. It gave Terian a chance to show Aubrie who he was on a personal level. It also allowed him an opportunity to get to know her.

Her laughter used to fill his heart with music, and that hadn't changed even now. He'd never known anyone like her before, a woman who possessed a steely strength and complete independence. Terian was captivated by her sharp mind and easy sense of humor.

He pushed away all thoughts of Aubrie as he adjusted the bow tie, which matched the gold-colored vest.

When he was dressed, he went to see if Aubrie had arrived. He was just in time to see her walk through the doors of the trade center with her cousin Phillip.

His breath caught in his throat. She looked stunning in a vivid purple dress, her long, flowing curls framing her oval face.

Terian decided not to make his presence known. He just wanted to stand there watching her, but he needed to get back to the dressing room. It was almost time for them to line up. The wedding would be starting soon.

He was glad that he'd trusted his instincts about Aubrie. Taking her on as a partner felt right. He was finally on a course to become the man he always wanted to be.

The groom and groomsmen were lining up

when he rounded the corner of the men's dressing room. Terian quickly took his place.

During the ceremony, he watched his twin begin her future with the man she loved. For a moment, Terian envied her. She'd never allowed their father to control her the way he had. Torrie loved the restaurant as much as he did, but she often told him she'd never let it rob her of peace and contentment.

He vowed to hold to that same policy going forward.

A CHAMPAGNE WALL welcomed guests as they entered the room where the reception was held. Both the ceremony and the reception were laden with fragrant flowers and candles.

Aubrie was still feeling emotional after witnessing Torrie and Luke's romantic union.

I might as well admit it. I'm a sap when it comes to weddings.

She always got emotional during the wedding dinners that were held at her restaurants. Aubrie especially loved it when a customer asked her assistance in planning the perfect way to propose during a romantic dinner. She was always eager to assist.

Phillip walked over with two glasses of Champagne, interrupting her musings.

"That was surely a nice wedding," he said.

"Simply beautiful," Aubrie responded as she accepted a flute. "If I ever get married, it will be here in New Orleans."

"Me, too," Phillip stated. "My ex wanted to have a destination wedding. She wanted to get married in Jamaica."

She eyed her cousin. "Is that why you two broke up?"

Phillip shrugged. "No, she decided I wasn't the one for her. She left me for some pro athlete, but I hear they're not together anymore."

"Well, it's her loss."

"Oh, I agree," he said with a chuckle. "I must tell you that I'm glad you and Terian have resolved your issues. I think he's a good guy."

"So do I," Aubrie responded.

Terian walked over. "Would you like to dance?" he asked her.

"Sure." She smiled at Phillip before taking Terian's arm.

"Now that all of the pictures have been taken, I can join you at your table," Terian said as he escorted her to the dance floor. "I never meant to abandon you, Aubrie."

"You didn't. I'm so glad I decided to come," she replied. "Torrie had a beautiful wedding and the reception…well, it was a party."

Terian chuckled. "That it was…"

They danced to two songs, one a slow, romantic medley.

When the music stopped, Terian wasn't ready to release Aubrie. He yearned to hold her even closer.

She was fanning herself. "It suddenly seemed to warm up in here," she murmured.

"Would you like something to drink?"

Aubrie nodded. "Yes. Thank you. Just some iced water with lime."

He needed a brief reprieve to sort the emotions swirling within.

When he returned to the table with their drinks, his racing heartbeat had returned to normal.

At the end of the evening, Terian drove her back to the hotel.

"It was nice to see your father enjoying himself." She chuckled. "He had a great time during the Second Line Parade. He can dance."

Terian laughed as he escorted her to her room. "He and my mother love dancing."

"I have to say that your father was much more welcoming than I was when you showed up with Phillip at our party on Polk Island."

He smiled at her. "You were definitely a bit cool to me, but I understood why."

"It was probably immature to wait so long before hearing you out."

"I should've talked to you after everything went down, but I was embarrassed."

"Actually, it never should have happened in the first place," Aubrie stated. "Terian, you should've come to me if you were struggling. I knew your grades weren't great, but not enough to make you quit. Maybe I could've helped you."

"You're right. Back then, I was too proud to ask for help."

"I hope you'll put aside your pride in the future if you ever need help."

"I did that, remember. I don't think we'd be partners otherwise. However, should that day come again, I'll rush straight to you."

"I'll do the same," Aubrie said.

His eyebrows rose in surprise. "Really?"

"Yes. Of course."

"You can't imagine how happy that makes me feel," Terian said. "I feel like the gulf between us is gone."

"It is," Aubrie confirmed. "I see how much you've grown. You own your mess and I like that."

She dared to look up and meet his gaze, the sight making her heart squeeze tight.

Aubrie reached up to trace the line of Terian's mouth with her finger, finally surrendering to what had been on her mind for a while.

His lips were firm and warm.

It was a good kiss—one that convinced her she'd made the right decision.

ON MONDAY MORNING, Terian had to drag himself out of bed. He and Aubrie had flown back to Charleston Sunday evening, then stayed up late at her place going over some business stuff. After seeing his father over the weekend, he wanted everything at Paradis to be perfect.

I can't fail.

He was dressed and on his way to the restaurant by the time the clock struck nine o'clock. He decided against going to the gym. He was looking forward to seeing Aubrie.

The kiss they shared in New Orleans was still at the forefront of his mind. He'd been both surprised and thrilled by the unexpected move on her part. He was left wondering if Aubrie was still attracted to him even though she fought against it. A part of him hoped that maybe there was a chance for them to be more than friends. Another thought came to him… maybe she'd just gotten carried away by the romantic setting.

Aubrie didn't arrive until a few minutes after eleven.

"How long have you been here?" she asked.

"Since nine. I expected you around ten."

"Why? I never said I was coming in that early."

He huffed. "We still have a lot that needs to be done, Aubrie. The appliances are being delivered today…"

"Whoa…" She frowned. "Terian, I'm not about to punch a time card. I had to stop at Bleu before coming here. I had bank deposits to make. Paradis is not my only responsibility."

He didn't respond.

"Another thing… I don't know what's going on with you, but I don't want to deal with your attitude." She glanced around the kitchen. "Things have been shaping up nicely. I'd really hate for us to start having issues now."

"We don't have an issue. I'm just feeling a lot of pressure."

"Does this have to do with your father?" she asked. "Or the fact that I have Rouge and Bleu. Do you believe my loyalty is more to my restaurants than to Paradis?"

"I've felt that way at times," Terian admitted. "But it's more of a passing thought."

Arms folded across her chest, Aubrie said, "Before we go any further—we need to discuss that *passing* thought."

He could tell she was upset with him. "There's not anything to talk about. It may have crossed my mind once or twice—that's it."

JACQUELIN THOMAS 273

"How could you even feel that way after everything I've done to help you? If anything, I neglected Bleu."

"I told you—it was a passing thought when we first started working together. You were still a bit cold where I was concerned. I haven't felt like that in a long while, Aubrie. Look, we're almost to the opening. We work well together. The last thing we need is a misunderstanding."

"I didn't start this."

Terian released a sigh. "I'm sorry for questioning your commitment. Can we please just start over?"

"Maybe we've been spending too much time together," she said. "I think I'll go back to Bleu."

He blocked her exit. "Don't go...please. I was behaving like a jerk, and it was wrong. I guess I'm feeling the stress of making Paradis the success I want it to be. And I admit that a chunk of that stress is proving to my father that I can do this. But I shouldn't have taken it out on you."

She didn't respond.

"Aubrie... I'm sorry. Can we please start over or move forward?"

"I know you're stressed. But try not to make me the enemy."

The conversation came to a halt when a deliveryman showed up. Terian went to let him inside the restaurant.

"I really like the new appliances," he said after the ovens and refrigerators were installed. "I wish my dad would consider updating his restaurant."

Aubrie glanced down at her phone. "The mixers and food processors will be delivered tomorrow. The slicers come on Wednesday."

His mood was suddenly much lighter. Terian broke into a grin. "This is really happening."

"Yes, it is," she murmured.

"I don't have the right to ask a favor after the way I acted earlier, but I'm going to give it a shot anyway. My house sold in New Orleans so I'm ready to buy something here on the island. Do you have some time to look at a couple of properties with me?"

Aubrie hesitated, and for a moment he thought she was going to refuse. But then her expression cleared, and she nodded. "I'll go with you."

"I appreciate it," he said. "Normally, Torrie would go with me, but she's on her honeymoon."

"It's not a problem. Have you looked at any listings?"

"A couple," Terian responded. "They looked good on paper, but I need to see them in person."

Aubrie followed him out to the car.

He held the front passenger door open for her. Terian closed it after she was safely inside, then walked around the SUV to the driver's side.

He drove to another neighborhood nearby.

"This part of the island is called the Victorian district," Aubrie said. "My cousin Trey lives in that next block. It's the house with the hanging baskets of Boston ferns on the porch."

"He's the marine, right? The one who runs the museum and is married to the physical therapist?"

"Yes, that's him."

"I heard he lost both his legs in Afghanistan. I have much respect for a man who inspires others."

"Trey's incredible."

"I look forward to getting to know him better."

"These are new," Aubrie said as they pulled into the parking lot of a cluster of Victorian-style condos. She admired the ornate exterior, the gabled roof and stone construction. "What do you think?"

"They look nice," Terian responded. "I like that they're new construction."

"Let's take a look at the model."

They got out of the car.

Once inside, Aubrie fell in love with the large sunny rooms, the gourmet kitchen and the decorative woodwork.

"I like it," Terian said. "I can see myself living here."

"This one has three bedrooms."

"That's what I want. I love that there's a flex room on the first floor for an office."

He walked over to a window and looked out for a couple of minutes. When he turned around, he said, "I'm going to put in an offer on one of these."

"Well, that was easy," Aubrie joked.

They headed to the condo office, where Terian filled out the necessary paperwork.

"Why don't we celebrate?" Aubrie suggested when he'd signed the last form. "We can have lunch at the Polk Island Bakery & Café."

He grinned. "Sure."

Terian didn't care where they went if he was with Aubrie.

"I'm glad Misty's taking some time off," Aubrie said a short time later as they took their seats in a booth near the large picture window facing Main Street. "I think she works as much as I do, only I don't have children or a husband."

"What would you do if you had a family?"

"I'd still work, but maybe not as many hours,"

Aubrie responded. "Especially if I have children. You know they grow up so fast. I want to witness all their special moments." She looked at him. "What about you?"

"Family will always come first," Terian said. "One thing about my father…he always put us before the restaurant. He made sure my work schedule never interfered with football practice…and he never missed any of my games."

"It's clear to me that despite what's going on between you two—you still love and respect your father. I think it's wonderful."

"I don't know why, but I would just feel better if I could get his blessing…"

Aubrie nodded in understanding.

Terian shifted in his seat. "I'm determined to succeed despite the lack of my father's support."

She glanced at her watch.

"Are you going to Manoir Bleu this evening?" Terian inquired.

"Yes. I have someone out sick, so I'll be working the kitchen."

"You're dedicated. I really like that."

"I have to be," Aubrie responded. "We have to be ready to step in when necessary. My restaurants mean the world to me. You'll feel the same way about Paradis."

"I already do," Terian said. "It's on my mind when I wake up and when I go to bed."

She smiled. "It's almost like the restaurants are our children. We give birth to them, nurture and help them grow..."

"I never really looked at it that way, but you're right."

"I have to get going, but I'll see you tomorrow," Aubrie told him. "And I still say that your father is going to surprise you. He'll come around because he loves you, Terian. Trust his love."

Terian wanted to believe her words. He hated being at odds with his father. He hated that he couldn't talk to him about Paradis to get advice or even to vent his frustrations. He was grateful to have Aubrie by his side.

"ROCHELLE, YOUR DAUGHTER is just lovely," Margo said when she called to update her friend. "You should've seen her and Terian together at the wedding. There's something there... I can tell from the way they look at one another."

"I always thought they'd make a cute couple—I just didn't voice it. Aubrie doesn't want me involved in her relationships. But I'm rooting for them."

"I normally don't butt in, but this is the first time I've ever seen Terian like this—he just couldn't keep his eyes off Aubrie. My son's eyes light up whenever she's around. He's in love with her."

"I believe my daughter feels the same way about him," Rochelle said. "But, Margo, we simply have to sit on the sidelines. We can't interfere. I've learned my lesson about that."

"I know you're right. I just hope they won't let work or Terrance get between them."

"You just keep your husband in check. Now that you can do—keep him from interfering with the kids' relationship."

"I'm hoping Terrance won't do something like that, but if he does—I'll take care of him. My son deserves to be happy."

"They have some great ideas for the new restaurant," Rochelle said.

"I'm proud of Terian."

"Margo, what do you think about joining me for a spa weekend at the beach?"

"I would love it… I need some time away just to focus on me for a change. Don't get me wrong—I love Terrance and we're good, but this rift between him and Terian really bothers me."

"Maybe you'll gain some perspective while we're relaxing."

"What dates do you have in mind?" Margo asked. "This is going to be so much fun."

CHAPTER TWENTY-TWO

"Chef..."

Aubrie came out of her reverie when one of the cooks called for her. "Huh?"

"Mise en place."

"Thank you," she murmured. Her cooks used the French term, which referred to the setup in the kitchen. All her ingredients had been measured, cut, peeled, sliced, grated, the pans and other equipment lined up. Tonight, she was filling in for her executive chef, who was out sick.

Aubrie spent most days at the restaurant taking care of the administrative side, creating specials, whipping up sauces and making sure there weren't any fires to put out. In the evenings, she often worked at the pass, personally inspecting and garnishing each dish before it was sent out. On weekends, Aubrie worked the dining room and bar area, greeting guests and explaining dishes. There were other times when she prepped food, washed dishes and whatever else needed to be done. She never asked anyone to do something that she wasn't willing to do herself.

"Chef LaCroix is in the dining area," Rachel announced. "I thought you'd like to know."

Aubrie was surprised since Terian never mentioned he was coming by. "Is he eating here?"

"Yes, I believe so. He's looking at the menu."

She walked to the entrance and peeked into the dining room.

He saw her and waved.

Smiling, she waved back.

When there were only a few guests left in the dining room and no more orders, Aubrie took off her chef's jacket, checked her reflection in the mirror, then made her way to Terian's table.

She sat down across from him. "How is your dinner?"

"It was superb," Terian responded with a grin. "The smoked salmon…it melts in your mouth."

Aubrie smiled. "Why didn't you tell me you were coming?"

"I honestly didn't know until I ended up here. I didn't feel like cooking tonight, so I went in search of food."

"It's nice of you to come all the way here. My cousin's place is just a few blocks from your condo."

"I thought about going to the café, but I just kept driving. My stomach was craving a really good meal."

Smiling, Aubrie rose to her feet. "I need to check on the kitchen."

"Do you mind if I wait for you?" Terian asked. "I'm not ready to go home."

"Not at all," she responded. Aubrie didn't mind his company.

After the restaurant closed, Terian followed her home.

Once inside the house, they settled down in the family room.

"Why did you really come to Manoir Bleu tonight?" Aubrie inquired. "I don't think it was the food that brought you there."

"I came to eat, but also because I wanted to see you."

"Oh," she murmured. "I would think you'd be tired of that, especially since we spent most of the day together."

"I enjoy spending time with you."

"Terian…" She wanted to believe that they were both feeling a bit lonely. Aubrie knew that he didn't really have any friends locally. But she didn't want to read more into it than it was.

She had to keep her emotions under wraps.

"I'm not trying to make you uncomfortable,

but I keep thinking about the kiss we shared… That meant something to both of us."

"We were in love once. It's only natural to just get caught up in the moment," she interjected quickly, hoping to convince Terian to see their kiss as simply that—a kiss. "You shouldn't perceive it as anything more."

"Aubrie, I know you. The kiss we shared did mean something."

"I do have some residual feelings for you, but the reality is that we're business partners. That's all we can ever be." Aubrie felt a tiny stab in her heart as she said those words. Despite her efforts, her feelings for Terian ran much deeper than she wanted.

"Why?"

"We're not the same people we were seven years ago, Terian."

He gave a tiny smile. "That's a good thing, don't you think?"

Aubrie looked at him. "I guess what I'm trying to say is that we shouldn't try to re-create the past."

"I've always cared deeply for you, Aubrie. That's never changed."

"Terian, let's just get through the opening of Paradis," she responded. "Things may look and feel different after that."

"I assure you my feelings won't ever change."

She reached over, taking his hand in hers. "We're becoming good friends. Let's not confuse things."

"I won't pressure you."

"Thank you, Terian."

When he left to go home, she sank down on the sofa, tears welling in her eyes. "I don't think I can do this," she whispered. "Why did I let him back in my life?"

TERIAN WALKED INTO the condo, grabbed a bottled water from the refrigerator, then dropped down on the sofa.

I hope I haven't ruined things between me and Aubrie. I never should've brought up the kiss. It was too soon.

He wasn't going to pressure her—he would just have to wait on Aubrie. He believed she still had feelings for him, but maybe it was just friendship, or worse—completely professional as she'd said. Maybe what she once felt was truly no more. He'd abused her feelings for him when they were in school.

Terian could only blame himself if she no longer loved him.

He shook away that last thought. Her kiss told him her feelings went beyond working together. He decided to hang his hope on that.

But deep down, his old insecurities bubbled.

Aubrie had always been out of his league. He was just too stupid to realize it back then. He knew that no matter how successful he was—he'd never be good enough for Aubrie Du-Grandpre. She was almost perfect, in his mind.

Terian was flawed—he knew it. But each day, he resolved to be the best person he could be. He wasn't doing it for Aubrie or his father—he was doing it for himself.

He couldn't let go of the hope placed in him by Aubrie's kiss. He wanted to hold on to it. It pushed him to do better…be better. Terian vowed that he would become the man who was worthy of Aubrie's love. She was worth fighting for. She was worth the wait.

THE NEXT DAY, Aubrie and Terian pretended the discussion from the night before never happened. They were able to get through the day without any uncomfortable silences.

"Phillip's in town," Aubrie announced when she finished her phone call. She was in the middle of some paperwork when he called. "He's here for a conference."

"Is he coming by to see Paradis?"

She nodded. "On Friday. He made sure to tell me that he's expecting a full tour of the restaurant."

Aubrie checked her watch. "I'm having an

early dinner with Michelle in an hour. I should probably head back to Charleston."

"Enjoy your evening," Terian said.

"Do you have any plans for tonight?" she asked.

"I'll be here for another hour or so, then it's home."

"After dinner, I'll be at Manoir Bleu until closing. If you're up for a late-night Netflix movie and dessert—come by the house. That's if you're okay with being friends."

He smiled. "I'll see you then."

She met Michelle at a Mexican restaurant two blocks from Bleu.

"What do you have planned for tonight?" Aubrie asked after they were seated. "You normally don't eat dinner this early."

"I'm meeting someone, but I also know that you have to work later."

Aubrie picked up the menu, scanning the offerings.

Michelle took a sip of her iced water, then said, "I think I'll get the pecan-crusted salmon."

"I might give it a try as well." She laid the menu on the table. "I invited Terian over for Netflix and dessert later tonight," Aubrie announced. "Michelle, I don't know what I was thinking."

"He's your business partner. Maybe you need

to do some bonding after all that's happened. How are you going to rebuild trust if you don't spend time together?"

"True," she murmured. "You're right. Terian and I agreed to be friends—that's what tonight is all about. *Two friends getting together.*"

Smiling, Michelle picked up her menu. "You over there doing a lot of rationalizing."

"No, I'm not. I'm just saying that nothing's going to happen between Terian and me."

"Nobody said anything like that." Her friend chuckled, then asked, "Why are you looking all flustered?"

"Let's talk about something else," Aubrie said. "Are you meeting with anyone interesting?"

"No. And you're not changing the subject. You and Terian had been getting along well before y'all went to New Orleans. Something shook you up. What happened?"

"We kissed," Aubrie responded. "I kissed him once after we went to the gym just to get it out of my system. But the kiss in New Orleans…it felt like more."

Michelle leaned forward in her seat. "*Really?* Well, I'm not surprised. I knew it was going to happen sooner or later."

"It was never supposed to happen. Terian and I can't go back down that road."

"Girl, that's the *only* road for you two. You might as well get ready to walk it out."

Michelle's words shook Aubrie to the core, although she tried not to show it.

They placed their orders when the server came to the table.

"We're really good as partners," Aubrie stated. "I don't want to mess it up by getting involved with Terian."

"I'm not one for repeating mistakes, but I just feel that you and Terian are supposed to be together. Give him a chance."

"That's rich coming from you. I remember if your date was more than fifteen minutes late, you would cancel the entire evening."

"Unless he had a good excuse," Michelle responded. "Like he was either dead or dying."

This made Aubrie laugh.

"We've been friends for a long time. We've seen each other through broken hearts and everything. Trust me when I say this…if you keep this wall up that you've built around your heart—you'll regret it one day. Just think about it."

"It took me a long time to get over Terian."

"I know it did. But you've said yourself that he's changed."

"He has," Aubrie confirmed. "He's more mature now than he was back then, but so am I."

"Take it one day at a time."

"I hear you, Michelle," she said with a soft sigh. "The thought of loving Terian scares me."

CHAPTER TWENTY-THREE

TERIAN ALWAYS ENJOYED spending time with Aubrie outside of the restaurant. He loved working with her as well, but she was different outside of business. It was those moments when she let her hair down that he glimpsed the old Aubrie—the one who captured his heart during their time in France.

He waited until she called to say she was on her way home before leaving the island.

"Normally, I don't like to eat this late," Aubrie said when he arrived. "But my mother would consider it bad form to invite you over and not have coffee and dessert."

"I'm not worried about my figure," Terian responded with a chuckle.

"Well, I *do* worry about mine. So, I made lemon and passion fruit pudding before I left the restaurant. It's delicious but low in calories. We just added it to the Manoir Rouge brunch menu. I'm going to test the chia and coconut pudding at Bleu."

"I'll pass on that one."

She laughed. "I know you don't really care for chia seeds."

"I can't believe you remembered that."

"Because you made a big deal about them when I put them in your smoothie. Do you remember any of the foods I dislike?"

"You think Brussels sprouts are the devil," he responded with a short laugh. "At least that's what you told Chef Renaud."

Aubrie made a face. "I've tried them but have never acquired a taste for them."

"I'll have to make some for you—once you taste mine, I think you'll change your mind."

Frowning, Aubrie shook her head. "I doubt that. They're just bitter to me. Salt reduces the bitterness but…"

Terian chuckled. "You've just made up your mind that you don't like them."

She looked at him doubtfully. "I *hate* Brussels sprouts."

He laughed, then sampled the dessert.

"This is good," Terian said after a spoonful.

"You can finish that while we watch a movie."

He followed her to the living room.

"Do I get to pick what we watch?" he asked.

"Nope. My house and my TV."

"I'll remember that when I have you over for a Netflix and chill night."

Aubrie chuckled. "That's fine."

Terian attempted to resist his urge to yawn. He didn't want Aubrie to think he was getting bored or sleepy. He simply wanted to relish being in her presence a bit longer.

When the clock neared 1:00 a.m., he decided to give up the fight. "I better head back across the bridge before I'm too sleepy to drive."

"I have a guest room down here if you need it," Aubrie said.

"I'm fine," Terian responded. "Thank you though." He was touched by her offer, but knew it was best that he go on home.

AUBRIE WAS RELIEVED when Terian decided not to take her up on her offer. Long after he left, she was still up. She was tired but had trouble falling asleep because of her unsettled emotions.

Humming softly, Aubrie picked up her tablet.

She had really enjoyed Terian's visit, but then again, that had always been the case.

However, spending more time together brought back feelings that she had buried a long time ago.

Aubrie had always been physically attracted to Terian, but that attraction ran more than skin-deep. She'd believed their relationship was a special one and that what she felt for him defied definition. It was one of the reasons she fought so hard to keep a wall erected between them. She glanced over at the clock and then pushed her puzzling thoughts aside because she needed to get some sleep.

It did not come easily, however, as she tossed and turned in bed.

Finally she sat up, propping her pillows behind her and tried to watch television. She chose a documentary that she hoped would put her to sleep.

An hour later, she was still wide-awake.

She tried listening to music.

She closed her eyes and hummed along as she felt the tension easing away from her body.

"WHAT'S THIS?" Aubrie asked when Terian walked out of the kitchen carrying a small plate laden with food the next day at Manoir Bleu.

"Roasted Brussels sprouts gratin," he responded. "At least that's what I call it."

She pushed away the plate. "I'm not eating that."

"Will you at least try it?"

"I'm going to hate it."

Terian broke into a grin. "I thought about blindfolding you, but decided it wasn't the best way to go."

"You're right about that."

"As a chef, we must remain open to new foods."

Arms folded across her chest, Aubrie said, "I can't believe you're quoting Chef Renaud."

"He's right."

"So, you're open to trying my chia and coconut pudding?" Aubrie asked. "I happen to have some in the refrigerator."

"Sure," he responded.

"Okay. I'll try this, but don't get your hopes up because I hate Brussels sprouts with a passion."

"Okay..." Terian prompted after she sampled the dish.

"It's actually not bad," she said before sticking a second forkful into her mouth. Aubrie chewed slowly, savoring the flavor.

She wiped her mouth on her napkin, then said, "You balanced the bitterness with salt, heavy cream, cheddar cheese—and what? Olive oil?"

He nodded. "The fats make it harder to detect the bitterness."

"Hmmm." Aubrie took another bite. "I'm still not crazy about Brussels sprouts, but I can tolerate them when cooked like this. You used just the right amount of breadcrumbs."

Pointing to the pudding she'd pulled out of the fridge, she asked, "So, what do you think?"

"I'm afraid I don't care for it. I liked the other one we had at your place. I'll have to pass on this one."

Aubrie chuckled. "Thank you for giving it a try."

"You tried mine. I had to sample yours."

They eyed one another before Aubrie turned away.

She cleared her throat softly, then said, "Let's get back to work."

Aubrie bit her lip until it throbbed like her pulse. It was becoming a real struggle to keep her feelings for Terian under control. He was beginning to dominate her thoughts whenever they weren't together. Their phone conversations were lasting longer and were less about business.

Their relationship had evolved, and Aubrie didn't really know when it changed.

She still needed some time to process her emotions, but at some point, they would have to sit down and have a discussion. Aubrie demanded honesty from Terian, so she had to give him the same.

Her phone rang.

"Hello," Aubrie said.

"Hey, it's Molly Lawson. I'm in town for a couple of days. I was wondering if you had some time to meet. I'd like to talk to you."

"Sure, I'll make time," she responded. "Why don't you come to the restaurant? I'd like to show you what we've done with the place."

"I can be there in twenty minutes."

"Great. I'll see you then."

Terian had run out before Molly arrived, but Aubrie hoped he would return before she left.

When Molly entered the restaurant, she exclaimed, "Oh my goodness! I love the decor. See, I knew you and Terian would make a great team."

"I'm glad you're here," Aubrie said. "I need to know. Why did you want us to partner?"

"Because you two reminded me of Larry and me. It was the best move we could've ever made. I don't know how much you know about this building, but every restaurant that's been in this location has done well when there were co-owners. We bought it from this guy who'd owned it for only six months, but never got a chance to open. He didn't have a partner."

"I wasn't aware of that."

"It's not that I'm superstitious, but I have this instinct about what works and doesn't. When I saw you and Terian—I knew there was history between you two. And from a marketing standpoint—it just makes sense. You're more seasoned in fine dining. Terian could make it work, but I didn't want to see him fail. I know his father well. He's very tough on Terian."

Aubrie nodded in understanding.

"So, tell me…was I wrong about you and Terian?" Molly asked.

"No, you weren't," Aubrie sighed. "Not about any of it."

"I hope you don't forget to send me an invite to the grand opening."

"We won't, Miss Molly."

"Mrs. Lawson, I didn't know you were coming by," Terian said from the doorway before walking inside.

"Please call me Molly," she said. "It's so good to see you. This place is absolutely stunning. I love the sapphire blue and silver color scheme. I like that you finished the second room for private dining. That was something Larry and I talked about before he got sick."

"Molly plans on coming back for the grand opening," Aubrie announced.

"I hope to bring my daughter with me. She's going to love it. You know we're planning to open a Lawson's Steakhouse in Texas. My daughter and son-in-law will be my partners."

"That's wonderful," she said.

Molly stayed for another thirty minutes talking with them.

When she left, Terian said, "I have a lot of respect for her. She is an astute businesswoman."

"She certainly is," Aubrie agreed.

CHAPTER TWENTY-FOUR

"ARE YOU IN a hurry to leave?" Terian asked a few days later at Paradis. He and Aubrie had gone there to make sure all the work orders had been completed.

The whole time they'd been there, he kept trying to come up with the best way to ask her to eat with him. They'd shared meals before, but Terian knew in his heart that this one was not going to be like the others. He wanted it to be special.

"No, I'm not going to Manoir Bleu tonight," Aubrie responded. "What's up?"

"I'd like you to have dinner with me."

"Where?"

"Right here. I'll cook. I'll make this dish I want to include on the menu."

Aubrie smiled. "I can't wait. Would you like me to help?"

He shook his head no. "Have a glass of wine and relax in the office. I'll call you when everything's ready."

He wanted this meal to be special, he thought

as he readied his cook area. He wanted to prepare it with love. To test the theory and see if Aubrie could tell the difference.

His grandmother, sister and Aubrie—they couldn't be wrong, but Terian wanted to see for himself if it were true.

He took his time as he cooked. He didn't want to rush the meal. While he waited for the food to finish cooking, he set a table for them and turned the lights down low, casting the dining room in a warm glow. The candlelight added to the romantic ambience, while soft, mellow jazz played in the background.

He glanced over his shoulder and released a short sigh of relief when there was no sighting of Aubrie. The door to the office was still closed. He prayed she'd stay there until he returned to get her.

He walked back to the kitchen to check on the food.

Everything had to be perfect.

TERIAN STOOD IN the doorway of the office. "Dinner is ready."

Aubrie rose and walked around the desk. "Great, because I'm hungry."

He escorted her to the linen-covered table set with flowers and candles.

Aubrie gasped in surprise. "Oh wow…how

beautiful," she murmured softly. "Did you do this?"

"I did." Terian held out a chair for her. "I might not be able to decorate a house, but I can put together a pretty nice table."

"Yes, you can. Everything looks really beautiful."

He strode into the kitchen and returned minutes later with a plate of appetizers.

"For starters, we're having salmon timbales," Terian announced. "I know you love smoked salmon."

Aubrie savored the flavors of smoked salmon, avocado, lemon, cucumber and fennel. "Oh, this is so good. I made a variation of this with crab meat for my mom's birthday celebration."

"I've made it once with lobster, and I did a vegetarian option with deseeded tomatoes, cooked asparagus, peppers and mushrooms," Terian responded.

"You'll have to make that for me one day."

He smiled. "I'd be happy to cook anything you want, Aubrie."

"What are we having for dinner?"

"Filet mignon, potato-celeriac gratin and steamed carrots."

She grinned. "You certainly know the way to a girl's heart. Did you have all this prepped and planned *before* you asked me to join you?"

"I was hoping," Terian responded. "I figured I'd be prepared just in case. Worst-case scenario is I'd have leftovers for dinner tomorrow."

"This is much better than the tuna salad I'd planned on eating tonight." When she finished the appetizer, she wiped her mouth on her napkin. "That was absolutely delicious, Terian."

"Thank you for joining me. I really don't enjoy eating alone."

"It's not the same whipping up a meal like this just for yourself."

"Exactly," Terian responded with a grin. Apparently, the theory about cooking with love was a viable one. Even he could taste a difference in the food.

They laughed and talked like old friends throughout the main course.

"Did you leave room for a white chocolate and raspberry blondie?" he asked.

Aubrie was surprised. "You found time to make dessert, too?"

"I made it earlier," he confessed.

Terian went to the kitchen, then returned with two plates.

"This reminds me of France," Aubrie said as she sliced into her dessert. "Remember when we'd be up late nights cooking and trying different recipes?"

"I do. Those are some of my favorite memories…studying and cooking with you."

"It was us against the rest of the world."

"I really missed our friendship, Aubrie."

"I did, too. But then I'd think about what you did, and I'd get angry all over again."

Terian opened his mouth to speak, but she stopped him.

"Let's not rehash the past," Aubrie said. "I've forgiven you and I mean it."

"The thing is… I don't just want you as a business partner," Terian stated. "I want more, and I really believe you feel the same way."

She eyed him but didn't respond.

"We work well together, don't you think?"

"Yes, but that doesn't mean that a romantic relationship will work between us."

"It doesn't mean that it won't either."

Aubrie nodded. She couldn't disagree with his statement.

"Let's just start with one date," Terian suggested. "A *real* one. Not two coworkers deciding to have dinner together."

"Like tonight," she said softly. "Because this sort of feels like a date."

"Does that bother you?"

"No, not really." For the first time in a long while, Aubrie decided to take this leap with Terian. It was harder to keep fighting her feelings for him. She decided to see where this would lead her.

"I would like you to join me aboard the *Charleston Princess*. I've heard some nice things about the Blues & BBQ Cruise."

Aubrie broke into a grin. "Sure."

"Really? It would be a real date."

"Yes, I know."

"Have you been on the ship before?" he asked.

"I haven't," she admitted. "I've wanted to, but never got around to it."

"We're really going on a date," Terian said almost to himself.

"Are you going to eat your dessert?" she asked. "If not, pack it up for me to take home."

AUBRIE WAS MESMERIZED by the way the beautiful coastline engaged the water's edge as the waves danced and merged. Her eyes caught sight of a boat near the seashore, painted in the colors of nature.

"It's a beautiful view from here," Terian said.

He stood beside her at the railing of the *Charleston Princess*. "I'm looking forward to seeing Fort Sumter and the *USS Yorktown*. According to the brochure, we sail by them. I have to say that Charleston's history is as fascinating as New Orleans."

Aubrie nodded. "I agree."

They headed to the dining area for the barbecue buffet, which consisted of pulled pork, smoked chicken, coleslaw and macaroni and cheese.

"The food looks and smells delicious," he said.

"Then let's find out how good it is."

They made small talk while enjoying their meal.

"I need to dance off some of this food," Terian said after they finished eating.

Aubrie took a sip of water. "Me, too."

She hadn't danced like this in a long time—well, since Torrie's wedding. Now that she wasn't trying to keep her guard up with Terian, she felt freer.

Terian kept his word and didn't try to pressure her. He didn't try to make anything happen—they just let the evening progress naturally.

"I had a great time tonight," Aubrie said as she unlocked the front door of her house at the end of the evening. "It brought back so many happy memories."

Terian followed her inside. "I'm glad to hear that."

They sat side by side on the sofa.

"My world feels whole again," he stated.

"After things ended between us, nothing ever felt right."

Aubrie took Terian's hand in her own. "In a way, I'm happy with the way it all turned out. I believe I'm a much better chef because of it. I was able to focus on building my businesses."

"You were pretty incredible in school. I should've just told you that I needed help."

"You treated everything like a competition. Always wanting to be the first to finish or taking shortcuts. It was all about being the best in the class."

"You're right. I was arrogant because I was Chef Terrance LaCroix's son, and my grades suffered because of it. Rather than have me fail publicly—my dad had me come home. I was too embarrassed to tell you, so I just left."

"We can take different paths and arrive at the same place. When we first started working together on Paradis, some of the old you started to emerge."

He chuckled. "You set me straight though. I appreciate you for it, too."

Aubrie smiled. "Sometimes we all need gentle reminders."

CHAPTER TWENTY-FIVE

TERIAN FELT LIGHTER than he had in years—free of the guilt he'd carried for seven years. He'd never been as happy as he was in this moment. He and Aubrie were a couple and their plans for the restaurant's grand opening were on target, despite a few hiccups.

Aubrie was having a positive effect on him. He no longer allowed the little things to bother him the way they used to—he simply let them roll off his shoulders. He wasn't as bothered by his father's lack of support. Well, the truth of it was that Terian was hurt and disappointed, but he no longer took it out on others.

He was also much better when it came to staying in his lane where the Bleu staff was concerned. Aubrie had her own way of running her kitchen. Terian quickly learned not to interfere.

When Aubrie told him that her trust and faith in him had been renewed—Terian's eyes watered. It was in that moment that the shadows of the past began to evaporate. He was finally free, and it felt *good*.

Terian wanted Aubrie as a partner for life. They were good together and he loved her. Always had, even though he was afraid to admit it to himself for a long time. They were a great team, which had him thinking of another proposal. He'd even stopped by a jewelry store a few days ago to look at engagement rings.

He didn't want to frighten Aubrie by moving too fast, but they'd waited seven years—he preferred not to wait any longer than necessary.

Nothing could mar his happiness.

"I HAD TO personally congratulate all of you for a job well done," Aubrie told her Manoir Rouge staff via Zoom. "We wouldn't be a Michelin Two Star Restaurant without y'all. I want you to know that I truly appreciate each of you."

When the meeting ended, she jumped out of her chair and did a little dance. Manoir Rouge had advanced from one to two stars, and she couldn't be happier. Her week was going quite well. Just this morning, she learned that Manoir Bleu was the recipient of the Grand Award from *Wine Spectator* magazine for their world-class wine list.

She couldn't wait to share the news with Terian.

These were the things they once dreamed about. This type of recognition meant more to Terian because he liked to win. Aubrie was appreciative of having her hard work and that of her staff publicly acknowledged, but she was intrinsically motivated—she gained the most pleasure from a job well done.

She hummed softly as she made her way to her bedroom, undressed and jumped into the shower.

An hour later, she walked through the doors of Manoir Bleu.

After verifying the deposit from the previous night, she took it to the bank.

When Aubrie returned twenty minutes later, she found Lance and three other kitchen staff doing inventory and setting up stations.

She decided to wait until later to share the news. She preferred to tell everyone at the same time. Besides, this would give her time to come up with some token of her appreciation for their hard work.

As she headed down to the wine cellar, she almost shivered at the drop in temperature. She wanted something special for a couple that would be coming in later for dinner. They'd celebrated their anniversary annually at the restaurant since it opened five years ago.

She selected a ten-year-old cabernet for the couple's tenth anniversary, then took it upstairs.

"This is for Tim Bradshaw and his wife," Aubrie told Rachel.

"That's right…it's their anniversary."

"Did he request anything special?" she asked.

Rachel checked her notes on the reservation. "He's updated her wedding ring. He would like for you to bring it out under a covered dish."

Aubrie smiled. "That's so sweet."

They discussed the reservations of diners celebrating special milestones.

"I need to leave for a couple of hours," she told Rachel.

Aubrie left the restaurant and drove to Polk Island. She wasn't going to see Terian—she was on another mission.

She walked into the bakery and café owned by Misty.

"Hey, cousin, I need a huge favor."

Misty broke into a smile. "What can I do for you?"

"I need a cake. Can you have it ready around four?"

"Sure."

"It's for my employees," Aubrie stated, then told her about the award.

"Congratulations," Misty said.

"Thank you. And I'm sorry about this being last-minute."

"It's fine, Aubrie. I'm sure there wasn't any way for you to anticipate this was going to happen. We'll have the cake ready by four. I'll come up with something special." She paused a moment, then said, "Leon has to be in Charleston at three thirty. I can have him bring it to you."

"That would be wonderful if he doesn't mind."

"He won't mind at all," Misty said.

Aubrie paid for the cake. "Thanks so much for this."

She considered stopping by Paradis to see Terian, but she really needed to get back across the bridge.

Although she wanted to tell him in person about the recognitions for both Rouge and Bleu, Aubrie decided it would have to wait until later.

TERIAN STARED AT the phone in his hand. He couldn't believe what he'd just been told by his mother. Margo called to inform him that their restaurant was destroyed by fire. He was grateful that no one was injured inside the building. However, it was ruled an accident, since one of the employees admitted to being outside smoking.

He made a call.

When Aubrie answered, he said, "I just got off the phone with my mom. LaCroix Restaurant is no more. It burned down this afternoon."

"I'm so sorry," she murmured. "How is your family?"

"They're all pretty upset right now, as you can imagine."

She nodded. "I'm sure."

"I need to go home," Terian stated.

"I'm going with you."

He was glad to hear Aubrie say this. "I'll get back to you with the flight information."

"How are you doing?" she asked.

"I don't know right now. Everything was going so well...now this..." Terian shook his head.

"Do you want me to come over?"

"No, I'll be fine."

"Have you talked to your father?" Aubrie asked.

"No, my mom said he wasn't up for a conversation. I know he has to be devastated. He loved that place."

"The restaurant can be rebuilt. Maybe I can help..."

"Thank you for wanting to help," Terian said. "I'm just not sure my dad will do it. From the way my mom made it sound—this may be the last straw for him."

"I truly hope that's not the case," she responded.

So did he.

Terian tried to think of how he could help his father. Right now, he was too numb to come up with anything. He just needed to be with his family.

THEIR PLANE LANDED shortly after 11:00 a.m. the next day.

Terian didn't talk much during the flight. He just sat there staring out the window. Aubrie didn't push him for conversation. She only wished she could find a way to make him feel better.

She still hadn't shared her news with him— it just didn't seem like the right time. It could wait, Aubrie decided. She'd also postponed the celebration with her staff. She wanted to be there for Terian.

She thought it best for her to drive after picking up the rental car.

They went to see his parents.

"Pop…"

"What are you doing here?" Terrance asked when his son walked into the living room.

Terian looked offended. "Did you really just ask me that? Pop, you know why I came home."

"I just figured you have it so good on that island…"

"I loved LaCroix…you know I did. I have so many wonderful memories of that place."

"So many that you decided to abandon it," Terrance uttered. "Maybe you're happy that the restaurant is gone. Now you're completely free of it. My employees knew I didn't allow no smoking. That guy you hired… Joey…he's the fella that burned down my restaurant."

Terian eyed his father in disbelief. "Are you trying to say that in some way, I'm to blame for what happened?"

"I didn't allow no smoking. Didn't hire no smokers."

"I haven't set foot in that restaurant since Torrie's wedding. How are you blaming me?"

"Terrance, what are you saying?" Margo asked. "Now, I'm not gonna let you do this to Terian. He's not at fault."

"If he'd been here, it wouldn't have happened."

"We can rebuild. We can make it better than it was before."

"I'm tired. It's gone, so we might as well move on."

"Pop, you don't mean that," Terian said.

"Yeah, I do."

Aubrie hated seeing Terian and his father both in such pain, but instead of coming together— they were arguing. If something ever happened to her restaurants, she would be just as upset— the loss was insurmountable. But she hoped she wouldn't lash out in anger and blame. If only Terian and Torrie could get their father to ride this storm—not be consumed by it.

The restaurant could rise from the ashes and be better than before. Aubrie was even willing to help in any way she could. She loved Terian and knew how much LaCroix meant to him. She'd always believed that Terrance and his son wanted the same thing—just had different ideas of how to achieve their goals for the restaurant.

I wish I could help, but there isn't any point in trying to talk to them now.

They wouldn't be able to hear her. Aubrie decided the best thing she could do for Terian was to leave. He and his family needed time to grieve together. Hopefully after everything settled down—they could discuss what to do next. She prayed most of all that Terrance would come to his senses and make peace with Terian.

He was doing well and was no longer under his father's thumb. Aubrie didn't want that to change.

CHAPTER TWENTY-SIX

"HE ACTUALLY BLAMES me for what happened," Terian stated. He was hurt by the things his father said.

"You know it's not your fault." Aubrie gave his hand a gentle squeeze. "Your father's very emotional right now. He doesn't really mean what he's saying."

Terian knew she meant well, but Aubrie didn't know his father. "Oh, he means it. I know the man."

Margo sat down on the other side of him. "Son, don't you dare take your father's words to heart. He's upset and striking out at everyone. He gave Torrie what for because she'd left the restaurant early. So you see, he's passing out blame to everyone, Terian. Before the day is over, he'll probably toss some my way. I'm ready for it."

"I hope he's taking some of it," he responded. "Maybe if he'd done the renovations I suggested, LaCroix wouldn't have been destroyed completely."

"We shouldn't be blaming one another," Torrie interjected. "This is the time we should be sticking together."

"I agree," Terian said.

He sat erect, his back straight, tense. It dawned on him that he was always like this whenever he was around his father. He could relax around his mother, but never with his dad. Since moving to Polk Island—that feeling had gone away. But an air of dread still surrounded him whenever he had to face Terrance.

This wasn't the way it should be with his own father. He loved him, sure enough, but Terian had a deep-seated fear of not being good enough to be his son. That's why having Terrance's blessing and approval meant so much to him.

Hot anger flooded through Terian like an ocean. He'd worked so hard to please his father over the years. He gave up a job he loved at a prestigious restaurant in Beverly Hills to come home at Terrance's request. He stayed when he knew it was past time for him to strike out on his own. There were a few other opportunities that came his way, but he couldn't disappoint his dad, so he turned them down.

After all those years of loyalty, his father blamed him for the restaurant's demise.

"I CALLED AN UBER," Aubrie told Terian. "I'm going to the hotel. Just text if you need me." She thought it best that she leave, so he and his family could have a conversation without an outsider.

"You don't have to go."

"I think it's the right thing for me to do, considering the situation, Terian."

"Are you worried that my dad would start blaming you?" He was trying to make light of the situation but failed. "Sorry, it was a terrible attempt at a joke."

"It wouldn't bother me if he did… I know it's not true."

"So why won't you stay?" Terian inquired.

"Because I think you and your family need space to deal with your emotions."

"I can drop you off or you can just take the car."

Aubrie shook her head. "I'll be fine, Terian. You stay here and focus on your family. I need to check in at the hotel anyway."

"I'll come by later."

"Okay," she responded before kissing him on the cheek. "Everything will be all right. We'll find a way to salvage your family's legacy."

Terian shook his head sadly. "I have to accept that the restaurant is gone for good. Aubrie, maybe what happened is for the best."

"I don't believe that, and I don't think you do either."

She felt horrible for Terian. He was trying to be strong and hold it together, but Aubrie knew that deep down, he was falling apart. Terrance was being unfair, but he was also devastated by the loss of the restaurant. They were in pain, and they needed each other.

They were just too stubborn to see it.

TERRANCE HAD RETREATED to his office and left instructions with Margo that he wasn't to be disturbed.

Terian sat with his mother in the den.

He heard the front door open and close, then footsteps clicking across the hardwood floors.

"Hey, where's Aubrie?" Torrie inquired. "I want to congratulate her."

Terian eyed his sister. "For what?"

"Manoir Rouge just became a Michelin Two Star restaurant," Torrie announced. "There was a nice write-up in the paper this morning."

He glanced at his mother, then back at his sister. Terian swallowed his hurt. *Why would she keep something like this from me?*

"Aubrie never mentioned it."

"I'm sure she'll get around to telling you,"

Torrie said. "I can't imagine why she'd want to keep that a secret."

"Aubrie knows we're dealing with a lot right now," his mother interjected. "She's probably just being sensitive to our feelings. Although we could surely use some good news."

Terian pondered the reason why Aubrie hadn't told him.

It's because she still doesn't trust me. Was she afraid hearing about her success would upset him?

He'd worked hard to prove himself to her and she'd disappointed him, too.

Terian had always believed that Aubrie was too good for him. They never should've crossed the line from business partners to dating. She'd been right about that.

As much as it was going to pierce him all the way to his soul, Terian knew what he had to do.

"I'm going to the hotel to see Aubrie," he announced. "I won't be gone long."

AUBRIE HADN'T REALLY expected to see Terian. "Hey…"

She stepped aside to let him enter the room. "Did you get a chance to sit down with your father?"

"No," he responded tersely. "I told you that he wasn't the type of man to change his mind."

When they were seated on the small sofa near the balcony, Terian asked, "Why didn't you tell me about Manoir Rouge?"

"It didn't seem like the right time," she replied. "You have a lot to deal with right now."

"And you thought I wouldn't be able to handle some great news?"

Aubrie scanned his face, trying to read his expression. "Why are you upset?"

"Because I'm tired of proving myself over and over only to have people like you and my dad continue to doubt me."

"I can't believe you just put me in the same category as your father," Aubrie said. "Terian, you're the one most like that man. Winning is everything to you and Terrance, despite who may get hurt in the process. They're just collateral damage. I'm just not like that."

"Naw... I guess you're not. I keep forgetting that you're Saint Aubrie."

She stood up at that comment and walked over to the sliding glass doors. Aubrie took a deep breath before turning to face him. "Look, I know you're upset over what happened, but I'm not going to let you take your anger out on me. I think you should leave, Terian."

"Just admit it, Aubrie... You felt you couldn't tell me about your latest achievements because you think I'd revert back to the old me."

"I know the type of person you are," she responded. "You're the one who hasn't fully let go of the past. You're the one who really doesn't believe in yourself. In your own talent."

"How can I when there are constant reminders about all my failures?" He paused a moment, then said, "Aubrie, you were right about one thing—we never should've gotten involved. We should've kept our relationship strictly business."

She kept her expression blank. She refused to let him see just how much his words wounded her. "That's an easy fix."

"I think it'll be for the best," Terian said quietly.

She got up and walked over to the closet.

"What are you doing?" he asked.

Aubrie blinked rapidly to keep her tears from escaping. She was not about to let him see her cry. "Packing. I've checked on Rouge, so there's no need for me to hang around. I'm going back to Charleston."

"Are you going to take Paradis from me?"

"Terian, I never wanted to *steal* your restaurant. We're partners unless you'd like to buy me out."

"You know I can't do that right now."

"I can wait until you're ready."

"Are you saying that you'll give up your share?"

"Yes. Why don't you talk to Torrie? She might want to buy me out." Aubrie tossed her clothes inside the luggage. "Until then, I'm willing to just be an investor. You can run Paradis however you see fit."

"I'm not trying to kick you out of the restaurant, Aubrie. I still want us to be partners. Even friends."

She rolled her eyes. "I don't want to be your friend, Terian. I don't want to have to look at your face."

His phone pinged and he glanced down at the message.

"Congratulations once again, Aubrie. I'm sure you know that you're a recipient of a *Wine Spectator* magazine award. I guess you didn't think it was a good time to mention that either."

She decided it was best not to respond while Terian was in this mood. He wasn't in the frame of mind to understand her reasons.

He headed to the door. "Have a safe flight."

As soon as Terian left the hotel room, Aubrie sank down on the bed in tears. Once again, he'd walked out of her life. Only this time, he'd at least told her he was doing so. Regardless, the pain that ripped through her did not hurt any less.

She wouldn't let this destroy her. With steely determination, Aubrie forced her tears back. She almost felt the ice spreading through her as she fought against her pain.

In time she would be able to erase the heartache. She'd survived seven years ago, and she could do it again.

MARGO WALKED INTO her bedroom. She found her husband sitting on the edge of the king-size bed.

"Are you happy with yourself?" she asked.

He looked at her, his expression one of confusion. "What are you talking about?"

"Terian never wanted to be a quarterback," Margo stated. "That was *your* dream."

"What's your point?"

"If you're not winning—you don't want to play anymore. That's what I'm talking about. The great Chef Terrance LaCroix is afraid of a little adversity."

"Margo…"

"No, you're gonna hear me out. I've kept my mouth shut but no more…"

"I've already had a bad day."

"And if you don't shut up and listen to me—it's gonna get worse."

Her hazel eyes flashed fire. Terrance knew she meant business. "Okay, I'm listening."

"Honey, I love you… I really do, but you're wrong. Our son deserves to follow his own path, even if it takes him away from us. I miss him, too. You've put so much pressure on Terian—I can understand why he left."

"All this is my fault. Is that what you're telling me?"

"How about it's nobody's fault?" Margo responded. "What you did—you did out of love for your son. I get it, but you went about it the wrong way."

"That sounds like it's my fault."

"Get over yourself, Terrance. Honey, what I'm trying to tell you is that you need to get to know your son. Listen to *his* dreams."

"Terian don't talk to me about stuff like that. He's always gone to you."

"Did you ever consider why?" Margo asked.

"The one thing I know about my son is that he's always wanted to follow in my footsteps. He told me so."

"I don't think he meant that literally."

Terrance massaged his temple. "I tried to be a good father."

"And you are a wonderful father. You're just controlling."

"I can't deny that," he responded. "My intentions were good…"

"I know, honey." She sat down beside him. "I've pretty much stayed out of the business, but that's changing. We are gonna rebuild La-Croix, and it's gonna be bigger and better. You and I will be in the background while Torrie takes over. She deserves it. Terian wants to help in any way he can and we're gonna let him."

Terrance didn't say a word. He just sat there listening.

Margo released the breath she'd been holding. "We can do this together. As a family."

He looked at her then. "I love you, Margo. I know I don't tell you often enough, but I do."

She kissed his cheek. "I see it in your eyes every time you look at me."

"Do you really think we can make LaCroix even better than before?" he asked.

"Yes, I do."

"I put my heart and soul into that restaurant. So did my parents."

"I know… That's why it's worth starting over and building it from the ground up."

"I guess I need to apologize to Terian."

"You do," Margo agreed. "He went to check out the damage."

She gave his hand a gentle squeeze. "Start out by telling him how much you love him. And tell your son that you're proud of him."

"Yes, ma'am, Mama."

Margo kissed him once more. "I just love you to pieces."

CHAPTER TWENTY-SEVEN

TERIAN REGRETTED HIS decision as soon as he walked out of the hotel. For a moment, he yearned to go back inside and convince Aubrie that he was wrong to end their relationship. He was in love with her and already his life felt miserable without her in it.

But the truth was that he was too messed up—he didn't deserve a woman like Aubrie. He did the very thing he'd promised never to do—break her heart a second time.

He drove to the location of their family restaurant. Only the charred bones remained. Terian stood there with tears in his eyes.

Just as he was about to leave, his father showed up.

They stood there staring at one another, not a word exchanged.

Terian turned to leave.

"Wait…" Terrance said. "I owe you an apology."

He was too shocked to respond.

"I admit to being stubborn, controlling and

always wanting things my way. I... You were right about the place needing renovations—maybe that's why it was so easily destroyed in the fire. I never should've blamed anybody for my negligence."

"All my life I've tried to please you, Pop." Terian sighed in resignation. "I'm tired of trying."

"I know I've been difficult and overbearing... I wanted the best for you, son. I laid the foundation..."

"You wanted me to be just like you. There was a time when I wanted to be a younger version of you, but not anymore. I just want to be *me*. The reason I wanted my own restaurant is to prove that I'm worthy of running a successful high-end business."

"I never thought you'd walk away from La-Croix."

"That's just it... It wasn't ours—it was *yours*, Pop. You made sure everybody knew it."

"I guess you feel that I wasn't a good father to you."

"I'd never say that," Terian stated. "You just wanted to control me. Pop, when I told you that I wanted to be a chef—you told me I'd go to school in France."

"It's one of the best culinary schools out there."

"But that wasn't good enough for you. You wanted me to be the top student, but I had a hard time keeping up with my studies. When I told you I might fail—you made me come home. I was too embarrassed to tell Aubrie, so I just packed up and left without telling her anything. I broke her heart."

"That explains why she came to New Orleans—she wanted to get revenge."

"It's not true," Terian interjected. "Pop, you know she has roots here. Besides, Aubrie isn't like that."

"I have to say I'm surprised she agreed to be your partner after all that."

"Trust me…it wasn't an easy feat."

"Son, how do you know Aubrie isn't out to sabotage you?"

"Because I trust her. I initially wanted to prove to Aubrie that I was a better chef, and that I could make Paradis better than her two restaurants. But once I found out about her connection to the island, I realized that it would be better with her as my partner. I wouldn't have been able to accomplish what I have without Aubrie."

"She's more than just your partner though."

"Aubrie was…" He shook his head. "Not any longer."

"When did that happen?" Terrance asked.

"She's flying home tonight."

"Whose decision was this?"

Terian eyed his father. "Mine. I thought it was for the best, Pop. Now I'm not so sure. To be honest, I really messed up."

"You love her."

He nodded. "I do."

"Then why are you giving up so easily?" Terrance asked.

"Maybe it is for the best." He didn't really believe this, but he had no other answers.

"What will happen to Paradis?"

"We're still going to be partners. At least until I can buy her out."

"Why don't we take the money we get from the insurance company and do just that?" his father said. "We don't need her. We don't have to rebuild here. We'll have Paradis."

"Paradis is mine," Terian stated.

"There's so much we can do together with that restaurant…"

"Pop, I don't need your help," he said, his tone firm.

"I see," Terrance responded.

"I have to prove to myself that I can do this."

"I felt that same way once. I had this same conversation with my own father. I wanted to breathe new life into the restaurant."

"I really think you should rebuild LaCroix."

"Your mother and sister feel the same way. They believe that we can restore the restaurant to its former beauty."

"I agree," Terian responded.

"I think it's time I retired. Torrie can take over the family business with you as a consultant. I know that you'll both do well."

He silently assessed his father. "What's going on with you? You're not the type of man who thinks of retiring."

"I have to have a hip replacement," Terrance announced. "I've been putting it off for two years now, but the pain... I want to have the surgery."

"Why haven't you mentioned this before?"

"I was hoping things wouldn't get worse."

"Torrie and Mom can handle the restaurant."

"I agree," Terrance responded.

Terian followed his father's car as they drove back to the house. They joined Torrie, Luke and Margo at the dining room table to discuss insurance and the next steps in rebuilding the restaurant.

A little later, Torrie took him aside and said, "I spoke with Aubrie briefly while she was at the airport. She's going back to Charleston."

"I know."

"What happened?"

"We decided it was best that we keep our relationship purely professional."

Torrie shook her head. "No, this was *you*. I guess my question is why? Because of the Michelin Star?"

"Did you know Manoir Bleu won a *Wine Spectator* award? The highest award they give. She will always be better than me, Torrie."

"If you feel this way about her, then why did you want to partner with her?"

"Torrie, we could buy her out. Paradis will belong to *us*."

"I'm really disappointed in you, Terian. Aubrie gave you a chance and this is what you do to her? She trusted you."

"Did she really?" Terian questioned. "I'm not so sure."

"Why don't you think about it?" she responded. "I'll talk to you later."

After Torrie and Luke left for home, Terian sat in the den alone, his thoughts consumed with Aubrie.

It made sense that she wouldn't mention the award or star of distinction because of the fire. Aubrie didn't want to appear insensitive. He'd been too angry and hurt to accept that until now. And as much as it pained Terian, he had to acknowledge that Paradis was as much a part of Aubrie as it was him, and not just in financial terms. The grand opening was a week away, and he was attempting to push her out after everything she'd done.

Shame washed over him. He'd been a real jerk.

"Your sister told me what happened between you and Aubrie," Margo said as she sat down beside him. "I can't believe you're trying to push her out."

"I'm not trying to push her out," Terian stated. "I just don't want it to be weird between us. So, if she *wants* to leave—I'll be prepared."

"Aubrie's not going anywhere. Maybe you should consider letting her buy you out instead of the other way around. You can close the door to that chapter without looking back. We can sure use your talents here to help us rebuild."

In that moment, Terian realized that his life in New Orleans was his past. His future was on Polk Island with Aubrie. However, he feared that he'd lost her forever.

"No, I can't, Mom. I've got to try and fix things. I only hope that it's not too late."

THE NEXT COUPLE of days went by in a blur. Aubrie refused to fall apart over her breakup with Terian. Instead, she kept herself busy.

The nights were the hardest. She'd released a few tears while lying in bed, but she refused to wallow in her pain. It was easier to do when she was at work.

Sensing someone standing in the doorway of her office at Bleu, she looked up from her computer to find Terian there. Aubrie gave him a withering stare before asking, "When did you get back?"

"This morning. I came because we needed to talk."

"I think you made yourself pretty clear."

"Aubrie, I'm sorry about the way I acted in New Orleans. I was confused and upset. After you left, I realized something important."

"And what was that?" she asked.

"I'm a fool for thinking I don't need you in my life."

"Okay, I'm not doing this with you," Aubrie said. "You really need to get over yourself, Terian. You walked out on me a second time. There won't be a third."

"I deserve that," he said. "But it doesn't change the fact that I love you."

Aubrie shook her head. "Nooo… Terian, I can't deal with this right now. We need to focus on the grand opening."

"My dad has to have a hip replacement. Whenever he has the surgery, I want to be there to help with his recovery," Terian announced.

"I understand completely," Aubrie said. "What do you need me to do?"

"Right now, I don't know when it will be scheduled, so we have some time to figure things out. We've worked so hard…"

"It's going to be fine," Aubrie assured him. "I'll take care of everything so you can focus on your father. Paradis will be fine."

"The grand opening is in a week. Are you nervous?" he asked.

"I am," Aubrie admitted. "But that's the case whenever I'm opening a new restaurant. I know we're ready and everything will go well, but my stomach is always in knots until after the first week." She eyed him. "How are you feeling about the opening?"

"I'm excited and nervous. I want everything to go perfectly."

"Even if it's not perfect, Terian—everything will be fine," she responded with a tender smile. "You're such a perfectionist."

"I guess I'm more like my father than I realized."

"You love cooking and you're a phenomenal chef. Have fun with it."

"I'm glad you'll be there cooking alongside me."

"Just remember it's not a competition. We're a team."

"I know."

"You say so," she responded. "But we'll see what happens that night when the pressure is on."

"Why do I feel like it's a test?"

"Because it is, Terian. That will be the true test of whether we can really work together."

"There's nothing to worry about," he stated.

"How's your father?"

"Much better. We decided as a family to re-build."

"That's wonderful news. I'm so glad to hear this. I meant what I said… I'll do what I can to help. When the restaurant reopens, I'll lend him some of Rouge's staff."

"You'd do that for us?" Even now, after the hurt he'd inflicted on Aubrie, she was still willing to come to their aid.

Aubrie nodded. "Of course."

"I appreciate that. I really do."

"I'd like to think you'd do it for me, if necessary," she replied.

"I would." Terian shifted his position in the chair. "I meant what I said, Aubrie. I love you."

"I have a lot of work to do, so if you can leave…"

"Aubrie, we need to talk."

"Not right now," she said. "Let's just focus on

the grand opening. You were right. We never should've crossed that line."

"I was wrong."

"I don't think so," Aubrie countered. "Right now, we need to get ready for the opening."

She loved him so much it hurt, but she had to forget about the way she felt in his arms and what it felt like to kiss him.

Some things just weren't meant to be.

FOR THE NEXT two days, the only time they talked was when they needed to discuss the restaurant. Terian had made a foolish mistake in ending his relationship with Aubrie, but he planned to rectify this as soon as he could. There was no way he was going to give up on her. He didn't after being apart seven years—there was no way he'd forget about her this time around. Aubrie was branded on his soul.

"What's going on in the LaCroix dining room?" Aubrie asked when she walked out of the office. They'd named a private room in honor of his father. She was about to head home. "Why are the lights on?"

"It's a surprise," Terian responded.

"For who?"

"You."

She glanced up at him. "We don't have time for surprises, Terian. We still have a lot to do."

"Although I don't deserve it, I'm asking you to trust me, Aubrie."

She walked into the private dining room. White candles of various heights were arranged around the floral centerpiece of a table in the middle of the room, creating a romantic, low-light atmosphere. The crystal rectangular chandelier added to the ambience.

She looked at him. "Terian…"

"I made a nice dinner for you. I'm asking that you please indulge me."

She shrugged. "I'm hungry, so fine."

Terian held out a chair for her to sit down. He joined her.

A server, one of the men they'd hired together, entered carrying two plates.

"This chicken is delicious," Aubrie said after trying it. "I love sun-dried tomatoes, mushrooms and red pepper. I see you added all three. What do you call this?"

"Marry me chicken," Terian responded.

Confused, she uttered, "Huh…?"

He grinned. "Aubrie, I've never loved any other woman. You are the only woman for me. I've known that since the day we met. Hurting you the way I did left a huge hole in my soul."

"I don't want to look backward anymore."

"Aubrie, I never got over losing you the first time. I didn't feel worthy of you. I guess I let my frustration with my father blind me where you were concerned, but I realize how wrong I was. I trust you with my life and my heart. I trust you with Paradis."

"A week ago, you ended things with me," Aubrie said. "I can't keep going back and forth with you. Terian, I won't do it. Maybe it's best to just remain friends and business partners."

"Aubrie, I love you. If you love me half as much as I love you, then I know we can make it work."

She didn't respond.

"Do you love me?" he asked. "Please answer me."

"Yes, I love you, Terian. But I'm not sure that we're good for each other outside of business."

"I believe that what we feel for each other is worth the risk. Aubrie, I'm proposing a new partnership." He paused a moment, then said, "Will you marry me? When I think of the future, I can't see my life without you in it."

As much as she wanted to keep her fragile heart protected, Aubrie couldn't disregard her feelings for him and how much she wanted to be his partner for life. "Terian, are you sure about this? You do realize that marriage is a lifetime commitment?"

"What I know for certain is that you're the only woman for me. I just need to know if you feel the same way about me. Do you love me enough to give me another chance?"

"What if my restaurants win another award? Can you be okay with this? Are you able to be my partner? Can you cheer for me on the side-lines, especially if it has nothing to do with you? Or the next time you're upset with your father—are you going to take it out on me?"

"Yes," Terian replied. "I can be your partner. I can cheer for you when I'm on the sidelines, and I won't take anything out on you if I have an issue with my dad. If you want to buy me out—it's yours, Aubrie."

"You don't mean that."

"Actually, I do," Terian responded. "A few months ago, I wouldn't have. I love you so much. If I have to choose between you and Paradis—I choose *you*."

CHAPTER TWENTY-EIGHT

AUBRIE KISSED HIM.

He grinned. "That was very nice, but I still need an answer."

"Yes. I'll marry you."

He pulled a small box out of his pocket and opened it to reveal a simple solitaire engagement ring. "I'll upgrade it later."

Aubrie shook her head no. "This ring is perfect, Terian. I'm not one for a lot of jewelry so I don't need anything extravagant."

He pulled her into his arms, kissing her again.

"You've made me one happy man," Terian said. "It feels like I've loved you my whole life."

She looked into his eyes. "I feel the same way."

He grinned. "I've finally got the woman."

Aubrie laughed. "You had to go and make it weird, didn't you?"

"Hey, I thought I was being romantic."

This sparked more laughter between them.

"Just be you, Terian. I love you just the way

you are—flaws and all. And you don't have to give up Paradis. We built it together—it's ours."

"You don't mean that. About the flaws, I mean." He wanted desperately to believe her.

"I do. Terian, I know the man you are, the good bits and the bad. But your good qualities truly outweigh the bad ones. I hope you can say the same of me."

"You're perfect, Aubrie."

Her smile disappeared. "No, I'm not. Terian, if you believe that, then this engagement will be over before it starts. Don't put me on a pedestal."

"What I meant is that you're perfect in my eyes, Aubrie. That's all that matters to me."

"I feel the same way."

Aubrie had found a home in his arms and yearned to stay there.

TERIAN FELT READY to take on the world. He was going to marry Aubrie and his dream would finally come true. While he wanted nothing more than to celebrate their engagement, they had to put all their focus on Paradis.

He woke up shortly after 7:00 a.m. the next day. Instead of turning away from the clock and going back to sleep, Terian decided to get up and get dressed. He was too excited to sleep, so he decided to get an early start on whatever tasks still needed to be done at Paradis.

Whistling softly, he left the condo and drove the short distance to the restaurant. Aubrie had to take care of some things at Manoir Bleu, so there was a chance they wouldn't see each other until later in the evening.

Terian found a small stack of RSVP's in the mailbox. He carried them inside with him.

In the office, he opened them, checking off each response. Everyone had replied yes except for one.

Terrance LaCroix.

Terian released a long sigh. *I still don't have my father's blessing.*

He decided in the moment that it no longer mattered. Terrance LaCroix was as stubborn as they came and would never change. Regardless, Terian loved his father unconditionally.

Two hours later, his phone rang.

Distracted by what he was doing, Terian answered without looking at the caller ID.

"Hey, son…"

"Pop," he responded. "How are you feeling?"

"Not in as much pain as before. That's why I'm calling. I didn't RSVP yes because I wasn't sure I'd be able to come at the time, but we're just leaving the doctor's office. I got a shot which seems to make the pain bearable. Terian, your mom and I will be there for your grand opening. I put the surgery off until the first of the year."

"That's good to hear, Pop. I'm so glad you're coming."

"I wouldn't miss this for the world. I'm proud of you, son."

Terian swallowed his emotions. "I can't wait to see you."

He wiped away a lone tear that escaped.

AUBRIE COULDN'T STOP staring at her ring. She'd put it back in the box while she was at work. They weren't ready to share their news just yet.

When Terian called a few minutes later, he said, "I just got off the phone with my dad. He's coming to the opening of Paradis."

She smiled. "I told you he'd be here."

"You did, and I wanted to believe you, but I know Terrance LaCroix. At least I thought I knew him. When he makes up his mind about something—he doesn't change it."

"He loves you, Terian. You're his son. Despite everything, I knew he wouldn't let you down."

"He wanted to wait until he saw his doctor to decide if he was going to come. I'd just made up my mind that I didn't need his blessing but turns out I've got it."

"I'm glad your parents will be here."

"Me, too," he responded. "Everyone that was on our list is coming. We're going to have a full house."

"That's what we want," she said.

"How's your day going?" Terian inquired.

"Great," Aubrie responded. "It's been busy in spurts." She fingered the black velvet box on her desk. "I can't stop looking at my ring. It's so beautiful. I keep thinking last night was just a beautiful dream."

"It's real," he said. "I proposed and you said yes... We're engaged."

She smiled. "It's surreal."

"All I know is that I'm the happiest man alive."

Aubrie laughed. "I'm overjoyed, but I'll be even happier when the grand opening is over."

"We only have four more days."

"I guess we need to get off this phone," she said. "Time to get back to work."

"I'll see you tonight."

Aubrie hung up, then turned her attention back to the computer screen, a smile tugging on her lips.

"TERIAN TOLD ME he and Aubrie are working things out," Margo told Rochelle. "They're still together."

"I'm glad to hear this. It was getting really hard not reaching out to Aubrie and knowing she was in such pain."

"I don't know how you do it."

"I told you... I stay in my lane until they need me. I don't know what's worse—independent children or needy ones."

Margo chuckled. "I know what you mean..."

"Are you and Terrance coming for the grand opening?" Rochelle asked. She hoped they would support Terian.

"Yes, we'll be there. We wouldn't miss it."

"Jacques and I are looking forward to seeing y'all. Don't worry about a hotel—you'll stay with us."

"Rochelle..."

"I mean it. We want you and Terrance to spend the weekend at our beach house."

"Torrie and her husband are staying with Terian... Rochelle, thank you for the offer—we accept."

"I hear Aubrie's voice. We're having lunch, so I'd better go. I'll call you back tonight."

"Talk to you later," Margo responded.

They'd agreed to keep their conversations just between them for now. Neither one of them wanted to be accused of matchmaking.

Still, she and Margo were rooting for Terian and Aubrie. They were perfect for one another.

CHAPTER TWENTY-NINE

AFTER MONTHS OF renovations and preparations, the doors to Paradis were finally open.

While waiting to be seated indoors, customers were treated to music by a sax musician outside. Aubrie and Terian personally greeted those waiting with a tray of appetizers.

She smiled when she glimpsed her Rothchild cousins waiting in line to be seated. "The gang's all here, I see."

"There's no way we'd miss this event," Trey said. He placed an arm around his wife, Gia. "We're very happy for you and Terian."

Aubrie hugged him. "Thank you."

Behind Trey was his brother Leon and Leon's wife, Misty.

"I'm so glad all of you are here." She embraced Aunt Eleanor. "Especially *you.*"

"I'm so proud of you, Aubrie. I remember when you would come to the island during summertime. You'd rather spend your time with me at the café than hang out with the others at the beach. You've always had a love for cooking."

She chuckled. "More like a love for food."

Her parents arrived with her aunt and uncle. Aubrie waved at them. It was time for her to put on her uniform. She was happy to see Terian's parents as well.

He walked out of the kitchen as she walked toward the back.

"You ready to do this?" she asked.

"I've never been more ready," Terian responded.

Aubrie kissed his cheek. "I'll see you in a few."

In the office, she adjusted the black skull-cap as she checked her reflection in the mirror. She made sure her hair was secured neatly in a bun at her nape and tugged her black double-breasted coat to straighten it.

How many hours had they spent preparing for this night? Planning the sixteen-course meal had taken meetings, late-night phone calls and lots of discussions about everything from logistics to recipes, to make sure their opening night went as smoothly and efficiently as possible. It had taken a lot of work, but was well worth it, Aubrie thought with satisfaction.

She walked out of the office and ran into Terian in the hallway.

"You look handsome in your uniform."

He grinned. "And you're stunning, my beautiful wife-to-be."

She put a hand to her lips. "Shhh…we don't want anyone learning about our engagement until after we tell the family."

"Okay," Terian said, a glint of humor in his gaze.

"It's showtime…"

Hector, their Maître d', approached them, saying, "Everyone has been seated."

Terian and Aubrie walked into the dining room together.

"Welcome to Paradis," he said. "We're so glad to have you join us for this special occasion. A full course menu can consist anywhere from five to sixteen courses—some menus have as many as twenty-one courses. Sounds like a lot of food…but it's not. The courses are smaller and spread out over the evening. I hope you brought your appetites because my partner, Chef Aubrie DuGrandpre, joins me to present a classic French sixteen-course dinner with a taste of Italy from appetizer to dessert and drinks."

Smiling, Aubrie added, *"Bon appetit…"*

Aubrie and Terian walked briskly into the kitchen.

"You've got this," she told him. "Have fun with it…"

"Chefs, the Melon Frappé is ready to be served," a cook announced.

"Let's get them to the guests," Terian responded.

Aubrie walked over to check on the consommé, which was going to be next. She sampled it and smiled. "Great job," she said to the station chef.

"This Spaghetti Bolognaise smells heavenly," she told another cook. Aubrie tasted the minced lean beef that was cooked in a rich brown sauce. "Oh yes… I can tell you that my mother is going to love this dish. This goes out after the consommé."

She glanced over at Terian, who had begun working on the dessert. After checking on the fish for the fifth course, Aubrie strode with purpose to her station to prepare the oxtails.

"Everything good?" Terian asked.

She nodded. "It's great. Oxtails in ten."

Aubrie had already started on the main course of the evening, braised duck and roast quail, which would be served after the sorbet. She and Terian had decided to serve the tenth course, sauteed spinach along with the meat.

When they got to the fifteenth course, Terian delighted everyone with his special cherry and rose éclairs for dessert. Hot and cold beverages completed the meal. Aubrie was exhausted but thrilled with the way the evening had gone.

All but their family members left the restaurant at the end of the night per Aubrie's request.

Terian locked the doors.

"Everything was delicious," Margo exclaimed. "You and Aubrie did a fantastic job."

Rochelle chimed in. "They sure did. When Terian announced that it was going to be a sixteen-course meal, I wasn't sure I'd be able to eat everything until I saw the portions. My favorite was the Spaghetti Bolognaise."

Aubrie chuckled. "I knew it would be."

"She insisted we put it on the menu," Terian stated. "My mom's favorite is oxtails."

Margo smiled. "Honey, they were delicious and so tender. Everything was just *magnifique*."

"Everything was cooked to perfection," Terrance said. "I'm proud of you both."

"Your son and I came up with an idea," Aubrie announced. "We'd like to feature you as one of our special guests. We'd like you to be the first. You'll help us create a special menu for that evening. Torrie, we want to do the same with you."

"That's different," Terrance said with a smile. "I'd be honored. Of course, it will have to wait until I'm fully recovered from my surgery. Maybe Torrie should be your first."

"Pop, I want you to be the first, so we'll wait. We plan to host guest chefs at least three or four times a year."

"That's actually a wonderful idea," Jacques said.

Aubrie smiled at her father. "We're so happy to share this night with all of you."

"Molly and her daughter had to leave," Rochelle stated, "but she said everything was superb and she'll call you next week."

Aubrie glanced over at Terian. "We did it," she said.

"THESE ARE THE private dining rooms—the La-Croix and the DuGrandpre to honor our fathers," Terian stated.

"I…I don't know what to say," his father responded. "Son, I told you that this restaurant would fail…" Terrance shook his head. "I was never more wrong. You and Aubrie have a winner in this place."

"Thank you, Dad. I can't fully express how much your words mean to me." Terian paused a moment, then said, "Aubrie and I have one more thing we'd like to share with all of you."

Everyone in the room looked at them expectantly.

"We're getting married."

"You're *engaged*?" Rochelle asked. "Are you telling me that my daughter is getting married?"

Aubrie laughed. "Yes, Mama. I know you've been waiting years for this day to come."

Rochelle and Margo jumped up and hugged one another. "Our prayers have been answered," they said in unison.

Terian looked at Aubrie. "What's that all about?"

"I'm guessing our mothers renewed their friendship at some point, but they failed to mention this to us," she responded with a smile.

"We're gonna be family now," Margo said. "This is just wonderful news."

Terian had servers bring out Champagne and sparkling wine to everyone in celebration of their engagement and a successful opening.

He could finally relax now that Paradis was officially open to the public. At least two of the guests earlier were food critics, but Terian wasn't worried. He was confident they would receive favorable reviews.

He'd learned not to expect things to always go as planned. He had to remain flexible. Aubrie was a pro when it came to adapting to changes and staying the course. Terian had learned a lot just by watching her.

She was good for him. Molly could see it and so could Torrie.

He was glad he didn't allow pride to keep him from pursuing a partnership with her. Paradis would not be what it was without her help.

Terian was eternally grateful to Aubrie for giving him another chance.

CHAPTER THIRTY

"I MISSED YOU TERRIBLY," Terian said when Aubrie walked out of the airport in New Orleans a few days before Valentine's Day. He came home two weeks ago to help his father after the surgery.

Aubrie savored the feel of his arms around her. "I missed you, too."

He placed her luggage in the trunk of the SUV.

She glanced over her shoulder. "Guess who I ran into at the airport?"

Terian followed her gaze, then chuckled as Michelle walked out with a suitcase, a weekender and backpack. "Are you moving here?" he asked.

"No, but a girl has to come prepared," she responded. "Aubrie, I didn't know you were coming to New Orleans."

"You never mentioned you were coming either. What brings you here?"

"I'm visiting a friend," Michelle responded.

"Would that friend be my cousin Phillip?"

Grinning, Michelle said, "Actually, yeah. How did you know?"

"Let's see…whenever he came to Charleston, you were busy. Then you had all these dates with a mystery guy. During those times, I couldn't reach my cousin… It was pretty obvious. Although you could've told me that you were seeing Phillip."

"We're friends. He invited me to a concert and to just hang out."

"You actually make a cute couple," Terian said.

"We're just friends," Michelle repeated. "You know I don't do long-distance relationships like that."

"For now," Aubrie said with a smile. "Is he coming to pick you up, or do you want us to drop you off?"

She glanced down at her phone. "He just texted me. Phillip's pulling in now."

"I had a feeling Phillip was interested in Michelle," Terian said in a low voice when she walked away.

Aubrie glanced at him. "Me, too. I could tell from their body language, but mostly the way Phillip was watching her during the gala. They just seemed to really connect. Besides, I knew he wasn't coming to Charleston that often to spend time with family." She paused a moment, then said, "Maybe that's why he's been talking so much about moving to Charleston? My mom mentioned that he's thinking of joining the firm."

"I guess we'll have to stay tuned."

"How is everything going with the insurance company?" Aubrie inquired.

"Everything is on track. The adjuster said there shouldn't be anything to hold up payment." Terian reached over and took her hand in his. "I'm so glad you're here, Aubrie."

In the car, he asked, "Everything running smoothly at Paradis?"

"Yes. There haven't been any complaints."

"That's always good to hear."

"You told me that surgery and his recovery are going well so far. I take it that things are good with you and your dad? I was so happy to hear that he's communicating more with you and asking your thoughts on the rebranding of LaCroix."

"He's been good about including me and Torrie...even my mom. Seems like Pop meant it when he said this time around was going to be more about family."

"That's great," Aubrie said. "It's everything you've always wanted."

"I have everything I want," he responded. "I

don't need to ask for anything else. I'm happy and content."

"Now you sound like me," Aubrie said with a chuckle. "I'm rubbing off on you."

"That's not a bad thing."

"Of course it isn't."

Terian laughed. "Looks like I'm rubbing off on you, too."

WHILE TERIAN WAS at rehab with his father, Aubrie and Torrie went shopping.

"I'm excited to find a bridesmaid dress," Torrie said. "I have a closet full of gowns I'll never wear again."

Aubrie chuckled. "I have a few of those as well. I'm glad you're here to help choose something that will get worn again."

"Is your cousin designing your wedding gown?"

"Yes. Renee's designed some of the most beautiful wedding dresses I've ever seen. I've always said that she would be the one to dress me if I ever married."

"I feel the same way," Torrie responded. "I love her designs. I had a chance to visit her boutique on the island and purchased a couple of pieces from her ready-to-wear collection."

"We're all very proud of her."

"What do you think of this one?" Torrie

asked while holding a pale blue gown against her body.

"I like it," Aubrie responded. "But you're the one who has to wear it. Why don't you try it on?"

"I think I will. It's a beautiful dress."

She sat down in a chair outside the dressing room and waited for Torrie to emerge.

After Torrie tried on four bridesmaid dresses, they left the shop and drove to meet up with Terian and Luke.

"DID YOU GET the tickets?" Aubrie asked.

Terian held up four movie tickets. "Right here."

She kissed his cheek. "Thanks, handsome."

They walked toward the entrance of the theater.

"I'm so looking forward to seeing this movie," Torrie said.

Aubrie agreed.

Terian looked over at his brother-in-law. "Can you believe they're this excited about a Spider-Man movie?"

Luke laughed. "You know Torrie still reads the comic books. I think she has every single one with Spider-Man."

"Some of those belong to me."

"I don't think you're going to get them back,"

Luke responded. "She's got them cataloged, labeled and numbered."

Terian wasn't surprised. He knew his sister. "I kept telling her that she and Aubrie would get along well."

It pleased him to see Torrie and Aubrie forging their own relationship. He and Ryker were beginning to do the same.

"Son, I appreciate everything you've done for me, but it's time for you to go home," Terrance said when he and Aubrie returned to the house after they left the movies. "You have a restaurant to run."

"I want to be here for you."

"I know, but I'm fine. I have your mama here with me—we can manage. I'll keep you posted on my condition."

"If we need you—I'll call you," his mother said.

"You had a strong start with Paradis. Don't make the mistakes I made, Terian. Keep your finger on the pulse."

He turned to Aubrie and said, "I guess I'll be flying back with you."

Grinning, she responded, "I don't have a problem with that."

CHAPTER THIRTY-ONE

OCTOBER WAS THE perfect month for a New Orleans wedding. Aubrie and Terian wanted their guests to experience the city without having to endure the sweltering summer heat. After planning for two years, their wedding day was less than twenty-four hours away.

Aubrie and her mother spent the morning going over last-minute details for the ceremony. They were now on their way to have lunch.

"Do you remember telling me that you'd get married at Southern Oaks one day?" Rochelle asked.

She eyed her mother. "I do and I meant it." She found everything about the Southern Oaks venue wonderful. The antebellum mansion, oversized oak trees, the breathtaking blue water in the pool, and the beautiful white horses named Magic and Majestic who would pull the carriage all provided the perfect backdrop for their wedding. She and Terian planned to have a couple of wedding photos staged with them.

"Yes, you did," Rochelle said. "It's a very

beautiful venue. I love the manicured lawns, the Chiavari chairs, the crystal chandeliers in that ballroom—they sparkle like diamonds... Everything is just perfect."

"I'm getting married tomorrow. For the longest time, I couldn't ever imagine that day happening. And I never thought I'd be marrying Terian LaCroix."

"Watching the two of you together... I wasn't surprised at all. I'm so proud of the way you supported Terian when he came back here to take care of his dad."

"It was challenging but we made it through. His dad says he now has the hip of a twenty-five-year-old."

"Maybe I need to get me one of those..."

Aubrie chuckled and embraced her mother. "I love you."

"I love you, too. Spending this week with you has been wonderful. It's a shame we had to come all the way to New Orleans to do it."

"Mama... I've been busy trying to make sure all the restaurants are doing well. I'm going to be more intentional about spending time with the family. Terian and I have already talked about it. We're going to take Sundays off for starters."

"I'm glad to hear it. Tomorrow isn't promised to anyone."

"I am so lucky to have all of you," Aubrie responded. "I'll do better."

"Don't be so hard on yourself, sweetie. We've seen you more since Paradis opened than with Rouge and Bleu. We're attorneys. We understand about long hours and having to make sacrifices when it comes to personal time. It's about quality—not quantity."

"I'm especially lucky to have you for a mom. I appreciate that you don't interfere in my life, but you have a way of making your point without crossing boundaries. Terian's mom is like that, too. I can see why you two are such good friends." Aubrie looped her arm through Rochelle's. "However, don't think I don't know that you and Mama LaCroix were busy somewhere in the background."

"Honey, I don't know what you're talking about. I learned to just stay in my lane, and I'm doing just that."

"Uh-huh…" Aubrie said with a laugh.

"TOMORROW'S YOUR BIG DAY," Torrie said to her brother.

"Yeah…"

"Terian, you're looking nervous."

"I am," he admitted. "I don't want to mess this up. I love Aubrie."

"Everything is going to be fine. She knows

you're not perfect—that you're going to make mistakes, but Aubrie loves you dearly."

"That's what she tells me," he responded. "My biggest fear is doing something to risk that love again."

"It's not going to happen, Terian. And if you do, it'll still be okay. That's what life is about. Learning from our mistakes."

"This is true. I almost lost Aubrie for good with mine."

"That's all over with. She's about to become your wife, brother. Hey, it's happening this weekend."

He grinned. "I can't wait."

"See… I always knew you were a romantic sap," Torrie teased.

"I am. I own it."

"Terian, I love you and I can't tell you how happy it makes me to see you like this—you've come into your own and it looks good on you."

He was watching her intently. "Is there something you want to tell me?"

"What are you talking about?"

"Twin…don't play… I feel something…"

Torrie burst into laughter. "I'm not sure this is a twin thing, but you always seem to know when there's something going on with me. It's weird."

"We shared a womb. It's a twin thing. So out

with it. When am I going to meet my niece, nephew, niece and nephew or…"

"I'm pregnant. I was waiting until after the wedding to make the announcement, so don't say anything—not even to Aubrie. I want to tell her."

"Do you know if you're having twins, triplets…?"

"Right now, it's just one as far as we know."

Terian embraced his sister. "Congratulations. You're going to be a fantastic mom."

"And you're going to be a great husband. Aubrie will see to it."

He laughed. "Yes, she will…"

SMILING, AUBRIE FINGERED the tulle overskirt of her lace bridal gown hanging on the door of the closet in the bedroom of an 1850s mansion on Royal Street her parents had rented for the week. Although there were eight bedrooms, her aunt Eleanor Louise and uncle Etienne rented another large house two blocks away for additional room to house the clan.

It had been a busy week for her and Terian from the moment they landed in New Orleans. They spent the first two days with his parents, making sure they had everything they needed for the wedding. On Wednesday, they met with a coordinator at Southern Oaks for a private rehearsal. The rest of the bridal party was scheduled to do a quick rehearsal an hour before the ceremony.

Tomorrow they would have three coordinators attending to them: one with the parents, groom, and groomsmen; one with the bridesmaids, flower girl and ring bearer; and one with Aubrie. Overall, she was pleased with how smoothly the wedding planning had gone.

A knock sounded on her door.

"Come in," she said.

"You feel like hanging with the girls for a little while?" Jadin asked.

"Of course," Aubrie responded. "It'll take my mind off of tomorrow."

She followed her cousin downstairs.

Jordin handed her a mug.

"What's this?"

"Warm milk. It should help you sleep."

"Thanks, but I doubt I'll get much sleep tonight," Aubrie stated. "I'm so excited about tomorrow."

"We are, too," Misty responded. "I'm so happy for you."

The doorbell sounded.

Jadin went to answer it.

Aubrie smiled when she saw Torrie and Michelle. "What have you two been up to?"

Holding up a couple of bags, her friend said, "What else?"

"This girl will always find a reason to shop," Aubrie said with a chuckle.

Michelle looked bewildered. "You make it sound as if that's strange. Shopping is what I do. One of my goals is to shop in every great mall in the country."

"She said every *great* mall," Jordin repeated.

"Now, you know not all malls are good ones." Michelle sat down beside Misty.

Gia took a sip of her bottled water. "I especially enjoy seeing how Terian gets this certain look on his face whenever you're around, Aubrie. He truly loves you."

"That's always nice to hear because I love him so much—more than I ever thought I could love someone. He's the only man I've ever loved."

Her cell phone rang.

"It's Terian," Aubrie said with a grin.

Renee frowned in confusion. "He's calling you from his bachelor party? I don't think I heard from Greg until the next night."

Aubrie stepped away from everyone to hear him better. "Hello…"

"Hey, beautiful."

"Aren't you at your party?"

"Yeah, but I had to call to say I love you and I can't wait to be your husband."

His words made her heart do a little flip.

"That's so sweet... I can't wait to marry you, too."

"I had no idea my brother could be this mushy," Torrie said.

Her comment sparked a round of laughter.

"I think he's playing it smart," Michelle responded. "Terian's stocking up some brownie points before the big day."

"Torrie, I must tell you that my daughter Talei really enjoyed the tea party you hosted for the children," Misty said after Aubrie finished her conversation.

"That was a wonderful idea for the restaurant," Aubrie stated as she returned to her seat. "Are you going to do more of them?"

"I thought it was a good way to include the girls in the prewedding celebrations," Torrie responded. "Especially since the boys were going to a football game. It went so well that I'm thinking of doing it annually."

"You should," Garland interjected. "Amya and Kai couldn't stop talking about it. They had so much fun. They were especially excited about getting dressed up, wearing hats and gloves."

They sat there talking and laughing until almost midnight.

Aubrie rose to her feet. "I don't want puffy eyes on my wedding day, so I'm going to bed. I'll see y'all in the morning."

"I need to get home to my hubby," Torrie said.

Aubrie walked her to the front door, then gave her a hug.

"See you tomorrow, *sister*," Torrie said.

"I'll be the one in the Champagne-colored gown. Don't forget to text to let me know that you made it home."

"I guess we're all going to bed," Jadin said. She tried to stifle her yawn but failed.

"None of us need to be walking around with bags under our eyes," Aubrie said as she led the way upstairs.

"Where's Mama Rochelle?" Michelle asked.

Aubrie replied, "She's out with Terian's mom. Those two have been inseparable since she arrived in New Orleans. I have a feeling I'm going to have to keep an eye on them."

Michelle burst into laughter. "Girl, they're living their best lives. You don't have to worry about them. Leave them alone."

"You're right. I just need to stay in my lane."

"Nope…you need to mind your own business," Michelle said. "That is all and goodnight."

EPILOGUE

THE CEREMONY WAS going to be held on the front lawn near the grand entrance of the antebellum mansion under the picturesque live oaks. The expansive grounds easily accommodated the two hundred guests in attendance.

Aubrie and her father arrived in a carriage pulled by horses Magic and Majestic.

"I can't tell you how long I've waited for this day to come," Jacques said. "To escort my beautiful daughter down the aisle."

"Nothing ever felt more right," she murmured.

Tears of happiness filled her eyes and threatened to spill as Aubrie made her way up the aisle toward Terian.

He looked so handsome in a Champagne and black paisley print tuxedo jacket over double-breasted waistcoat and pants in solid black. All the groomsmen looked straight off the cover of a magazine in black tuxedos and cummerbunds matching the rose-gold dresses worn by her bridesmaids.

She glanced at Michelle, her maid of honor, who winked.

Aubrie didn't take her eyes off Terian as they stood face-to-face minutes later. This was the very moment she'd dreamed about when they were in school. She couldn't keep the tears from falling any longer.

The minister began speaking. "Welcome to this day of celebration. It's great to have all of you here to witness the union of Aubrie Du-Grandpre and Terian LaCroix as wife and husband before God. On this day, we will forever bind Aubrie and Terian together." His gaze landed on them.

"Aubrie and Terian, you two are blessed to share this experience with your friends and family gathered here to support you as you embark on this journey together."

Misty read a passage of scripture from 1 Corinthians.

"Love is patient, love is kind. It does not envy, it does not boast, it is not proud. It is not rude, it is not self-seeking, it is not easily angered, it keeps no record of wrongs. Love does not delight in evil but rejoices with the truth. It always protects, always trusts, always hopes, and always perseveres. Love never fails."

When Misty returned to her seat, the minister began speaking once more. "Marriage is more than a simple exchanging of rings or combining of material assets. Rather, it is an indescribably powerful shared commitment. Your marriage is the foundation upon which you will build the rest of your lives and, despite any adversity, will always be there to sustain you. Aubrie and Terian, take a moment to sense the tremendous amount of love radiating throughout this space…"

Aubrie considered the words spoken, capturing them and committing them to memory. She knew from observing the couples in her own family that marriage had the capacity to deepen, challenge and strengthen her relationship with Terian in ways that she never thought possible. She prayed that the joy she felt now would serve as fuel to face head-on any challenges they might encounter in the future.

WE LEARNED TO work together, to laugh together and to love together, Terian thought as he listened to the minister's wise counsel. He wanted his marriage to work and vowed to avoid getting caught up in anything that would draw Aubrie and him apart. Instead, he intended to focus on their love. It was a remarkable love, one abundantly given and freely accepted.

Aubrie was a vision in her wedding gown.

It was time for them to exchange vows. He and Aubrie decided to write their own. It had taken them almost a week to come up with the right words to express their feelings.

Aubrie spoke first.

"Terian, today I take you to be my husband. I join my life with yours. I promise to love and honor you, to treasure and respect you, to be by your side in joy and sorrow. I vow to be caring, supportive and truthful, to love you as you are, and not as I want you to be. I promise to grow old by your side as your lover and best friend. I give you my hand, my heart and my love, from this day forward."

Caught up by his emotions, Terian swallowed hard while staring into her loving gaze. "Aubrie, I take you to be my wife. Today I join my life with yours. I promise to love and honor you, to treasure you and respect you, to walk with you in joy and sorrow. I vow to always be caring, supportive and truthful, to love you as you are, and not as I want you to be. I vow to grow old by your side as your lover and best friend. I give you my hand, my heart and my love, from this day forward."

After the declaration of intent and exchange of rings, the minister said, "You may now kiss your bride."

At the end, the minister held up a ceremonial broom saying, "Aubrie and Terian, while the words you have spoken have sealed your union, it is in jumping over this broom that you truly transition into your new combined lives together."

Terian took Aubrie's hand in his own and they jumped over the broom that had been placed on the ground.

"Family and friends, by the power vested in me by the state of Louisiana, I am pleased to pronounce Terian and Aubrie as husband and wife, sealed together today both in law and in love.

"For the first time, *Mr. and Mrs. LaCroix...*"

Applause rang out all around them.

AUBRIE REMOVED HER veil and the tulle overskirt of her wedding ensemble, enabling her to move more freely in the fitted lace gown.

"You look so beautiful," Talei said as she fingered the veil. "Can I wear this on my wedding day?"

"You sure can, sweetie," she responded. "Let's pack it up nice and neat for when you're ready for it."

Aubrie took Talei by the hand. "Thanks for helping me. Now it's time for us to join the others."

"You have to make an entrance, Mrs. La-Croix."

She laughed. "You've attended quite a few weddings, haven't you?"

Talei nodded. "I love them. They're so romantic."

"I feel the same way," Aubrie said. "Maybe when you're older, you can assist me at the restaurant whenever we host a reception."

"I'd love that. Don't forget, Aubrie."

"I won't."

They met Terian in the hallway.

"I'm a lucky man to have the most beautiful woman and young lady on my arms."

Talei giggled. "I'm gonna go sit with my parents so I can take a picture of y'all when you make your entrance."

"We'll see you soon," Aubrie said.

"She's a sweetheart," Terian stated.

She agreed.

"You're exquisite, Aubrie. And now I get to call you *wife*."

He kissed her.

"Husband, it's time for us to make our entrance, as Talei called it."

He grinned. "Let's do it."

When the doors opened, they were greeted by sparkling chandeliers, LED lights, twinkling candles along with applause from their guests.

She and Terian were led to their table.

Their guests were treated to an array of diverse foods hand-passed throughout the evening while a DJ played music in the background.

Aubrie couldn't stop smiling. She was happy. Maybe more than happy. Beyond happy. She loved Terian beyond measure.

He looked at her and grinned. "I've dreamed of this day for nine years and now it's come true. You're my wife."

She leaned against him. "I love you, Terian," she said in a low voice. "More than I could ever tell you. I loved you from the moment we met. It's as if my heart knew you were the one for me."

"Whenever you look at me like that—you make me believe that all things are possible, Aubrie. I love you, too."

Her eyes traveled the ballroom, landing on Phillip and Michelle, who were deep in conversation.

Terian followed her gaze. "You think they're serious about each other?"

"I know Michelle is… My cousin Phillip's working in Charleston now with the family. I'd say it's pretty serious."

"Make sure you throw the bouquet in her direction."

She chuckled. "I was thinking of just walking it over to her."

After they ate, Aubrie and Terian walked together around the room, to acknowledge each of their guests.

It was soon time for the Second Line Parade.

The first line consisted of a brass band as well as Terian and Aubrie. Their friends, family and wedding guests made up the second line.

Aubrie twirled a custom parasol, which matched her dress, to the sound of the band as she and Terian made their way along the parade route, a wedding tradition in New Orleans. Behind her, she heard the laughter of the children as they danced and waved white handkerchiefs.

She looked over her shoulder to see her parents dancing. Aubrie imagined this was how they must have looked during the Second Line Parade celebrating their own wedding. Even Rusty and Aunt Eleanor appeared to be having a great time.

Aubrie knew in her heart that she would never forget this day. It would be forever imprinted in her memory.

* * * * *

Get 4 FREE REWARDS!

We'll send you 2 FREE Books plus 2 FREE Mystery Gifts.

FREE
Value Over
$20

Both the **Harlequin® Special Edition** and **Harlequin® Heartwarming™** series feature compelling novels filled with stories of love and strength where the bonds of friendship, family and community unite.

YES! Please send me 2 FREE novels from the Harlequin Special Edition or Harlequin Heartwarming series and my 2 FREE gifts (gifts are worth about $10 retail). After receiving them, if I don't wish to receive any more books, I can return the shipping statement marked "cancel." If I don't cancel, I will receive 6 brand-new Harlequin Special Edition books every month and be billed just $5.49 each in the U.S. or $6.24 each in Canada, a savings of at least 12% off the cover price, or 4 brand-new Harlequin Heartwarming Larger-Print books every month and be billed just $6.24 each in the U.S. or $6.74 each in Canada, a savings of at least 19% off the cover price. It's quite a bargain! Shipping and handling is just 50¢ per book in the U.S. and $1.25 per book in Canada.* I understand that accepting the 2 free books and gifts places me under no obligation to buy anything. I can always return a shipment and cancel at any time by calling the number below. The free books and gifts are mine to keep no matter what I decide.

Choose one: ☐ **Harlequin Special Edition** ☐ **Harlequin Heartwarming**
(235/335 HDN GRJV)   **Larger-Print**
                             (161/361 HDN GRJV)

Name (please print)

Address   Apt. #

City   State/Province   Zip/Postal Code

Email: Please check this box ☐ if you would like to receive newsletters and promotional emails from Harlequin Enterprises ULC and its affiliates. You can unsubscribe anytime.

Mail to the Harlequin Reader Service:
IN U.S.A.: P.O. Box 1341, Buffalo, NY 14240-8531
IN CANADA: P.O. Box 603, Fort Erie, Ontario L2A 5X3

Want to try 2 free books from another series! Call 1-800-873-8635 or visit www.ReaderService.com.

*Terms and prices subject to change without notice. Prices do not include sales taxes, which will be charged (if applicable) based on your state or country of residence. Canadian residents will be charged applicable taxes. Offer not valid in Quebec. This offer is limited to one order per household. Books received may not be as shown. Not valid for current subscribers to the Harlequin Special Edition or Harlequin Heartwarming series. All orders subject to approval. Credit or debit balances in a customer's account(s) may be offset by any other outstanding balance owed by or to the customer. Please allow 4 to 6 weeks for delivery. Offer available while quantities last.

Your Privacy—Your information is being collected by Harlequin Enterprises ULC, operating as Harlequin Reader Service. For a complete summary of the information we collect, how we use this information and to whom it is disclosed, please visit our privacy notice located at corporate.harlequin.com/privacy-notice. From time to time we may also exchange your personal information with reputable third parties. If you wish to opt out of this sharing of your personal information, please visit readerservice.com/consumerschoice or call 1-800-873-8635. **Notice to California Residents**—Under California law, you have specific rights to control and access your data. For more information on these rights and how to exercise them, visit corporate.harlequin.com/california-privacy.

HSEHW22R3

THE 2022 ROMANCE CHRISTMAS COLLECTION

6 FREE TRADE-SIZE BOOKS IN ALL!

NEW YORK TIMES BESTSELLING AUTHOR
RAEANNE THAYNE
ALL IS BRIGHT

MAISEY YATES
Merry Christmas Cowboy

JENNIFER SNOW
Alaska in Christmas

In this loveliest of seasons may you find many reasons for happiness, magic and love, and what better way to fill your heart with the magic of Christmas than with an unforgettable romance from our specially curated holiday collection.

YES! Please send me the first shipment of **The 2022 Romance Christmas Collection**. This collection begins with 1 FREE TRADE SIZE BOOK and 2 FREE gifts in the first shipment. Along with my free book, I'll also get 2 additional mass-market paperback books. If I do not cancel, I will continue to receive three books a month for five additional months. My first four shipments will be billed at the discount price of $19.98 U.S./$25.98 CAN., plus $1.99 U.S./$3.99 CAN. for shipping and handling*. My last two shipments will be billed at the discount price of $17.98 U.S./$23.98 CAN., plus $1.99 U.S./$3.99 CAN. for shipping and handling*. I understand that accepting the free books and gifts places me under no obligation to buy anything. I can always return a shipment and cancel at any time. My free books and gifts are mine to keep no matter what I decide.

☐ 269 HCK 1875   ☐ 469 HCK 1875

Name (please print)

Address   Apt. #

City   State/Province   Zip/Postal Code

Mail to the Harlequin Reader Service:
IN U.S.A.: P.O. Box 1341, Buffalo, NY 14240-8531
IN CANADA: P.O. Box 603, Fort Erie, ON L2A 5X3

Get 4 FREE REWARDS!

We'll send you 2 FREE Books **plus** 2 FREE Mystery Gifts.

FREE Value Over **$20**

Both the **Romance** and **Suspense** collections feature compelling novels written by many of today's bestselling authors.

YES! Please send me 2 FREE novels from the Essential Romance or Essential Suspense Collection and my 2 FREE gifts (gifts are worth about $10 retail). After receiving them, if I don't wish to receive any more books, I can return the shipping statement marked "cancel." If I don't cancel, I will receive 4 brand-new novels every month and be billed just $7.49 each in the U.S. or $7.74 each in Canada. That's a savings of at least 17% off the cover price. It's quite a bargain! Shipping and handling is just 50¢ per book in the U.S. and $1.25 per book in Canada.* I understand that accepting the 2 free books and gifts places me under no obligation to buy anything. I can always return a shipment and cancel at any time by calling the number below. The free books and gifts are mine to keep no matter what I decide.

Choose one: ☐ **Essential Romance**
(194/394 MDN GRHV)

☐ **Essential Suspense**
(191/391 MDN GRHV)

Name (please print)

Address   Apt. #

City   State/Province   Zip/Postal Code

Email: Please check this box ☐ if you would like to receive newsletters and promotional emails from Harlequin Enterprises ULC and its affiliates. You can unsubscribe anytime.

Mail to the **Harlequin Reader Service:**
IN U.S.A.: P.O. Box 1341, Buffalo, NY 14240-8531
IN CANADA: P.O. Box 603, Fort Erie, Ontario L2A 5X3

Want to try 2 free books from another series! Call 1-800-873-8635 or visit www.ReaderService.com.

STRS22R3